Up until now Annie'd been getting a kind of grim satisfaction from pouring Max's aftershave down the plughole and fantasizing about sending his Ralph Lauren suits to the local Oxfam shop.

'Anyway, I think you should meet this guy,' Julia went on. 'And I happen to know he'll be at Alex Wingate's party tonight. I haven't told him about you yet. I thought if you could just casually turn up and bump into him –'

But Annie wasn't listening. 'A party? Tonight?' She accidentally inhaled the Strawberry Creme. 'But I can't!'

'Of course you can.' Julia laughed. 'For heaven's sake, it's only a party.'

Only a party. She couldn't have been more terrified if Julia had invited her to take part in a Satanic bonding ritual. At least then she wouldn't have been faced with the awful, insurmountable task of making herself look decent. 'I can't do it,' she whispered, shrinking back into the sofa cushions. 'It's too soon, I – I'm not ready for it.'

'For God's sake, Annie, stop acting like a grief-stricken widow! Max has walked out, he hasn't died.'

More's the pity, Annie thought, gripping the phone. It might have been easier if he had died. At least then she wouldn't have to face the thought of him being happy with someone else.

Donna Hay is a TV journalist. For the past eight years she has been regular soaps correspondent of *What's On* TV magazine, inteviewing the stars and writing features, and since 1998 she has had her own column in *TV Times*. In 1999 she won the Romantic Novelists' Association New Writers' Award. Donna Hay lives in York with her husband, daughter and two cats, Matilda and Ebony. *Waiting in the Wings* is her first novel.

Waiting in
the Wings

~

DONNA HAY

ORION

An Orion paperback
First published in Great Britain by Orion in 2000
This paperback edition published in 2000 by
Orion Books Ltd,
Orion House, 5 Upper St Martin's Lane, London WC2H 9EA

A CIP catalogue record for this book
is available from the British Library.

Printed in Great Britain by
Clays Ltd, St Ives plc

For Ken and Harriet

Acknowledgements

First of all, to Marina Oliver and everyone at the RNA for their help, advice and encouragement. Also to my pals on the New Writers' Scheme, especially Val McManus, Pauline Case and Heather Jan Brunt. Even if all this had never happened, it would have been worth it just to get to know them.

To my agent Sarah Molloy, and to Jane Wood and Selina Walker at Orion, for taking me on, for never being too busy to answer stupid questions and for knowing a lot more than I do.

To the many actors and actresses who have graciously offered me insights into everything from auditions to first-night nerves.

To my best friend June Smith Sheppard, because I promised if I ever wrote a book I'd mention her (although I absolutely refuse to put 'the wind beneath my wings', as she insisted I should).

Last but by no means least, to my husband Ken and daughter Harriet, the unsung heroes who lived through every agonising page of this book, and without whose endless support and sacrifice it would never have been written.

London

Chapter 1

According to *Every Woman's Self Help Guide to Relationships*, there were four stages to the classic break-up: Denial, Self-Recrimination, Anger and Resolution.

Strange they didn't mention Compulsive Eating, Annie reflected, delving into the box of Coco Pops she clutched to her bosom like a much-loved teddy bear. Max had only been gone three weeks and she'd already worn quite a furrow in the stretch of carpet from the sofa to the fridge. At this rate, by the time she got to the Resolution bit she'd look like she'd swallowed a duvet.

If she ever got there. At the moment she was still hanging on by what was left of her finger-nails to Denial, before she made the long, dismal freefall into Self-Recrimination.

Julia had been typically blunt. 'You're letting yourself go,' she'd bawled down the telephone earlier. 'I bet you're wearing that sad old cardigan, aren't you? And when was the last time you washed your hair?'

Annie ran a hand through her tangled curls. 'Mind your own business. You're my agent, not my mother.'

'I'm just protecting my investment. Carry on like this

and I'll be lucky to get you a guest appearance as a dosser on *Casualty*.'

'Look, I just want to be left alone, okay? I'm depressed.'

'And don't we know it.' Julia sighed.

'I think I've got a right to be slightly cheesed off. My husband walked out on me three weeks ago.'

'Exactly,' Julia snapped. 'Three weeks ago. So don't you think it's time you pulled yourself together?'

Annie picked at a chocolate stain on her shapeless grey cardie. How could she expect Julia to understand? When it came to the men in her life, she had the boredom threshold of a black widow spider. Her idea of commitment was to give a man her phone number. And half the time it wasn't her real one.

Whereas Annie was more like a swan, mating for life. Or so she'd thought, until Max swam off in search of a new, more attractive pond.

'I know what you need,' Julia said.

Annie groaned. Julia Gold had a serious interferiority complex. She could just imagine her sitting at her desk overlooking Soho Square, lighting up her twentieth Silk Cut of the morning, strong black Java blend coursing through her veins. 'I'm not interested in your cast-off men, if that's what you mean.'

'And I dare say they wouldn't be interested in you, either. Let's face it, you're hardly Claudia Schiffer at the moment, are you?'

Julia could be very cruel sometimes. She was a frighteningly elegant forty-something, with a Nicky Clarke blonde bob and a designer wardrobe to die for. She also had two divorces behind her and a contacts book that read like a *Who's Who* of British theatre. It had been fear at first sight when Annie met her straight from drama

4

school. After seven years together Julia still refused to treat her like a grown-up.

'No,' she went on briskly, 'what you need is a job. And I've got just the one for you.'

Annie shovelled down another handful of Coco Pops as Julia described the 'fantastic new opportunity' she'd lined up for her. Some downbeat repertory theatre in an unheard-of part of Yorkshire was reopening after many years and the new artistic director was casting for its opening production.

And for some reason Julia seemed to think it was just what she needed.

'I know it's not exactly the RSC, darling, but it's six weeks' work,' she'd purred down the phone.

Annie straightened her shoulders. Her husband might have run off with her best friend, leaving her with a mortgage to pay, a terrifyingly huge Barclaycard bill and the self-esteem of the last sandwich in a railway buffet, but professionally speaking she still had her pride. 'I couldn't possibly do it,' she said, with as much hauteur as she could muster through a mouthful of breakfast cereal.

'Don't be silly, darling, I'm sure it won't be that difficult.' Annie listened as Julia drew long and hard on her ciggie. 'Besides, even if you do make a complete arse of yourself, no one will see it, will they? I mean, who'd be desperate enough to go all that way?'

'How reassuring.'

'Seriously, this guy's an absolute genius, so they say.' Julia had obviously realised she wasn't doing too good a sales job. 'He's got some fantastic ideas for the first season. They're opening with *Much Ado*. You know you've always wanted to play Beatrice.'

'I don't think I could any more.' Once she might have

taken Beatrice's sparky, feisty character in her stride. These days, it was all she could do to fetch in the milk from the front step.

'Nonsense, you could do it with your eyes closed,' Julia insisted. 'And you've got too much talent to waste it sitting around stuffing your face and waiting for that bastard to come home.'

'What makes you think I'm doing that?' Annie shoved a half-empty Quality Street box under the sofa with her foot.

'Because I know you. You won't get him back by eating yourself into blimpdom, you know.'

Too late for that, Annie thought, plucking at the baggy knees of her leggings, which were well into their fourth day of wear and looking the worse for it. 'Who says I want him back?'

'You mean if he came through that door now you wouldn't welcome him back with open arms?'

'Not necessarily.' Annie crossed her fingers.

'And you don't jump on the phone every time it rings?'

'Oh, please!' No need to tell her she took it to bed every night, along with an old flannel shirt that still held lingering traces of his CKBe.

'So you're not just existing from day to day, hanging on to the hope that he'll come back?'

'I do have my own life to live, you know.' Annie abandoned the Coco Pops and foraged under the sofa for the Quality Street box. So what if she chose to spend it huddled up on the sofa with the curtains closed, eating chocolate and watching Richard and Judy phone-ins.

'I'm glad to hear it. So there's nothing to stop you taking this job then, is there?'

There was a penetrating silence. Julia was extremely good at them.

Annie wasn't. 'I'm grieving,' she mumbled.

'What on earth for?'

'My marriage.' She felt tears rising again and sniffed them back.

'Oh, for God's sake!' Julia snapped. 'Anyone can see you're better off without that egotistical little shit. If I were you I'd be changing the locks and hanging out the bloody flags.'

As Julia launched into her well-rehearsed speech on Why Max Kennedy Wasn't Worth Spitting On, Annie tuned out, her gaze drifting around her strangely sparse living-room. Max had already removed most traces of himself – his books, his CDs and his collection of priceless Broadway sound-tracks. But he'd left behind a freakish piece of modern art, a twisted mass of knotted perspex and metal that occupied far too large a space in one corner of the room. Annie loathed it, but he'd always been extremely fond of the piece – called, inexplicably, *Freedom*. Now she latched on to it as a vital sign that one day he would come home.

Since Max had gone she'd become obsessed with signs and portents. She devoured her horoscope every day, searching for clues that he might return. She even made bets with herself. If she could get through *Coronation Street* without a ciggie he'd come back. If Trevor McDonald scratched his ear during the news he wouldn't. Sometimes she wondered if her grief had unhinged her.

And here was another sign. A narrow shaft of July sunlight had managed to edge its way through the closed curtains, illuminating their wedding photo, propped up on the half-empty bookshelves. Max had also left that behind,

7

although he had taken the framed photo of him meeting Lord Attenborough – or Dickie, as he called him – that had once stood beside it.

Annie smiled at the photo. Max grinned back at her from outside Chelsea Register Office, that slow, sexy smile that still made her stomach curl. He was reaching up to push his flopping blond hair out of those denim-blue eyes. She was clinging to his arm and looking slightly startled, as if she couldn't believe her luck in landing such a beautiful man.

She felt the hot sting of tears behind her eyes again. She knew Julia was right: he was a shit and she was better off without him. But even with all her drama school training she still couldn't summon up the appropriate emotions.

'God knows what possessed you to marry him in the first place,' Julia droned on. 'He held you back from the moment you met. You could have taken that RSC contract and become a huge star if he hadn't stood in your way.'

'He didn't stand in my way.' Annie wedged the phone between her chin and shoulder as she unwrapped a Strawberry Creme. 'It was my decision not to take that job.'

'Only because he said he wouldn't marry you if you did!'

'He didn't want us to start our married life apart –'

'Bollocks! He just didn't want you to outshine him. Not that it's too difficult,' Julia added waspishly. 'A twenty-watt bulb could outshine that talentless—'

'Is that all you wanted?' Annie cut her off.

There was another long silence. This time Annie bit her lip to stop herself breaking it.

'What you need is a complete change.' Having failed

8

with bullying, Julia decided to try conciliation. 'That's what's so wonderful about this job. You can go away for six weeks, put your career back on track, get your personal life sorted out. And you know what they say: success is the best revenge.'

'Is it?' Annie said bleakly. Up until now she'd been getting a kind of grim satisfaction from pouring Max's aftershave down the plughole and fantasizing about sending his Ralph Lauren suits to the local Oxfam shop.

'Anyway, I think you should meet this guy,' Julia went on. 'And I happen to know he'll be at Alex Wingate's party tonight. I haven't told him about you yet. I thought if you could just casually turn up and bump into him –'

But Annie wasn't listening. 'A party? Tonight?' She accidentally inhaled the Strawberry Creme. 'But I can't!'

'Of course you can.' Julia laughed. 'For heaven's sake, it's only a party.'

Only a party. She couldn't have been more terrified if Julia had invited her to take part in a Satanic bonding ritual. At least then she wouldn't have been faced with the awful, insurmountable task of making herself look decent. 'I can't do it,' she whispered, shrinking back into the sofa cushions. 'It's too soon. I – I'm not ready for it.'

'For God's sake, Annie, stop acting like a grief-stricken widow! Max has walked out, he hasn't died.'

More's the pity, Annie thought, gripping the phone. It might have been easier if he had died. At least then she wouldn't have to face the thought of him being happy with someone else. 'But what if everyone knows?' she wailed. 'I couldn't stand it if they were all looking at me, talking about me –'

'You should be so lucky! Besides, that didn't seem to

worry you at the Lloyd Webber party, when you stood on that table and –'

'That was different. I was drunk.'

'Well, for God's sake don't get drunk tonight,' Julia warned. 'I want this guy to know what a highly talented and consummate professional you are. That's not going to happen if you start doing one of your party pieces.'

'No chance of that,' Annie said firmly. 'I'm not going.'

'But you must. You don't know how hard I've worked to pin him down –'

'Well, you can call and unpin him, can't you?'

'Actually, I can't,' Julia said. 'He's in meetings all day and his mobile is switched off.'

'Liar.'

'And even if I could I'm not going to.' Julia ignored her. 'Because frankly you owe it to yourself and to me to stop being such a complete pain in the backside and get your life together. I know no one else would say this to you, but the fact is you've become extremely boring since this break-up business. And let's face it, the chances of Max coming back are about the same as me playing prop forward for Wigan Athletic, so it's about time you got used to it.' She paused. 'I'm only telling you as a friend.'

'Thanks a lot,' Annie said bitterly. Why did people think that gave them the right to deliver such devastating insults? As far as she was concerned, 'I'm only telling you as a friend' rated as almost the worst seven words in the English language. Just ahead of 'Don't worry it will soon grow back' and, shortly behind, 'I just thought you ought to know . . .'

That was what Suzy Carrington had said just before she broke the news that she had stolen her husband. Annie could still picture her standing in the kitchen, holding the cup of coffee that she had just made for her, her blue eyes wide and earnest in her porcelain-pretty face. She'd made it sound as if she was doing Annie a favour, telling her. What she didn't say was that the whole story would be appearing in Nigel Dempster the following morning, alongside a photo of Max and Suzy hand in hand slipping out of Joe Allen's together, and a hideously unflattering one of Annie when she played Lady Macbeth, plastered in heavy white make-up and looking about a hundred and fifty.

Later that day Max had slunk home, packed a bag and moved out of the house, leaving a huge gap in their wardrobe and an even bigger one in her heart. Annie cringed to think how she'd begged and pleaded with him not to go, how she'd clung to him, tearfully promising to change, to do anything he wanted, as long as he didn't leave her. All the while Max had gone on emptying his cupboards, stony-faced, not even looking at her.

That night he and Suzy had escaped to her father's house in Provence, leaving Annie to cope alone with the hordes of press men camping in her tiny front garden, trampling her herbaceous border and poking their zoom lenses through the letter-box.

For a full forty-eight hours she had crouched on the bed, whimpering with terror as she listened to the hammering on the door, hugging her knees under her chin, afraid to move because it hurt so much.

It was two days before she could summon the strength to venture downstairs, by which time a fresh scandal had broken and the paparazzi had scooted off to stake out an MP who'd been having an affair with a teenage call-girl in Hackney.

Gradually, moving slowly and painfully, she'd started to

get on with her daily life. She'd put the phone back on the hook. She'd done her best to reassure her anxious parents down in Sussex that she wasn't about to kill herself and that there was no need for them to catch the next train to London. The last thing she needed was to spend a week putting on a brave face when she was dying inside.

It had taken her two weeks to pluck up the nerve to go to the supermarket. Asking her to go to a party was like inviting an agoraphobic to a beach barbecue.

'Annie? Are you still there?' Julia's voice rang out on the other end of the phone. 'I'll expect you at nine, shall I?'

'Do what you like, I'm not coming,' Annie said sulkily.

'You won't forget, will you? The Mortimer Gallery at nine. I'll bike your invitation round to you.'

'I told you, I'm not coming.'

Julia sighed. 'If you don't, you can find yourself another bloody agent.'

'Suits me.'

There was a long pause. 'Actually, I think I might bring along one of my cast-off men after all,' Julia said. 'A decent, uncomplicated one-night stand with a real man might be just what you need. Maybe then you'll realise what you've been missing, married to that self-centred bastard all these years.'

'Julia –'

'I'll see you at nine.' She laughed and rang off.

Chapter 2

Alex Wingate's parties were legendary, at least to the readers of *Hello!* magazine and anyone who cared whether they were invited to them. Wingate Management was one of the biggest theatrical agencies in the country. Every summer Alex threw what he called with ironic modesty a 'little office bash' for his clients. But this was no run-of-the-mill office party: the guest list included directors, producers, Hollywood megastars who happened to be in town, plus anyone Alex wanted to poach from other agencies. This was where influential people met, talked and did their deals. Stratospheric careers had been launched over the champagne and canapés. It was a standing joke in the business that Wingate's party could start phones ringing all over the West End by the next morning.

No wonder invitations were difficult to come by. But Julia, of course, had managed to pull a few strings and wangle a couple.

Annie wished she hadn't bothered as, under the watchful eye of the cloakroom attendant, she reapplied her lipstick for the third time. She'd been hiding out in the

Ladies for so long she'd almost become rooted to the polished marble tiles.

The party was exactly the nightmare she'd feared it would be. It was being held in a fashionable Mayfair art gallery, very minimalist and monochrome on a Japanese theme. Oriental waiters, dressed in black, moved through the room with the swift, silent intent of Ninja assassins armed with trays of sushi.

Because she was so terrified of walking into a crowded room, Annie had deliberately got there early. But as soon as she arrived she'd realised the tactical error she'd made. At least in a crowd she could pass unnoticed. As she walked into that vast, echoing white space, her Doc Martens squeaking on the polished maple floor, all eyes turned to follow her. They went on following her as she grabbed a drink from a passing tray and fled to the loo.

And there she stayed. Her pounding heart had slowed down, but her sense of foreboding was still there.

Why had she ever agreed to come? At the time it seemed less exhausting than a full-scale argument with Julia. Now she was beginning to wish she'd stuck to her guns and stayed at home. She didn't want the bloody job anyway. How could she ever hope to win Max back when she was two hundred miles up the A1? And that's what she wanted to do, although she would never admit it to Julia. Julia would just tell her he wasn't worth it, or that she was wasting her time. All of which she already knew, but it didn't stop her clinging to that last shred of hope, like a *Titanic* survivor holding on to a lump of wreckage in a freezing ocean.

Julia kept talking about her rebuilding her life, but as far as she was concerned, she didn't want a life without Max.

Annie jumped as the door opened and a thin Sloaney

type came in. From beyond, the sound of laughter grated across her exposed nerves. She probably wouldn't get the job anyway. This director would take one look at her and decide she was too tall, or too gawky, or just too suicidal-looking for a merry romantic comedy. And he'd be right. She stared gloomily at her reflection. And she was dressed all wrong. Why hadn't Julia warned her everyone else would be sporting the understated designer look? Not that it would have made much difference, since she didn't own anything designer or understated. But in her dark-green velvet hippy-chic dress and jangling ethnic jewellery she stood out among the Amanda Wakeleys like a morris dancer at a funeral.

She offered the cloakroom attendant an ingratiating smile. The woman glared back, her meaty arms folded across her chest, as if she suspected Annie might at any moment try to make off with the paper towels, or attempt a smash-and-grab raid on the condom machine.

Behind her the toilet flushed and the Sloane emerged. Suddenly the cloakroom attendant underwent a dramatic transformation, smiling and fawning. 'Perfume, madam?' she asked. 'We have quite a selection.' Elbowing Annie aside, she threw open the door of the cupboard and drew out a tray full of goodies that looked like a small-scale version of Harrods' perfumery department.

'No, thanks.' The woman sent them all a dismissive look, dropped a pound coin in the saucer and headed off back to the party. Annie smiled again at the cloakroom attendant. Again, she glared back.

Annie's shoulders slumped. God, what chance did she have of networking when she couldn't even get the loo attendant to like her?

She jammed the top back on her lipstick and dropped it

into her bag. She didn't have to do this. She could just walk out and go home. In half an hour she could be watching *Inspector Morse* and eating cold rice pudding out of the tin.

'Bugger it,' she said out loud. Alarmed, the attendant took a step backwards. Annie seized her opportunity, lunged at the perfume display and gave herself a generous spritz of Escape.

Very appropriate under the circumstances, she thought, making for the door.

The room had filled up while she'd been lurking in the Ladies. She got halfway across the room and stopped dead. There was Julia, standing by the entrance, looking sharply elegant in a cream Jasper Conran trouser-suit, her shiny blonde bob swinging as she chatted to a man.

The dreaded director, no doubt. Annie studied the back of his head. Bulbous, balding and hunched inside a rather nasty houndstooth-check jacket. Her heart plummeted to her DMs. She didn't need to go any closer to know that he would have damp, sweating palms and eyes that would spend the whole evening searching out her cleavage like a heat-seeking missile.

Not that it mattered. He could have had the body of a love god and she still wouldn't be able to face him.

Annie swiped another glass from a passing Ninja waiter and tried to work out her next move. She'd never get past Julia's eagle eye. In fact, she'd probably situated herself by the door for that very reason. She searched the room for another route. Should she sidle around the room until she got on Julia's blind side, then make a dash for the door? Too risky. Should she create a diversion? She shuddered. Just what she wanted to avoid.

Or should she just approach Julia and say, straight out,

16

'Sorry, I've changed my mind'? That would be the sensible, grown-up thing to do. She dismissed it instantly.

Then she saw that a pair of fire-exit doors, discreetly masked by a Japanese paper screen, had been left half open to let in the warm summer air. With another quick glance around the room to make sure no one was watching, Annie edged towards them and slipped behind the screen.

She found herself amid the overflowing dustbins in a narrow back alley. She leaned against the wall, the balmy evening breeze cooling her face. The sound of crashing plates and pots came from the open back door of the Italian restaurant opposite, mingling with the impatient noise of the busy West End traffic streaming past the end of the alleyway.

Annie sighed with pleasure and relief. Alone at last.

She searched in her bag for a cigarette to calm her nerves. She found the packet, then delved again for her lighter. It wasn't there. She trawled through the mire of old bus tickets, Tampax, festering sweeties and other assorted gunge at the bottom of her bag, muttering under her breath.

'Allow me.' There was a soft click and a tiny flame flickered towards her.

Annie hesitated for a moment. A mugger? Not in a designer suit, surely. 'Um . . . thanks.' She leaned towards the lighter.

'Annie? Annie Mitchell?' His voice was deep, husky and strangely familiar.

Annie jerked back so quickly she nearly singed her eyebrow on the stranger's lighter. 'Who –'

'Don't tell me you don't remember me?'

Of course she remembered. The voice might have eluded her, but those eyes didn't. They were as dark as sloes, warm, kind and, at that moment, on the verge of laughter. She could already see the faint crinkles forming at the corners the way they always used to.

'Hello, Annie,' said Nick Ryan, the man she'd jilted six years previously.

Chapter 3

Talk about out of the frying pan! Annie looked at him in horror. Performing a naked one-woman conga through the party crowd couldn't be as embarrassing as this.

Her brain groped for some appropriate greeting. But what could you say to the man you'd abandoned to run off with someone else? 'Long time no see' was a bit flippant under the circumstances.

He put her out of her misery. 'Small world.'

Annie squinted up at his white teeth, glinting in the fading light. Was he smiling, or just baring them? She gulped. 'Isn't it?'

'So are you with Wingate Management, then?'

'You must be joking! My agent would kill me if I ever left her.' Actually, Julia would probably kill her anyway, after tonight. 'Er – how about you?'

Nick shook his head. 'I'm just here to rub shoulders with the rich and famous, like everyone else.'

'Ah. Right.' The embarrassed silence between them lengthened. God, this was painful.

'Do you still want that light?'

She looked up, startled. 'Sorry?'

'For your cigarette.' She followed his gaze to the ciggie

she'd been nervously pleating between her fingers. Shit. And it was her last one.

As if he'd read her thoughts, Nick drew out a packet of Marlboros from his pocket. 'Here. Have one of mine,' he offered.

'Thanks.' As he leaned forward to light it for her, Annie couldn't resist giving him a quick once-over. He didn't look like the Nick she'd once known. The Scruffy Out of Work Actor Look had given way to the Man Who Can Afford Casual but Probably Expensive Italian Linen Suits Look. Even his tousled dark hair had been tamed with an expert trim. But as he glanced up and met her gaze she caught a glimpse of the old Nick. Those dark eyes, that strong-featured face, the shadowing of stubble around his jawline, that faint, irresistible citrus smell of his aftershave . . .

The last time she'd seen him he'd just splurged his life savings on a couple of one-way tickets to New York. But on the day they were supposed to be flying out to start their new life she'd married someone else.

She looked away guiltily and took a quick, nervous puff on her cigarette. 'I'm trying to give them up,' she gabbled. 'I've started limiting them to after meals.'

'And does it work?'

'Oh, yes. Except I'm on twenty meals a day now.' Oh, God, why did she always make stupid jokes when she was nervous?

Nick's dark eyes crinkled. 'Same old Annie,' he said softly. 'So what are you doing with yourself these days?'

'Oh, you know. This and that.'

'Still acting?'

'When I can get the work. That's why I'm here,

actually.' She could feel herself gabbling again. 'My agent is trying to fix me up with some rep company.'

'You don't sound too keen?'

'Hardly!' She curled her lip. 'I'm only here to keep her happy.'

She glanced up at him from under her lashes. It was quite disturbing, meeting up with him again after all these years. She could feel the burden of what she'd done to him like a great weight on her shoulders, making it difficult for her to look him in the eye.

Yet once they'd been really close. So close that there was even a time when Annie thought they might have become more than friends. Maybe they would have, if Max hadn't come along.

They had met seven years ago when Annie, fresh out of drama school, had joined Nick's community theatre company. Although 'company' was perhaps too strong a word for half a dozen actors who bummed around the country in a beaten-up old van, performing Shakespeare workshops in schools.

They all knew they were never going to get rich or famous doing it. They were supposed to split the profits, but after they'd paid for petrol there was usually hardly any left. Often they were so broke they had to sleep in the back of the van, curling up among the diesel-scented tarpaulins and scenery flats. But they'd laughed a lot and it was good experience. Annie had only joined to get her Equity card. But she ended up staying for nearly a year. Mainly because of Nick.

He was four years older than her and good-looking in a casual sort of way. But they were never lovers. It was difficult to become intimate with someone when you were sharing the back of a battered old Bedford van with four other people every night. The others used to tease them about their closeness and Annie knew one or two of the girls were jealous. But she never thought of Nick like that. To her, he was more like a best friend. She could talk to him about anything and know he'd understand. They'd lie awake on warm summer nights, talking, laughing, sharing their dreams while the others snored in the back of the van.

It was hearing Sinatra singing 'New York, New York' late one night on the van's crackly radio on the way down the M6 that gave them the idea to seek their fortunes in the States. Somehow Broadway seemed more glamorous than the West End.

They planned it all. They would head for New York, find a cheap apartment and get stop-gap jobs to support themselves until they found acting work.

And then along came the *Pericles* tour. Annie hadn't wanted to take the job, but her new agent had cajoled her into it. 'It's about time you did some proper acting,' Julia had said scathingly. 'Doing Ophelia to a bunch of sixth formers isn't going to get your name in lights.'

Ironically it was Nick who finally persuaded her to do it. As he pointed out, in three months she would have saved enough to tide them over for their first few weeks in the States. So they made a deal. She would take the job, go on tour and save her money. Meanwhile Nick would use his savings to buy the plane tickets. As soon as she came home they would be off.

Except she never came home. She met Max, fell in love and married him instead.

Cowardly to the end, she couldn't face Nick with the truth. Instead she'd sent him an invitation to the wedding.

He'd sent it back with a barbed refusal and their paths hadn't crossed since. Until tonight.

'So – er – are you still acting?' she asked.

Nick shook his head. 'I gave up that idea years ago. I'm more on the technical side now.' He smiled wryly. 'Let's face it, I was never going to make it as an actor.'

'But you were really good.'

'No, I wasn't. Six months out of work in New York soon cured me of any illusions I might have had.' He glanced at her. 'You were the one with all the talent, as I recall.'

Annie felt herself blushing. 'So are you still living in the States?'

'I was, until last week. I've got a new job over here.' He looked her up and down. 'You're looking great, by the way. How's married life?'

She opened her mouth, then closed it again. Of course, Nick wouldn't know about her break-up. So all encompassing was her pain that she somehow imagined it must show on her face. 'Fine,' she lied. 'Absolutely fine.'

They stood in awkward silence. Annie contemplated the glowing tip of her cigarette, willing it to burn faster. 'I like your suit,' she said at last.

'Thanks. My wife bought it for me. She said she'd rather I looked fashionably crumpled than just plain scruffy.'

But Annie wasn't listening. 'Your wife? You got married?'

'Don't look so surprised.' Nick grinned ruefully. 'I'm not that bad, am I?'

'No! Not at all. It's just – I can't imagine you with a wife.'

'Actually, I'm divorced. Nearly two years ago now.'

'Oh, I'm sorry.'

Nick shrugged. 'It was fairly amicable. Elizabeth's married to a doctor in Connecticut now. She seemed very happy last time I saw her.'

Annie's jaw dropped. 'You still see her?'

'Occasionally,' Nick said. 'Most of the time we phone, or write. She and Gil are hoping to come over, once I'm settled in my new place.'

Annie searched for signs of hidden anguish, some tell-tale glint in his eye that told her he would really like to drop-kick this Gil character's head off his shoulders. She couldn't see any.

Was there really such a thing as an amicable separation, she wondered? Would she ever reach the point where she could mention Max's and Suzy's names in the same breath without wanting to burst into tears? She could certainly never see herself exchanging Christmas cards or, heaven forbid, going round for a cosy dinner at their Chelsea love nest.

'Actually, Max and I —' She stopped. She couldn't tell him. Not now. Five minutes ago she'd been boasting everything was rosy. 'Actually, Max and I are very happy,' she finished, realising how awful and smug it sounded, especially after Nick had just been talking about his divorce. 'Very, very happy,' she added, unable to stop herself.

'Good for you.' Nick looked at her strangely.

Another silence. 'So you're not interested in this rep job, then?' he said finally. 'I thought you enjoyed working in the theatre.'

'That depends.' She stuck out her chin. 'If it were the West End I might consider it.'

'And there speaks a girl who once played Juliet in a

rugby club beer tent!' He grinned. 'Do you know, I can never watch the balcony scene without thinking of you dodging those empty lager cans.'

She smiled reluctantly. 'Why do you think I don't want to go back to it?'

Just then the back door of the Italian restaurant was flung open by one of the cooks, filling the warm evening air with the scent of garlic and flooding the gloomy alleyway with light. It was like the moment at the school dance when all the lights went on and you were confronted with the acne-ridden specimen you'd been canoodling with all evening. Annie stole a quick glance at Nick's rugged profile. If this had been a school dance, she thought, she wouldn't have been too disappointed.

The cook emptied a bowlful of vegetable peelings into the dustbin and retreated back inside, plunging them into darkness once more.

'Well,' Nick said briskly, 'I suppose I'd better be making a move.'

'You're not going back to the party?'

'I don't think there's much point in hanging around. Besides, I've got an early start in the morning.' He glanced at his watch, then at her. 'How about you? Shouldn't you go in and tell your agent you've changed your mind about that job?'

'No, thanks.' Annie shuddered. 'If Julia's going to tell me off, I'd rather be on the other end of a telephone.'

'In that case, can I offer you a lift home?'

She hesitated. 'I wouldn't want to put you to any trouble. I can easily catch the tube —'

'It's no trouble. My car's just around the corner.'

Why did I think this was a good idea, Annie wondered, as

the gleaming BMW made its way across Vauxhall Bridge. She sat rigidly upright, her hands knotted in her lap. She stared at the moonlight on the Thames and trawled her brain for something useful to say. Something that wouldn't touch on the last six years and all that had gone before. 'Nice car,' she said finally.

'Isn't it? It's only hired, unfortunately. But I could certainly get used to it.'

'It's got a lot of – er – buttons and things.'

'God knows what half of them do. But I did find this one.' Nick flicked a switch on the impressive-looking console and the sexy, smoky sound of Aretha Franklin drifted out. 'What do you think?' he asked.

She thought she'd like to close her eyes, sink into the soft leather seat and let the sheer luxury of it all wash over her. But she didn't. 'Very nice. It's certainly a lot better than that old heap you used to drive –' She closed her eyes. Oh, God, why did she say that?

Nick smiled. 'Your taste wasn't much better, I seem to remember. What about that ghastly old VW you had? It was forever conking out on you.'

It still is, Annie said silently, thinking of Beryl the Beetle which was at that moment rusting away quietly outside her house.

She cleared her throat. 'So – er – where are you living now you're back in England?'

'I'm kind of between addresses at the moment. I'm staying with a friend until I move into my new place. Do you remember Rob Masters?'

Of course I remember him, she was about to exclaim. Then her mouth closed like a trap. 'Can't say I do,' she mumbled.

'You must know Rob. We started up the theatre

26

company together. Tall, skinny guy? A bit hippyish. It was his old van we –'

'Doesn't ring any bells.' Annie cut him off abruptly. Just to press home the point, she leaned across and turned Aretha's volume up.

Nick's jaw was clenched, although whether this was from annoyance or because he was negotiating the Wandsworth one-way system she couldn't be sure.

Annie had her key in her hand by the time they pulled up outside the terraced cottage. Without thinking, she glanced up at the windows, looking as she always did for the light that would tell her Max was home. The little house slumbered in darkness under its shaggy ramparts of clematis.

She stifled a sigh. 'Well, thanks for the lift. I'd invite you in for coffee –' But I can't wait to get away from you, she added silently.

'No problem. It's getting late.' He peered out of the windscreen. 'Nice place,' he remarked. 'It must be great at this time of year, being so close to the river.'

'We like it.' She groped around in the darkness for the door handle.

'I see you've still got that car.'

'Yes, well, it's more out of pity these days. I can't sell her and I can't bring myself to send her to the scrapyard. She's like an ageing relative I've been saddled with.' At last! She found the door handle and yanked at it. Nothing happened.

'Here, let me.' Nick leaned across and lifted the lock. Annie shrank away as his arm brushed hers. He turned his face towards her, until she could feel his warm breath fanning her cheek. He's going to kiss me, she thought in panic.

The next moment the door was open, Nick was back in his seat and Annie was wondering if she'd imagined the whole thing.

'Well, it was nice seeing you again,' he said calmly.

'And you.' She got out of the car and looked up at the little house, with its dark windows. Suddenly she had a horrible vision of herself, huddled in her dressing-gown, watching *Newsnight* all alone. Just her and Jeremy Paxman.

'Nick!' He was pulling away from the kerb. She flung herself at the car and wrenched the door open. He slammed on the brake so hard she would have been catapulted on to the bonnet if she hadn't been clinging to the handle.

He leaned across, his face pale in the lamplight. 'Christ, Annie, you certainly know how to get someone's attention. What is it?'

'I was just wondering –' She did her best to sound casual. 'Maybe you'd like coffee after all?'

Chapter 4

'Won't Max mind?' Nick asked.

'Max doesn't care what I do.' That was the truth, at any rate. 'The sitting-room's through here.'

As Annie flicked on the lamp she remembered the mess she'd left behind. She saw the room through Nick's eyes, littered with coffee cups and discarded chocolate wrappers. On the coffee table an unfinished bowl of cereal provided an attractive centrepiece.

'Sorry about the mess.' She rescued a banana skin from behind the cushion just as Nick sat down. 'Max is away at the moment, so I've let the housework slide. Well, not so much a slide as an avalanche, really.' She smiled apologetically.

'It looks very – lived in.' Nick's gaze roamed around the room, then stopped abruptly when it reached the corner. 'My God, what's that?' he said, staring at *Freedom*. It was looking particularly gruesome, the lamplight striking off its many sharp angles.

Annie stuck out her chin defensively. 'It belongs to Max. It's Art.'

'It looks like a road accident.'

'It's a very significant new work.' Annie parroted Max's own words. 'It's a shocking metaphor of –'

'It's shocking, all right.' Nick frowned at her. 'Don't tell you me you actually like it?'

'Of course.' Since it was Max's she was prepared to defend it as if it were her first-born.

'Then you two must really be made for each other.'

'We are. We're happy. Very, very happy,' she said firmly.

'So you keep telling me.'

She caught the sardonic glint in his eyes, and felt herself blushing. 'I'll make that coffee,' she mumbled and fled.

In the kitchen she put the kettle on and stood for a while to collect herself. What was she doing? She didn't want Nick here. She didn't want anyone. She liked being alone. She didn't have to smile, or pretend to function. She could slob around on the sofa, eating junk food and wallowing in her own self-pity.

And even if she did want company there were plenty of friends she could call on. She certainly didn't need Nick Ryan. She couldn't look at him without feeling swamped with guilt. More than that, he reminded her of how incredibly, over the moon in love she and Max had once been.

Like every other female in the *Pericles* company, Annie had developed a huge crush on Max Kennedy. But she never dreamed he'd look at her twice. He was everything she wasn't – outspoken, self-assured, extremely ambitious. He had a gorgeous body, irresistible faded-blue eyes, a devastatingly sexy smile and the kind of aristocratic cheek-bones most women would go under the knife for. He also had an entourage of beautiful women whom he treated with casual neglect. He was always taking calls from some frustrated, abandoned girlfriend on his mobile. Occasionally one would turn up tearfully at the stage door to confront him. Depending on his mood, Max would either whisk them off to bed or instruct the stage doorkeeper to turn them away.

'Scenes are so boring,' he'd drawl in that world-weary way of his. Annie would be torn between pity for them and quiet satisfaction that there was one less rival to worry about.

She was determined not to make a fool of herself. Worried that her every move and glance might give her away, she steered clear of him. After each performance she would scurry back to her digs, avoiding the clique that drifted down to the pub for last orders. Little did she realise that her unwitting indifference was just the kind of behaviour guaranteed to pique Max's interest. He wasn't used to women turning their backs on him. He was intrigued.

Annie never imagined anything would happen between them. She was playing Marina to his Lysimachus but, despite refusing to surrender her virginity to him on-stage every night, she was stunned and delighted when it happened for real in a grotty seafront hotel in Brighton.

From that moment she was lost. She had never been so hopelessly and passionately in love before. It almost hurt. She couldn't eat, she couldn't sleep. Sometimes, when Max was on the phone to one of his female friends, or flirting with one of the other women in the cast, she could hardly breathe. One minute her emotions were soaring and she felt light-headed with happiness that he wanted her, the next she was writhing in a pit of black despair, terrified of losing him. For the first time in her life she found herself feeling jealous of every woman who crossed his path.

Max did little to ease her agony. He could see what she was going through, but he carried on flirting and teasing regardless. Sometimes she wondered if he got some kind of perverse satisfaction from seeing her suffer. She longed for him to give up his other women, but she didn't have the courage to ask him. She knew how Max hated possessiveness and the last thing she wanted was to be seen as clingy.

And then, one night in Bath, Nick turned up. The curtain had just come down and Annie was in her dressing-room taking off her make-up when the stage doorkeeper called.

She felt the cold grip of panic in her chest. Oh, God. This was it. The moment she'd been dreading. She'd been feeling vaguely guilty about Nick ever since she and Max got together. She had kept meaning to write to him, but it was easier not to get round to it. Now he was here and there was no putting it off any longer.

In a panic, she rushed to Max's dressing-room. She wanted advice, moral support. Most of all, she wanted him to offer to do her dirty work for her.

But he didn't. 'Just don't see him,' he said flatly.

'But I've got to,' Annie reasoned. 'I promised I'd go to America with him. He's bought the tickets. I owe him an explanation, at least.'

'You don't owe him anything. You and I are together now. That's all there is to it.'

He turned away and she stared in frustration at the back of his head. It might be that simple for Max, who discarded girlfriends like other people threw away paper hankies. But she'd never been in this situation before. Nick was her friend and she didn't want to hurt him.

'Couldn't you come with me?' she pleaded.

'God, no! I'm not going anywhere near him. And I don't think you should either.' He reached for his cigarettes and lit one up. 'You know what will happen, darling. He'll make you feel guilty and the next thing you know you'll be right back where he wants you, in that grubby little theatre group.'

'That won't happen,' Annie said, but Max wasn't listening.

'You're too good for him,' he drawled. 'Anyone can see he's going nowhere. He even has to put on his own tinpot little shows because no one will employ him.'

His laughter grated. She might not love Nick the way she loved Max, but he deserved her loyalty. 'It's not like that. He runs that theatre group because he believes in it. He likes to have artistic control.'

'Well, he's certainly got control of you, hasn't he?' Max's eyes narrowed. 'The way you're talking, anyone would think you had the hots for him.'

'I don't!' Annie protested. 'I just want to be fair –'

'What about being fair to me?' His voice rose. 'You say you love me, but the minute this guy turns up you're falling over yourself to see him.'

'That's not true.'

'Prove it.' He snatched up his mobile and thrust it into her face. 'Send him away.'

'I can't –'

'You mean you won't.' He sent the phone skittering across his dressing-table. 'So bloody well go to him, if that's what you want.'

He gazed moodily at his reflection in the mirror.

Annie stared at him, shocked. Then it dawned on her. 'You're jealous,' she whispered.

'So what if I am?' He jabbed his cigarette out on the dressing-table, not caring that he missed the ashtray. 'Look, this isn't bloody easy for me. You know I hate possessiveness. I just never thought I'd feel like this myself.' He glared at her. 'I love you. I'm scared of losing you. And I know that's what will happen if you see him again. Okay?'

It was the first time he'd ever shown how he really felt and it was as if a great bubble had suddenly exploded in her chest, filling her with so much warmth and happiness she could hardly breathe. 'It won't happen,' she said gently, reaching for his hand. Max's fingers closed around hers. 'But I've got to talk to him,' she pleaded. 'He's come all this way —'

The hand was quickly withdrawn. Annie suddenly felt cold, as if he'd taken his love away too.

'Go, then,' he snapped. 'Bugger off to America with him.'

'Max —' She stood for a moment, staring at his stubbornly turned back. Then, with a defeated sigh, she turned away.

She was almost at the door when Max said, 'Marry me.'

He whispered it so quietly she stopped dead, wondering if she'd really heard him. Slowly she turned to face him.

'Marry me,' he repeated. His blue eyes searched hers. 'Please?'

Somehow, after that, Nick just didn't seem important any more.

She was just spooning out the coffee when the phone

rang, followed a moment later by her own cheery voice inviting the caller to leave a message.

It was bound to be Julia, calling to give her an earful for not turning up. That particular conversation could wait until morning.

Then she heard Max's familiar drawl on the machine and a surge of panic ran through her. Dropping the spoon, she ran into the living-room. But it was too late. Before she could reach the answer-machine, Max was already announcing loud and clear that he would be round to pick up the rest of his stuff the following day.

'I think it's best if you're not around when I get there,' he concluded. 'We don't want another scene like last time, do we?'

She couldn't bring herself to look at Nick. Instead she kept her gaze fixed on the answer-machine long after the message had clicked off, staring hard at the tiny flashing red light.

'Why didn't you tell me?' Nick broke the silence.

'There's nothing to tell.' She forced a shrug. 'It's – it's just a temporary separation. No big deal.'

'When did he leave?'

'A couple of weeks ago. I can't remember.' Annie shook her hair back impatiently. 'Like I said, it's no big deal.' She turned away and fled back to the kitchen.

Chapter 5

There was a bottle of brandy somewhere, long buried at the back of a kitchen cupboard. Annie clawed her way among the bottled fruits and jars of pasta sauce and dug it out. Sod the coffee. She needed something stronger. She dusted off the bottle, sloshed some brandy into a glass and downed it in one.

'Oh, my God!' She clutched her throat as the first fiery mouthful seared its way down her windpipe, making her gasp for breath. She stopped spluttering, wiped her streaming eyes on her sleeve and topped up her glass defiantly.

She slumped against the cupboard door. So now it was official. Her life couldn't get any worse. Not only did Nick know that Max had abandoned her, he also thought she was a compulsive liar and mentally unhinged into the bargain.

Screwing her eyes shut, Annie took another gulp of the brandy. Actually, it wasn't so bad once she got used to it. The first lot must have burned away her throat lining, so this went down quite easily, spreading a pleasant warmth through her limbs and bringing barely a tear to her eye.

She peered into the depths of her glass, distracted for a

moment from the terrible mess that was her life. She couldn't face Nick. If she stayed here long enough, perhaps he'd take the hint and go away.

No such luck.

'Annie?'

She sensed him standing there in the doorway behind her. 'Go away.'

'Does this mean I don't get my coffee?'

'There's an all-night café on the corner if you're that desperate.' She didn't move. Neither did Nick. 'Look, I just want to be alone, okay?'

'So you can drink yourself into a stupor? I don't think that's going to help.'

'Well, I do.' She poured another brandy, threw back her head defiantly and gulped the lot. It went down with barely a shudder this time. She was getting good at this.

She could feel Nick watching her with disapproval. 'So I take it this isn't just a temporary separation?' he said at last.

'No, it isn't. He's gone. For good. With my best friend, if you must know.' She fired out every word like bullets from a gun.

That shocked him. 'Jesus,' he whispered. 'I'm sorry. Why didn't you tell me?'

She stared down at his well-polished brogues. 'I don't know,' she admitted. 'Maybe I just wanted to go on pretending for a little while longer. Or perhaps I was afraid you'd laugh.'

'Why should I do that?'

'Because I deserve it.' She forced herself to look at him. 'I did the same to you, didn't I? I let you down when I went off with Max. What goes around comes around and all that.'

Nick ran his hand through his dark hair, so it stood up in cropped spikes. 'Let me get this straight,' he said slowly. 'You reckon I could get some kind of satisfaction out of seeing you suffer, just because you dumped me?'

Annie looked into her glass. 'Why not? I couldn't blame you, after what I did.'

'But that was years ago. I'd have to lead a pretty sad and empty life to harbour a grudge against you for all this time.'

Annie scuffed her boots on the polished wood floor. Put like that it did seem slightly foolish. 'But we were going to America,' she said. 'You'd bought the tickets and everything –'

'Yes and I was pretty pissed off when you didn't turn up. But do you really think I'd spend six years brooding over it?' He shook his head. 'Life goes on, Annie.'

She pushed her hair uncertainly out of her eyes. 'So everyone keeps telling me.'

Annie settled back into the squashy comfort of her sofa and topped up her glass again, marvelling at how steady her hand seemed, considering the paralysis creeping up her arm. The hellish fire of the brandy had faded quickly into an agreeable warmth, which spread through her limbs, giving her an inner glow.

It was nice to have someone to talk to, she reflected, beaming at Nick across the room. Someone who actually wanted to listen. Most of her friends had got so bored with her pouring out her troubles that now they either changed the subject or just left the room whenever Max's name was mentioned.

Not that she really needed anyone around when she wanted to talk. She could unburden herself emotionally to a plant stand if she was desperate enough. When it came to her marriage break-up, Annie knew she could bore for England.

But Nick was really interested. At least he *seemed* interested. Although after all that brandy it was difficult to see whether his eyes had glazed over or not. Annie squinted at him. It was hard to make out if he even had eyes any more.

She'd already given him the full, unexpurgated story of how Max and Suzy had gone on that *Separate Tables* tour. How she'd fretted about him being away, how she'd even begged Suzy to keep an eye on him for her.

'I might have known,' she muttered. 'It was like asking a wolf to watch over a flock of sheep.' And Max was like a lamb to the slaughter.

Everyone knew, it seemed, except her. Max had come home every weekend with a bag full of dirty socks and underwear, and she'd never suspected a thing. Until the tour ended.

Annie had spent all day planning a special romantic evening to welcome him home. She had Marks & Spencer beef *medallions* in the oven, Krug in the fridge and a sensational La Perla bustier under her dress when Suzy turned up. Alone.

Even then she'd been stupidly blind. She'd made Suzy a cup of coffee and settled down for a gossip, never imagining that the juicy titbit her friend had to tell her was about her own husband.

Nick listened to the whole sorry story. Although he might have been nodding off, she couldn't really be sure.

'It's my fault. I shouldn't have let him go.'

'You weren't to know,' Nick said.

'That's just it,' Annie insisted. 'I did know.' In her heart of hearts she had always known. Just as she'd always known it was only sheer fluke that had won her Max in the first place. And she also knew it was only a matter of time before someone more worthy claimed him.

She just never imagined it would be her best friend.

Strange, really, when she'd been so watchful of other women throughout their marriage, that she should ignore the danger on her own doorstep. She remembered Suzy's pole-axed expression when she met Max for the first time. Up until then, Suzy had always been the one with the fabulous boyfriends. At drama school she was known as the Gorgeous Blonde. Annie was Her Friend. Tall, gawky and tawny-haired, Annie had felt she was destined for a lifetime of blind dates with the friends of whichever Adonis happened to be after Suzy at the time.

But then along came Max and suddenly it was as if, in the Great Game Show of Love, Annie had swanned off with the holiday in St Lucia, while Suzy had been left with the Crackerjack pencil.

She took a steadying gulp of her drink. She could feel herself sliding dangerously towards self-pity. 'I've always known I'd lose him in the end. He was so sexy and gorgeous –'

'Really? He sounds a bit of a bastard to me.'

Annie's head jerked back. 'How can you say that? You don't even know him.'

'I know any man who can sleep with his wife's best friend is hardly going to be an all-round nice guy.'

'It was her fault. She lured him into it.'

'I don't suppose he took much luring. Seems like he was about as hard to get as a flu bug.'

Annie ignored him. 'You don't know what she's like,' she protested. 'Max didn't stand a chance.'

She took another swig of her drink. When it came to men, her career or anything else, 'No' wasn't a word in Suzy's limited vocabulary. That fluffy blonde exterior hid a steely inner core. She was like a lump of granite wrapped in candyfloss.

'She's beautiful. And successful. How can I compete with that?'

'You could be successful too, if you wanted to be.' Annie noticed with a touch of annoyance that he didn't mention the beautiful bit. 'You've got tons of talent.'

'I'd rather be gorgeous,' she muttered into her glass.

'You are.'

'Oh, please!'

'I mean it. Any man would fancy you.'

She squinted at him across the room, just to make sure he wasn't making fun of her. His gaze was as direct and honest as she'd always remembered. She could feel herself blushing. 'Thanks,' she whispered. But as she lifted her drink, her hand was shaking so much the glass rattled against her teeth. 'You too. Not that men would fancy you, of course,' she added hastily. 'I mean they might, but I'm not saying you're gay or anything. Not that there's anything wrong with being gay, but –'

'I know what you mean.' Nick grinned as she floundered helplessly.

I'm bloody glad someone does, Annie thought, crashing the bottle against her glass as she refilled it. It was true what they said about brandy being good in a crisis. Very calming and relaxing. In fact, she was so relaxed she was in danger of sliding off the sofa and straight into a coma under the coffee table.

She stared across at Nick, trying to focus on him. He

seemed to have sprouted three wavering heads. And none of them was drinking. 'Drink up,' she encouraged.

'I'm driving.'

'Oh. Oh well, that means more for me.'

'Don't you think you've had enough?'

'God no. There's still tons left.' She held up the bottle and squinted into it.

'That doesn't mean you have to drink it all.'

'I'm drowning my sorrows,' she told him huffily.

'I reckon they're well and truly drowned by now, don't you?'

'Actually, no,' she said. 'They're just coming up for air again. My sorrows are very strong swimmers, if you must know. Every time I think I've drowned the little buggers they surface again.'

'I see.' Nick smiled once more. He had a wonderful, warm smile, she reflected squiffily. And gorgeous eyes, very dark and soulful. She racked her brains, trying to remember if they were brown or very dark grey. In her current state she couldn't even remember what colour her own eyes were.

And Nick listened. He'd always been a good listener. Not like Max, who would rather have undergone colonic irrigation than discuss matters of the heart. In fact, all their most meaningful conversations had been conducted with him safely hidden behind a copy of *The Stage*.

'How did someone like you ever end up getting divorced?' She looked round, wondering who'd had the cheek to ask such a question. And why were they shouting?

'It's a long story.'

'You can tell me if you like,' Annie offered. 'I mean,

I've been boring you all evening. Now it's your turn.' Her eyes widened. Had she really just said that?

'Some other time, maybe. Anyway, it's all ancient history now. Elizabeth and I have come out of it good friends and that's all that matters.'

'I can't imagine ever being good friends with Max.' Annie shuddered.

'I know. The emotions are too raw at the moment. But you'll get over it, I promise.'

'That's what people keep telling me. But I don't want to get over it. I just want Max!'

'Even after everything he's done?'

'I told you, it wasn't his fault.'

Nick looked as if he was about to say something, then thought better of it.

Annie finished her drink. The pleasant warm feeling was starting to give way to an alarming numbness. She could feel the paralysis spreading up through her feet. What would happen when it reached her brain?

She looked at Nick lopsidedly. He was definitely attractive, in a dark, rugged kind of way. Not like Max, of course, who was as flawlessly beautiful as a Greek god. She frowned. Was she always going to measure every man she met against him? 'I suppose you must have masses of girl-friends?' she asked.

'A few. No one serious.'

'I should never have dumped you like that.'

'Oh, I don't know. As Dear John letters go, a wedding invitation was pretty original.'

'I mean, maybe we should have stayed together. After all, we've both made a mess of our other relationships, haven't we?' Her mouth seemed to have declared UDI from her brain. It couldn't be trusted. 'Do you ever wonder what would have happened if I'd come with you to America?'

'It's not something that keeps me awake at nights.' She noticed he wasn't smiling any more, but that didn't stop her.

'Do you think we would have stayed together? It might have been fun –'

'We'll never know, will we?' Nick cut her off abruptly.

He put down his glass and stood up. Annie looked at him in panic. 'You're not going?'

'I've got to go. Like I said, I've got an early start in the morning.'

A flash of perception pierced the alcoholic fog in her brain. 'I've upset you, haven't I?' she said. 'Talking about us . . .'

'It's not a good idea to rake up the past, Annie.' So much for him still carrying a torch for her after all these years. Their brief friendship was obviously so meaningless he could hardly bring himself to think about it. She fought the urge to offer him another drink, or coffee, or anything at all to make him stay. She might be paralytic, but even she could recognise a brush-off when she saw it.

Well, if he was going she could at least be dignified about it. But as Annie hauled herself off the sofa she felt a huge rush of blood to her head and a simultaneous rush of alcohol to her legs. She turned, took a step forward, tripped over the coffee table and fell headlong towards the door. There was a painful crash, and she found herself lying dazed and confused amid a tangle of metal.

'Are you okay?' Nick's face swam into focus above her.

'I've flattened *Freedom*,' she wailed, disentangling herself with difficulty from the clawing metal arms. Max's pride and joy. He would never forgive her.

'It's about time someone did.' Nick held out his hand.

'But you don't understand.' She allowed him to haul her to her feet. 'It was Art. It was conceptual –' It also cost more than the average family saloon.

They both stood there for a moment, staring in solemn silence at the squashed jumble of metal.

'Actually, I think you've improved it,' Nick remarked at last.

Annie glanced at his twitching smile, then suddenly the absurdity of it all hit her and she started laughing too. At the same moment her legs inexplicably turned to elastic, pitching her forward into Nick's arms. They closed around her, crushing her to him. At nearly five feet nine, it took quite a man to make her feel small and fragile, but somehow he managed it.

She looked up into his face. His eyes were charcoal grey, almost black, she remembered. 'Nick?' she whispered.

He frowned down at her. 'What?'

She closed her eyes. 'Kiss me,' she said. And passed out.

Chapter 6

She woke up several hours later, sprawled across the bed, sweating and shivering in the chilly grey light of dawn, and realised she was dead.

She couldn't feel like this and still be living. Her body had been crushed by a Chieftain tank. A whole regiment of them, in fact. The regiment in question was still in her head now, doing drill practice. And, oh God, they'd been cleaning their filthy boots on her tongue.

Annie opened her eyes and wished she hadn't, as her eyeballs ricocheted around in their sockets. For a minute or two she lay, clutching her head. She would never, ever drink brandy again. In fact, she would never drink anything again. The way she felt, she would probably never move again. This was God's punishment to her for – she frowned. For what, exactly?

Slowly, painfully, she tried to piece together what had happened the night before. She remembered being stupendously drunk, of course. She remembered falling over, and Nick picking her up, and then –

Annie caught sight of her bra dangling from the bedpost and groaned. It was all coming back to her now. That kiss. She couldn't remember the actual details, but it must have been quite something because she'd passed out. She remembered coming round just as Nick was putting her – well, all right, dumping her – on the bed. She'd reached up for him, pulled him down on top of her, and they'd both collapsed in a frenzy of pent-up passion . . . Or had they?

She sat up quickly – a bad mistake, as her stomach shot to her throat like a high-speed lift – and looked around. All that remained of the previous night were her own clothes, scattered with wild abandon around the room. There was no sign of Nick.

He'd done a runner. Annie didn't blame him. She would have fled too, if some complete and utter berk had launched a drunken pass at her.

Then she spotted the note on the bedside table. It was propped up against a glass of water, beside a packet of Nurofen. Annie groped for it, her hand shaking.

'*Dear Annie,*' it said, '*thought you might need these. Nick.*'

She didn't know whether to feel relieved or just mortified. Surely the only thing worse than waking up after a one-night stand was waking up and realising you'd been turned down.

She rolled over, clutching her head and groaning with pain and misery. Not only had she failed dismally at marriage, she couldn't even manage a night of casual sex.

Julia would have been ashamed of her.

Julia, as it turned out, was more furious than ashamed. 'You blew it,' she yelled, when Annie finally summoned up the strength to answer the phone later that morning. 'For God's sake, what happened to you last night?'

'I – I couldn't make it.'

'You mean, you bottled out!'

Annie clutched her head against the verbal onslaught, too sick to fight back. A handful of Nurofen, a piece of dry toast and several cups of strong black coffee had failed to stem her relentless hangover. A feeble 'sorry' was all she could manage in her defence.

'You will be,' Julia threatened. 'And why are you mumbling? You sound like Marlon Brando.'

'I don't feel very well.'

'Well, you'd better make a quick recovery. Your audition's at eleven.'

'What audition?'

'The one I've just fixed you up with. For the rep company. You wouldn't believe the trouble I've had to go to. He practically refused to see you, after last night.'

'But I can't,' Annie croaked. 'I'm dying.'

'Nonsense. Have a stiff drink and you'll be fine.'

Annie's stomach lurched protestingly. She took a deep breath and braced herself. 'Look, Julia, I've been thinking about this and I really don't want the job –'

'I know you don't, but you need it,' Julia said. 'Besides, you owe me. I had to do a lot of heavy-duty grovelling for this. The least you can do is turn up and meet the man.'

'I suppose so.' So much for being assertive.

'At least you're thinking clearly.'

I don't know about that, Annie thought as she scribbled down the details Julia gave her.

'So what did happen to you last night?' Julia asked suddenly.

'You wouldn't believe me if I told you.'

'Let me guess. You chickened out and rushed home to your lonely marital bed with just a photo of darling Max for company.'

'Actually, I picked up a gorgeous man and brought him home.'

There was a shocked silence, then an insulting laugh rang out from the other end of the phone.

I told you you wouldn't believe me, Annie thought, putting down the receiver.

Chapter 7

It was a warm July morning outside, but the draughty church hall had all the welcoming cheer of a morgue. With its peeling paintwork and musty smell of old hymn books, it was like every other rehearsal room Annie had ever been in.

Around the room people were talking about work: discussing who was and who wasn't, comparing notes on recent auditions, gossiping about other people and furtively scribbling down potential leads in their address books. Annie, meanwhile, sat shivering on her hard plastic chair, sheltering behind her Ray-Bans and wondering if anyone would notice if she was sick into her rucksack.

In spite of endless pain-killers washed down with coffee, her monster hangover still hadn't abated. Neither had her burning sense of shame.

She couldn't help replaying last night's horrific scene over and over in her head. And every time her brain hit the rewind button, some fresh and humiliating detail appeared.

Like the way she'd toyed with the curling hair at the nape of Nick's neck as he hauled her up the stairs. And how she'd dragged him down on top of her as she lay on the bed. And the moment when he'd averted his face as she tried to kiss him.

She shifted in her seat and closed her eyes with a shudder. Her only consolation was that she would never, ever have to see him again.

'Well, of course I could go into mainstream West End if I wanted to, but I actually prefer experimental theatre.' A woman's voice sliced into her troubled thoughts. 'It's much more broadening, don't you think?'

There was a general murmur of agreement. Annie smiled to herself. She knew that, like everyone else, the woman would gladly have given up wearing bin bags and smearing herself with axle grease in the name of art for a sniff at the new Tom Stoppard.

Like most other auditions, the room was pretty evenly divided into the Haves and the Have Nots. The Haves, who already had a job or at least a couple of hopeful call-backs, exuded an air of blasé confidence, as they gossiped to each other about work. The Have Nots, whose phones had remained stubbornly silent for too long, gave off a nervous, sweating despair. Annie gazed sympathetically at the lanky young man opposite her. From his bobbing Adam's apple and the bony, white-knuckled hands clutching his CV, it was clear the only role he'd played recently was Man in Dole Queue.

Not that she looked much better. Her face had the greyish pallor of unbaked dough, in stark contrast to the huge black circles under her eyes. Her hair, which she couldn't bring herself to wash, was scraped back in a rubber band. If they'd been auditioning for one of the witches in *Macbeth* she would have walked it.

The door to the audition room opened and a woman with cropped two-tone hair and a black *Les Miserables*

T-shirt stuck her head out and announced they were running forty-five minutes late. Everyone groaned. Annie closed her eyes against the throbbing pain in her head and wondered if she had alcohol poisoning. Perhaps she would die. If so, she hoped it would be soon.

She began to day-dream that Max found out she was dead and was filled with remorse. Would alcohol poisoning be romantic enough, she wondered? Perhaps it should be something else. A lingering but rather beautiful illness, like Greta Garbo in *Camille*. Then Max could sob at her bedside while she made a touching farewell speech, bestowing love and forgiveness, while at the same time making sure he was too grief-stricken and guilty ever to go near Suzy Carrington again.

Annie frowned. What was it Garbo had in that film? Consumption, maybe? Although didn't that involve coughing up blood? She winced. Hardly romantic. She could just imagine what Max's reaction to that might be.

She moved on to her funeral. Small and dignified, yet big enough for Max to see how much she was adored, by everyone else if not by him. There would be touching eulogies from her friends. Then someone, probably Julia, would say they should be celebrating her life, not mourning her death. She'd tell some suitable anecdotes, revealing Annie's sensitive, caring side as well as her sense of humour (she would have to check these in advance, just to make sure none started with 'I remember when Annie was so pissed . . .'). Then someone else would whip out a guitar and play some heart-breaking music, everyone would sob and Suzy Carrington would become a social leper from that day on.

'Tip? I'll give you a tip, mate. Don't come via the bloody North Circular next time.' Everyone exchanged glances as heavy footsteps thudded up the stairs. Moments later the doors burst open and a diminutive figure fell through them, staggering under the weight of several Pied A Terre carriers.

'Shit,' she muttered, as the doors swung closed on her, trapping her bags. 'Shit, shit, shit!' She wrenched them impatiently, ripping the handles.

Annie blinked in recognition at the flushed angry urchin face framed by cropped black hair. It couldn't be, could it?

Who else but Caroline Wilde could make an entrance like that? Chaos was her middle name. The last year at drama school when they'd shared a flat it had been like living in a soap opera, with its relationship dramas, financial crises and general angst, not to mention a supporting cast of bastard boyfriends and eccentric relatives. The quiet life it wasn't, but it had certainly been fun.

Needless to say, Caz was one of the many aspects of her former life of which Max didn't approve. And the feeling was obviously mutual. Annie had done her best to make them like each other, but after one too many tense dinner parties even she had to admit defeat. Gradually their girls' nights out had dwindled to exchanging Christmas cards.

She'd often thought of picking up the phone and making contact again, especially since Max had walked out. But she was too afraid of what Caz's response would be.

She snatched up her magazine and ducked her head behind it, just as Caz flopped into the chair beside her. Great, just great. Now she'd have to spend the next hour hunched motionless behind *Hello!*.

'I don't know why you're bothering to hide. With that

53

hair and those legs you're about as inconspicuous as a nun on a hen night,' Caz said after about ten minutes.

'Hmm?' Annie squeaked.

'Oh, for God's sake!' Caz snatched the magazine out of her hands. 'I don't know about you, but I'm dying for a ciggie.'

'Me too.' They grinned at each other and suddenly it was as if the years separating them hadn't happened. They were final-year students again, nipping out of the mime and mask workshop for a sly smoke.

Caz propped her feet up on the seat opposite and lit up a Marlboro Light, casually ignoring the No Smoking signs. She was as small and slender as a dancer, but there was nothing fragile about her tight black Levis and leather biker's jacket. 'I hear you've given that bastard the push,' she said bluntly. 'About bloody time too.'

Annie glanced around the room. Suddenly everyone seemed to be looking at her. 'It was more the other way round,' she admitted sheepishly.

'I know.' Caz blew a perfect smoke ring into the air. 'I bet that's the first time Suzy Carrington's ever done anyone a favour. If you ask me, those two deserve each other.'

Annie fiddled with the zip on her rucksack, wishing Caz would shut up. If she'd wanted her private life dissected in public, she could have gone on the *Vanessa* show. But at least she wasn't avoiding her, like most people. Annie had known old friends cross the street when they saw her coming. Overnight she'd become a social embarrassment.

'Anyway, he'll regret it,' Caroline went on. 'Once he finds out what a bitch she really is.'

'Do you think so?' Annie ventured.

"Course.' Caz shrugged. 'And she's a crap actress. Everyone knows she only gets work because of her family.'

That was true. Suzy came from an acting dynasty that made the Redgraves look positively *arriviste*. Her grandparents were veterans of the British theatre, her uncle a film director, her father a famous TV detective. The Carringtons practically had their own section in *Spotlight*.

Suzy had cornered the market playing demure young heroines in lavish costume dramas. No Dickens or Hardy adaptation was complete without her, blonde tendrils framing her innocent face, her bosom spilling out of sprigged muslin. It was kind of ironic, Annie thought, that her husband had run off with a professional virgin.

'I mean, did you see her in that Jane Austen?' Caz went on, warming to her subject. 'She was so bloody wooden the director had to keep moving her around in case someone mistook her for a chest of drawers.'

Annie grinned. She hadn't had a decent bitching session in ages. Nor had she realised how much she'd missed her old friend.

'Been working?' Caz changed the subject.

'Oh, you know. This and that. How about you?'

'Don't ask.' She aimed another moody smoke ring at the ceiling. 'I've been working as a children's entertainer. You know, kids' parties and stuff?'

'That must be – er – nice.'

'No, it bloody well isn't.' Caz looked indignant. 'Have you ever been shut in with a bunch of hyperactive six-year-olds with only a comedy wig and a box of magic tricks for protection?'

'Can't say I have.'

'Well, it's no joke, I can tell you. Do you know, I once

spent two hours locked in an airing cupboard while the little buggers ran riot?'

Annie was horrified. 'They locked you in?'

'Did they, hell! I locked myself in.'

'Still, it must pay well?' Annie eyed the carrier bags around Caz's feet.

'This is retail therapy. I need it to survive.' Caz shifted her shoulders with a creak of ancient leather. 'The more depressed I'm feeling, the more I get this urge to go out and buy shoes. I reckon a quick splurge in Pied A Terre is better than a couple of Prozac any day.' She stubbed out her cigarette. 'Although I must say, my bank balance is beginning to suffer. That's why I need this job. It sounds really interesting, don't you think?'

Annie did her best to look interested.

'I haven't done any Shakespeare for ages. And my agent reckons there's a good chance he'll be looking for people for the rest of the season. Just think — no more kids' parties.'

Annie listened with a growing sense of guilt as she nattered on about the theatre's forthcoming season. Poor Caz was desperate for this job. Unlike her, who'd only turned up because her agent had threatened her with a fatwah if she didn't.

Although, listening to Caroline, it did sound interesting. She hadn't done any theatre for a long time. And she'd always enjoyed Shakespeare. Perhaps Julia was right. Maybe this job might be just what she needed. It wouldn't be for ever. And it might even do Max some good to see her getting on with her life. Sitting at home moping was all very well, but there was nothing sexy about a doormat.

She was running through her audition piece in her head when the door opened and the woman with two-tone hair stuck out her head and yelled, 'Annie Mitchell, please.'

Annie's stomach lurched. Suddenly she was desperate for the loo. 'I'm going to be sick,' she muttered through clenched teeth.

'You haven't got time,' Caroline hissed back, giving her a shove.

The woman introduced herself as Mel Bushell, the Assistant Director. Annie remembered to wipe her clammy palms down her jeans before shaking hands.

'Don't be nervous,' Mel reassured her. 'We've heard great things about you.'

Annie smiled back. Holding on to the contents of her stomach grimly, she followed Mel into the audition room. The squeak of her boots on the polished floorboards echoed up into the cavernous ceiling.

'Take a seat, would you?' Mel pointed to chair in front of a long trestle table, but Annie didn't move.

Her eyes were fixed on the line of faces seated on the other side of the table. There was an efficient-looking girl with mousy hair held in place by a black velvet Alice band. Her clipboard was poised. At the other end of the table another girl with blonde hair in drastic need of a roots job doodled with great concentration on hers.

And between them, his scuffed Timberland boots up on the table, was Nick Ryan.

Chapter 8

He'd swopped his designer suit for faded Levis and an ancient grey sweat-shirt, but she'd know those dark eyes and that sardonic grin anywhere.

Annie hardly listened as Mel introduced the girl in the Alice band as Fliss, the Deputy Stage Manager, and the messy blonde as Debbie, the Casting Assistant. She tried to concentrate, but horrifying images of herself, half dressed and completely plastered, trying to lasso Nick with her bra, kept rising up to haunt her.

'And this is Nick Ryan, our Artistic Director.' Mel smiled. 'But of course, you two know each other already, don't you?'

'What?' Annie stared at him in panic.

Nick's eyes twinkled. 'I told Mel we once worked together.'

'Oh. Yes. Worked together. Of course.' Annie's tongue clung to the roof of her mouth in terror.

'Nick tells us you're quite something,' Mel said.

Annie glanced at Nick. He was studying his notes, but she could see his lips twitching as his dark head bent over his clipboard.

He was enjoying this, the bastard! She closed her eyes. It

could only happen to her. Other women had one-night stands that disappeared with the dawn. Hers came back to haunt her.

'Annie?' Mel sounded concerned. 'Are you okay?' she asked. 'You look a bit pale.'

'I'm fine,' Annie lied. 'Only a bit of a headache, that's all.'

'Probably just audition nerves,' Mel said. 'I used to suffer terribly.'

Annie felt a stab of fury. This was all Nick's fault. Why hadn't he told her who he was last night? He could have saved her from all this embarrassment, instead of letting her make a complete fool of herself. She cringed. Well, even if she did want this job, she'd more than talked herself out of it.

Mel began to ask her about her background and experience. As Annie mumbled her replies, she kept catching the glances Fliss was giving her. God knows what she must have thought of her, slumped zombie-like in the chair, reeking of stale booze and ciggies. If only she'd done something with her hair. Or put on some make-up. Or never been born.

Once the interview was over, it was time for her audition piece. Annie rose to her feet, sweat prickling on her upper lip as she tried to stop the room spinning. Nick wasn't even looking at her, as he flicked through his notes. Annie felt another surge of rage that cleared her head. How dare he ignore her! She knew there was no way he was going to give her a job, but she could still make him sit up and take notice.

She'd chosen a speech from *A Midsummer Night's Dream*, where the spurned Helena confronts her love rival Hermia. It wasn't until she began to speak that she realised how appallingly appropriate it was. There was Helena, full of jealousy that the man she adored was in love with another woman. Every word she uttered could have come straight from Annie's own wounded heart.

'"O teach me how you look, and with what art you sway the motion of Demetrius' heart."' She'd never made this speech with so much real feeling. If she could be more like Suzy, maybe she could sway Max's heart too.

The room was still for a moment after she'd finished. Annie knew she'd impressed them. Even Nick was looking at her with respect. 'Thank you,' he said softly.

There was a quick, huddled conference. Annie tried to compose herself and push all thoughts of Max aside. It was like trying to stop herself breathing.

Then Nick looked up. 'Would you mind sight-reading something for us?' he asked.

'Of course.' Why was he doing this to her? They both knew he had no intention of hiring her.

The piece was from *Much Ado*, taken from the opening scene. 'I'll read Benedick,' Nick said, coming from behind the table to stand in front of her.

'Great.' Annie took the text from him, her hands shaking.

Nick peered into her face. 'Are you okay?'

'Fine. Let's get on with it, shall we?'

She might have known he wouldn't. Nick was a perfectionist. Every couple of lines he stopped her, pointing out some new expression he wanted her to try. 'Let's have a bit more bantering,' he suggested. 'This is meant to be a battle of wits, remember?'

Annie nodded. She had never felt less witty and bantering in her life. Now she'd started thinking about Max again, she couldn't seem to stop.

"'Then is Courtesy a turn-coat. But it is certain I am loved of all ladies, only you excepted.'" Nick was looking at her. "'And I would I could find it in my heart that I had not a hard heart, for truly I love none.'"

"'I thank God and my cold blood I am of your humour for that.'" Annie bent her head over her script. "'I had rather hear my dog bark at a crow than a man swear he loves me.'" Her voice caught on the words. She would never hear Max swearing he loved her again.

"'God keep your ladyship still—'" Nick broke off. As she looked up at him, a tear escaped and rolled down her cheek. 'Annie?' he whispered. He reached out to brush it off, but she flinched away from him.

'I'm sorry,' she blurted out. 'I – I can't do this.' She looked at the bemused faces of Mel, Debbie and Fliss. 'I'm really, really—' But her last words were choked on a sob as she fled from the room.

'Perhaps it wasn't as bad as you thought?' Caz said encouragingly, as they perched on high stools in the Costa Coffee at Waterloo station an hour later.

Annie shook her head. 'Believe me, it was.'

'You wait, these things are never the way they seem –'

'Caz, I cried my eyes out! How much worse can it get?' She buried her face in her hands, trying to shut out the awful picture. The last twelve hours had been the most mortifying of her life and it was only lunch-time. 'God knows what he must think of me.'

'Perhaps he'll see the funny side,' Caz suggested.

Annie pushed a handful of curls out of her eyes. 'There wasn't one,' she said gloomily.

'But it could happen to anyone.'

'Has it ever happened to you?'

'Well, no, but –'

'There you are then.' Her hands trembled as she wrapped them around her black coffee. 'He probably thinks I'm having some kind of nervous breakdown. What with that, and –' She slammed her mouth shut.

It was too much to hope Caz wouldn't notice. 'Is there something you're not telling me?' she asked, eyes narrowed.

Reluctantly, Annie admitted the whole story. How she'd once dumped Nick and how disastrously their paths had crossed again the night before. By the time she'd finished, Caz was wiping away the tears.

'It's not funny,' Annie grumbled, toying with a sugar lump.

'Are you kidding? It's the funniest thing I've heard all year.' Caz shook her head. 'And you're actually telling me you ditched him for Max?'

Annie's chin rose defensively. 'What's that supposed to mean?'

'Nothing.' But she could see the incredulous look on Caz's face. She knew not everyone liked Max. He could be quite outspoken at times, but it was hardly his fault if people mistook it for arrogance. And Caz wasn't the only one of her friends who'd been edged out of their social life. Annie could still remember a couple of excruciating nights out when Max had watched her friends' antics in haughty silence. But his honesty was something she had always appreciated.

And it wasn't as if he was antisocial. God no, he had a huge circle of friends. He was forever talking about the mates he'd met at first night parties – Ken and Helena, Ralphie Fiennes, Judi and Mike. He used to show off the phone numbers he'd collected. So what if some people found him a bit pompous? Annie thought he was adorable.

She still did. She took a huge gulp of scalding coffee, which did nothing to ease the lump of misery in her throat.

'He's gorgeous though, isn't he?' Caz skimmed the froth off her cappuccino. 'Very sexy in a world-weary kind of way, don't you think?'

'Who?'

'Nick Ryan, of course. I'm not surprised you tried to get him into bed last night.'

'I didn't!'

'Oh, right. So dragging him up the stairs was you playing hard to get, was it?' Caz sent her a sly look. 'I don't think you've got anything to worry about, anyway. Nick's bound to give you a job. Even if it is out of pity.'

'Somehow I don't think so.' It was a good thing she hadn't set her heart on it.

'I know what you need,' Caz said later as they were leaving the café.

'What?' A nose job? A personality transplant? Annie was prepared to try anything.

'Some retail therapy.' Caz grinned. 'How about going on a mad splurge in South Molton Street?'

Annie shook her head. 'No, thanks. I've got next month's mortgage to think about.' That was something else pecking away at her troubled mind. Max had always handled the finances. How was she going to cope with paying the bills, especially if she didn't have a job?

'Suit yourself.' Caz planted a kiss on her cheek. 'Take care of yourself, won't you? And don't forget to let me know if you hear from the lovely Nick.'

'I will.' Although she was already expecting the 'thanks

but no thanks' message to be waiting on her answering-machine when she got home.

'Anyway, cheer up!' Caz called over her shoulder as she headed towards the Northern Line. 'Things could be worse.'

Annie thought about it as she made her way home. She had been dumped by her husband and betrayed by her best friend. She was out of work, out of luck and out of cash. Short of being struck down by some rare virus that caused her to gain three stone and lose all her hair, could her life really get any worse?

Then she let herself into the house, saw Max standing there, and realised it probably could.

Chapter 9

It wasn't meant to be like this. When she met Max again in her day-dreams she was always cool, poised and desirable. She was not hungover and wearing a *Rocky Horror Show* T-shirt that could have doubled as a dishrag.

He was standing at the hall table, flicking through his post. Annie took one look at him in his white polo shirt and faded Levis, streaky blond and gorgeous, and felt her stomach contract with lust.

He glanced up at her. 'Did you know this Barclaycard bill was due last Friday?' His voice was clipped with irritation. 'Why didn't you send it on to me?'

'I had other things on my mind.' She walked past him quickly, hoping he wouldn't detect the whiff of stale ciggies. 'What are you doing here, anyway?'

'Collecting the rest of my things. I called last night, remember?'

Did she ever! 'You should have waited until I got back. You can't just walk in here whenever you feel like it, you know.'

'What's the problem?' His lip curled. 'You haven't got a man here, have you?'

'I might have.'

'Yeah, right.' He grinned. 'That's why you're all dressed up.' He looked her up and down insultingly.

'Oh, fuck off!' She was too tired to fight him. After dreaming for three weeks of this moment, suddenly all she wanted him to do was to go away. 'I'd still rather you waited until I was here.'

'Why? So you can make another scene?'

'What scene? I don't make scenes.'

'You're making one now.'

She opened her mouth, then closed it again.

'Anyway, my name's still on the mortgage,' Max went on. 'So this place is still technically half mine, remember?'

'In that case, you still technically owe me half the phone bill.'

He smiled that maddeningly handsome smile of his and pushed the blond hair out of his eyes. 'I'll write you a cheque, shall I? Only I'll have to send it on. I'm changing bank accounts at the moment. Which reminds me, there are some papers you've got to sign. About closing our joint account.'

Annie felt her lip trembling. 'The joint account?'

'Well, it makes sense, doesn't it?' Max said briskly. 'We don't need it now we're separated.'

Annie wasn't listening. The joint bank account was one of the last shreds of hope she was clinging on to. Like his Ralph Lauren boxer shorts in the chest of drawers, it was a sign that one day Max might, just might, come back to her.

'I hope you're going to be sensible about this?' he warned. 'My God, it's only a bank account.'

She stared at his back as he turned away to flick through his post. Only a bank account. Like their marriage certificate was only a piece of paper.

66

'So what happened to *Freedom*?' he asked. Annie felt confused. Was he after some kind of philosophical discussion? '*Freedom*,' he repeated slowly, as if talking to a backward child. 'The Art. It's wrecked.'

How can you tell, she wanted to ask. 'It was an accident.'

'Of course it was.' He smiled knowingly.

'I didn't do it on purpose, if that's what you're thinking. If you must know, I got pissed and fell on it.' She saw his face fall and added weakly, 'I'll pay for it, of course. I know how much you loved it –'

'Forget it.' Max aimed a *Reader's Digest* Prize Draw letter at the waste-paper bin. 'Suzy wouldn't have it in the house anyway. She reckons all that post-Modernist stuff's crap.'

Annie breathed in sharply. She'd always thought it was crap too, but that hadn't stopped Max insisting it take up half the sitting-room.

She went into the kitchen. Max followed her. Too late, she remembered the unwashed dishes festering in a sinkful of cold, greasy water.

'I see the place has gone to pot since I left.' Max leaned against the doorway, his mocking eyes taking in the scene.

'And Suzy's utterly perfect, I suppose.' Annie snatched up the kettle with unnecessary force. 'Don't tell me, she gets up at dawn to serve you breakfast with a rose between her teeth?'

Max grinned. 'Actually, it's me who usually gets up first. Suzy's hopeless until she's had her first cup of Earl Grey.'

Annie crashed cups around. How dare he swan in and start discussing his domestic arrangements with her. Did he honestly think she wanted to hear what he and Suzy got up to in the bedroom, or anywhere else for that matter?

And when was the last time he'd brought her tea in bed? Not once, in six years of marriage. She could have been struck down with the bubonic plague and he wouldn't have offered her so much as a Lemsip. And yet Suzy got the star treatment every day.

She caught sight of herself in the mirror over the sink and flinched. Bloody Suzy, she thought. And bloody Max, too. Why did he have to turn up now, when she was looking like something other people scraped off their boots?

'So have you finished packing the rest of your things?'

'Not yet.' He folded his arms. 'What's the rush? Anyone would think you wanted to get rid of me.'

'Well spotted.' She banged the kettle down on the work top and fumbled for the switch. 'If you must know, I want to go to bed. I didn't sleep too well last night.'

'Not because of me, I hope?'

'Don't flatter yourself! I happen to have a hellish hangover.'

'Oh, I get it.' He grinned knowingly. 'I suppose you've had the coven round for a few girly bitching sessions? I thought my ears were burning.'

'Actually there were only two of us,' she said haughtily. 'And we had better things to talk about.'

'I see.' His gaze fell on the two glasses sitting side by side on the draining board, waiting to be washed. 'So this friend of yours,' he said casually. 'Anyone I know?'

'No.'

'Male or female?'

'What's that got to do with you?'

'I just wondered, that's all.'

She glared at him. 'It was a man. Is that a problem?'

'No,' he said quickly. 'No, not at all.' But he looked shaken, she noticed.

'Good,' she said. 'I mean, it would be a bit rich under the circumstances, wouldn't it?' She raised her chin. 'I am a free woman. What's sauce for the goose and all that.'

They stood in silence for a moment, both watching the kettle as it failed to boil. Finally Annie sighed. 'I don't think I'll bother with the coffee after all. I'm going for a bath instead.' She eyed him coldly. 'Don't forget to lock the door on your way out, will you?'

It was amazing what a generous slosh of Body Shop Aromatherapy Bath Oil could do, she reflected some time later, as she sank beneath the hot, steaming water. Already she could feel her headache easing and the life slowly ebbing back into her aching limbs. Any minute now she might start to feel almost human again.

She could hear Max moving around downstairs. She was beginning to regret being so offhand with him. Not that he didn't deserve it, but she wondered if she hadn't gone too far. Being cool was one thing, but she didn't want to put him off completely.

She grabbed a towel off the rail. She would catch him before he left, try to make amends. God knows when she'd get another chance.

She was out of the bath when she heard footsteps on the stairs. She barely had time to wrap the towel around herself before the door opened and Max appeared, mug in hand.

'You could have knocked.' She pushed her damp hair out of her eyes.

'Why? It's not as if I haven't seen you naked before.' He ran his eyes slowly and disturbingly down her body.

She distracted herself quickly. 'I see you've made yourself at home. Who said you could use my coffee?'

'Actually, it's for you. I thought it might help the hangover.'

She inhaled sharply in disbelief. Max making coffee? She wasn't sure he even knew how. 'Thanks,' she muttered, fumbling with the towel. Should she pull it down so it decently covered her thighs and risk leaving too much bosom exposed, or should she tweak it up so it covered her boobs but barely skimmed her bottom? And did it really matter when every inch of her was blushing furiously?

'Just take the bloody thing off.' Max was watching her with amusement. Annie trembled. If only he weren't so gorgeous it might be a lot easier to hate him.

He took a step closer. She could feel the heat of his body. 'Where do you want it?' he whispered.

'What?'

'Your coffee.' His smile was sexy and knowing. 'Shall I leave it here, or would you rather have it in the bedroom?'

'I'll take it,' Annie said shakily. Clutching her towel with one hand, she made a hasty grab for the mug.

'You look like a mermaid, with your hair like that.' Max reached out to touch a damp curl. 'It's beautiful, like the colour of sherry. The finest Oloroso –'

His touch was electric. Annie flinched away, splashing hot coffee over her hand. 'I thought you preferred blondes these days,' she snapped.

Max smiled. '*Touché.*'

Annie suddenly felt as self-conscious as a teenager. 'I'll go and get dressed,' she muttered, moving to push past him.

Max stood in her way. 'Do you have to? I prefer you the way you are. All kind of sexy and rumpled.'

She felt her knees buckling and her carefully built-up defences melting like wax. In spite of her pain and anger, he could still do it to her.

'Annie –' Next moment his hands were cupping her face, drawing her towards him.

'What about Suzy?' she whispered. Max's face was so close to hers she could see the dark-blue flecks in his eyes.

'What about her?'

What indeed, Annie thought, as he began to trace a tingling line of kisses along her collarbone. Had Suzy spared a thought for her while she and Max were cavorting in her dressing-room after the curtain came down?

Next moment the towel was at her feet and she was in Max's arms, kissing him hungrily, ripping at the buttons on his shirt, desperate to touch him, to feel the warmth of his skin under her fingers.

'What about your boyfriend?' he asked suddenly.

'Hmm?' She went on fumbling at his shirt buttons.

'The guy from last night?' Max caught her wrists, pulling her away from him.

She felt cold and shivery. All she could think about was getting back into his arms. 'What boyfriend?' she mumbled.

It seemed like the right answer. Max smiled an odd little smile, almost triumphant, before his mouth claimed hers again.

They'd made it all the way to the bedroom and collapsed on to the bed when the phone rang, shattering the mood. At first Annie ignored it.

It was Max who pulled away. 'Aren't you going to answer it?' he asked.

'No.' Annie dragged his mouth back to hers. She couldn't have stopped even if she'd wanted to. Her whole body was molten with lust.

Max jerked away, lifting himself up on to his elbow. He could never ignore a ringing phone. 'But it might be important,' he insisted.

Annie stretched out for the receiver, picked it up, then slammed it down again. The sudden silence was deafening.

'They hung up.' She grinned mischievously, reaching for him. Almost immediately it rang again.

'Look, you'd better answer it.' Max picked up his shirt.

Annie began to panic. 'You're not going?' She raised her voice above the insistent ringing.

'I've got to.'

She touched his skin, feeling its warmth under her hand. 'Stay,' she pleaded.

'I can't.'

Annie watched him button up his shirt. 'You're going back to her,' she said in a small, flat voice.

And still the phone kept ringing. 'Can't you answer that bloody thing?' he shouted.

She picked it up and slammed it down again, her eyes never leaving his face. 'How can you go back to her, after – after what we've just done?'

Max sighed. 'I don't want to, but – it's complicated.'

'What do you mean?'

'I mean it's just – complicated, that's all.' He cupped her chin in his hand. 'Look, I don't know how I feel at the moment. Everything's totally confused.'

You're confused? Annie pulled the duvet around her.

He wasn't the one being abandoned one minute and seduced the next.

Her throat felt tight. 'So are you coming back?' she whispered. She hated herself for sounding so pathetic, but she had to know.

'I –' The wretched phone started ringing again. Max glanced at it, then at her. He bent down, dropped a quick kiss on the top of her head, then ruffled her hair affectionately. 'I'll call you,' he promised.

'Max –' But she was already talking to his retreating back as it disappeared through the door.

'We'll talk later,' he yelled. 'Now answer that bloody thing!'

As his footsteps echoed down the stairs, Annie reached across and snatched up the phone. 'Yes?' she hissed. If it was a double-glazing salesman, he was in serious trouble.

But it wasn't.

Chapter 10

'Have I called at a bad time?' Nick asked.

Downstairs the front door banged shut. Max was gone. Annie swung round and directed all her frustration down the phone. 'What do you want?'

'How are you feeling?'

Annie gritted her teeth. 'Fine.'

Gathering the duvet round her she went over to the window and looked into the narrow, tree-lined street, trying to catch a glimpse of Max. But he'd already gone.

If only the wretched phone hadn't rung, she might have held on to him long enough to make him change his mind. This was all Nick's fault. And if Max never came back, if he stayed with Suzy bloody Carrington, that would be all his fault too.

'Are you sure? It's just the way you left –'

'I told you, I'm fine.' Max wouldn't really stay with Suzy, would he? Not after what had happened.

'I was surprised to see you at the audition today,' Nick was saying.

'I could say the same thing!' Annie dragged her thoughts away from Max. 'You could have told me who you were last night. It might have saved us both a lot of embarrass-ment.'

'How was I to know you were the one I was supposed to be meeting? All I knew was that when Julia Gold phoned, begging me to meet her client, she made it sound like you were the greatest thing since Kate Winslet. I never imagined it would be you.'

'Thanks a lot,' Annie muttered.

'That's not what I meant, and you know it. Anyway, by the time I realised it was you, you'd made it so clear you didn't want the job I decided it was best not to mention it. I was trying not to embarrass you,' he said pointedly. 'I didn't know your agent would be on the phone the next morning, begging me to give you an audition.'

Annie rolled over on the bed and caught a glimpse of herself in the wardrobe mirror. Her cheek-bones were stained with hectic colour, her eyes as brilliant as topaz. It was an after-sex face. Almost.

Now that the post-Max euphoria was beginning to fade she felt cold and uncertain. She'd nearly let him make love to her and now he was gone. What did that tell her?

'So why did you do it?' Nick asked.

Annie stared at the phone, startled. 'What?'

'The audition. What made you change your mind?'

'Julia.' She bit her lip. Where had she gone wrong? Had she made it too easy for Max? She had a vague idea that falling into bed with him wasn't the shrewdest move she'd ever made. But he only had to touch her and she melted. God, why was she such a wimp?

'Ah, yes, I can understand that. Very – er – forceful, isn't she?'

'She could bully for Britain.' But maybe she'd got it wrong? Maybe Max really did want to come home?

Perhaps living with Suzy had made him realise how much he'd missed her. Quite how that could have happened she didn't know, but didn't Max say he was confused? A small bubble of hope rose within her.

'Annie? Are you still there?'

She realised that she hadn't heard a word Nick had said for the last two minutes. 'Sorry, what was that?'

'It doesn't matter. Look, are you sure I haven't called at a bad time? I can ring back if it isn't convenient.'

'No, no. Now is fine.' She didn't want to risk tying up the phone lines if Max was trying to get through later on.

Besides, she felt she owed him some kind of apology. A pretty big one, in fact.

'I'm sorry about last night.' She blurted out the words, gripping the phone cord tighter.

'Oh, that.' She could hear the smile in his voice again.

'I don't know what made me do it.'

'A gallon of brandy might have helped.'

Annie pressed her lips together in annoyance. 'Anyway, I'm sorry it happened.'

'Forget it,' Nick said. 'I hope you understand that it was nothing personal – me turning you down like that?'

'No.' She could feel the blush creeping up from her ankles.

'It's just when I go to bed with a woman I prefer her to remember it in the morning.'

Oh, I remember it all right, Annie thought. Was she ever going to be able to forget it?

She reached across for her dressing-gown and glanced at the bedside clock. Three thirty-seven. Maybe Max was already trying to get through?

'Well,' she said briskly, 'if that's all you wanted, I'm pretty busy –'

'Wait,' said Nick. 'There was something else.'

She stifled a sigh. 'What?'

'How would you like to play Beatrice?'

Annie froze, the phone wedged against her shoulder, one arm in her dressing-gown. 'You're not serious? But my audition –'

'– was one of the best I've seen in a very long time,' Nick finished for her. 'Although to be honest, I would have offered you the job anyway.'

'Because you feel sorry for me?'

'Because you're good. I've seen you work. I know what you can do.'

He began to outline his offer. The Phoenix Theatre, Middlethorpe, was due to reopen in early September. Rehearsals for *Much Ado* would begin in a fortnight, with four weeks' rehearsal before they opened. As Caz had predicted, Nick was also casting for the rest of the season and there was a good chance that she would be offered more work if things turned out well.

The whole time he was talking, Annie's mind was racing. A few hours ago she might have been tempted. But Max's unexpected reappearance had thrown everything into chaos.

'Well?' Nick's voice broke into her thoughts. 'What do you say?'

Annie twisted the phone cord in her hands. 'Look, it's very sweet of you to offer,' she said, biting her lip. 'But I can't do it.'

There was a long silence. 'You're turning it down?'

'Yes.'

'I see.' His voice could have frozen the phone line. 'So why did you bother turning up for the audition if you think this job's so far beneath you?'

'It's not that –' Annie took a deep breath. She would have to tell him, she decided. After the way she'd poured her heart out to him he'd want to know. 'It's Max,' she said.

'What about him?'

'I think –' oh, God, please don't let her be wrong '– I think he's decided to come home.'

There. She'd said it. For a minute she thought Nick had hung up.

'What makes you think that?' he said at last.

'He was here. Just now. When you rang. And he's changed. I really think he knows he's made a mistake –'

'Did he tell you that?' Nick cut her off abruptly.

'What?'

'Did he tell you he'd made a terrible mistake? Did he beg you to take him back?'

'Not exactly –'

'So where is he now?'

'I – I don't know,' she faltered. 'He had to leave.'

'I see.'

'At least I know he still cares,' Annie protested. The chill of the wooden floor was beginning to seep through her bare feet. 'I thought you'd be happy for me.'

Nick sighed wearily. 'I am,' he said. 'If that's what you really want.'

'It is.'

There was a heavy silence. 'Then I wish you luck,' Nick said, and put down the phone.

Annie held on to the dead line, her happiness evaporating like mist. How dare Nick go and spoil it all? He was only put out because she'd turned down his stupid job offer.

She put down the receiver and sat for a moment, half

expecting Max to ring back straight away. But he didn't. Annie spent the rest of the day and evening in a state of agitation, full of restless energy, waiting for him to call. She sorted through her knicker drawer, cleaned the kitchen floor and even found herself washing the windows so she could keep an eye on the road. She would have weeded the window boxes too, but she was worried about getting soil under what was left of her nails.

And all the time she prowled around the phone, waiting for it to ring.

Her nerves were in tatters by the time it did ring, just after nine. She was flopped in front of the *Nine O'Clock News*, watching Michael Buerk with the sound turned down.

She pounced on the receiver. 'Thank God!' she cried. 'I've been waiting hours. Max, what's going on?'

'I was rather hoping you could tell me that.' Suzy's voice was cool on the other end of the line. 'I think it's time we met, don't you?'

Chapter 11

They arranged to have lunch in the Garden restaurant the next day. They'd often met there in the past, but this time Annie doubted if girly gossip would be on the menu.

She sat at the corner table, staring out over the sunny Covent Garden piazza and wondering what Max had told Suzy. She'd tried to call him, but his mobile had been switched off all morning.

Whatever he'd said, Suzy had been tight-lipped on the phone. Had he told her he was leaving? Annie tried to quell the unworthy surge of spiteful triumph at the thought of Suzy pacing tearfully around her Chelsea love nest, shredding soggy tissues and chewing her manicured nails.

She mustn't gloat, she told herself firmly, as she tried to catch a passing waiter's eye. She would have Max back and that was all that mattered. Although maybe Dempster should be told, just to set the record straight.

She'd arrived at the restaurant a fashionable fifteen minutes late, only to find Suzy still wasn't there. Maybe she wasn't coming? Perhaps she was still at home, desperately trying to repair her tear-ravaged face?

Annie took out her mirror and cautiously examined her

own appearance. She'd taken hours to get ready and for once she was satisfied with herself. Her war-paint was just right, the blend of gold shadows bringing out the tigerish amber in her eyes, which was reflected in her tobacco-coloured silk shirt. Her hair had been moussed, serumed and pinned into submission. She snapped her mirror shut, feeling confident. Then the waiter arrived.

Annie could tell that, like most of the staff, he was an out-of-work actor. As he appeared at her table his restless gaze was skimming the crowd, searching for the famous face who might offer him his big break. He'd already given Annie her place in his sucking-up order. And by the impatient way he was tapping his pen against his order book it wasn't near the top.

She dithered over the drinks menu. Should she have a glass of wine to steady her nerves? Or should she keep a clear head and order mineral water?

In the end she opted for the water. 'Yeah, go mad, why don't you?' the waiter said in a bored voice, scribbling on his pad before drifting off to the bar.

Five minutes later he was still leaning there, deep in conversation with two other waitresses, while Annie waited for her drink. She'd just lit a cigarette in desperation when Suzy turned up.

She looked blonde, glowing and not the least bit heart-broken. She was wearing a brief white lacy top and skin-tight pink pedal pushers which should have looked idiotic on anyone over seven years old, but on her looked irritatingly cute and sex kittenish.

Annie was so shocked to see her she took a wrongly judged puff and swallowed a lungful of smoke.

'Oh, my God, are you all right?' Suzy banged her on the back, taking the rest of her breath away.

'I'm fine.' Annie shook her off. So much for being cool, she thought, mopping her streaming eyes with her sleeve.

'Are you sure? Let me get you a glass of water.'

You'll be lucky, Annie was about to gasp. But Suzy had barely raised her finger the merest fraction of an inch before the waiter came scampering over, his notebook poised. Annie felt sick, and not because she'd just swallowed half her cigarette.

Suzy ordered the water, then turned back to Annie. 'Haven't I told you smoking's bad for you?' She smiled. It wasn't the smile of someone who had just been dumped by her lover. It was more the supremely confident, hundred-kilowatt, teeth-dazzling smile of someone who knew she had the upper hand.

Annie fumbled in her bag for a tissue. Typically, all she could find was a tattered, disconcertingly crispy scrap she'd once used to wipe the mud off her boots. She was just wondering if she could get away with using an old bus ticket when Suzy handed over a pristine hankie.

'Here, have one of mine,' she offered. 'Don't worry, I haven't got any germs.'

I bet you haven't, Annie thought, dabbing her eyes. Everything about Suzy was as squeaky clean and fresh as an advert for bathroom cleaner. Except her conscience.

The waiter came scuttling back with the water. He stood over Suzy as she dithered prettily over the menu. Any minute now he'd be on his back, begging her to tickle his tummy, Annie thought bitchily.

Normally at such a lunch Annie would have demolished the day's special and still found room for the chocolate fudge brownie with extra whipped cream. But today her stomach was knotted with tension. Gloomily she closed her menu and ordered a salad.

'Do you want fries with that?' the waiter asked, eyeing her thighs unkindly. Annie glared at him.

'How about some wine?' Suzy suggested.

'Why not?' Annie sipped her water grimly. Forget abstinence. It would take more than a bottle of Perrier to get her through this ordeal.

Suzy ordered house white and a fresh orange juice for herself. 'I'm not drinking at the moment,' she said smugly. 'But I'm sure you won't have any trouble finishing the bottle.'

Annie stared at Suzy's nauseatingly perfect face and wondered how she had ever considered her a friend. Not only was she a cheating, man-stealing cow, but she was also without a shred of human failing. She was the only person Annie knew who not only belonged to a gym, but actually went there regularly. She'd never demolished a family-sized bar of Whole Nut in one sitting. In fact, she was unnaturally perfect. How could she have ever felt close to a woman for whom cellulite was something that only happened to other people?

'So.' Suzy leaned forward with the hushed, concerned tone normally reserved for visiting patients in secure establishments. 'How are you?'

'Fine. Never better.' Annie tossed her curls defiantly.

'That's good.' Suzy leaned even further. 'You know, I've really missed you,' she confided. 'It's been awful, not being able to call you for a gossip like I used to.'

Was she for real? 'Well, yes, it did make things a teeny bit awkward,' Annie said. 'You running off with my husband like that.'

Suzy nodded earnestly. She wouldn't have recognised sarcasm if it turned round and bit her on her sickeningly pert backside. She sat across the table, her smooth skin the colour of orange-blossom honey, her rosebud mouth a little circle of concern. 'That's why I'm here,' she said. 'To get things sorted out between us. I hope when this is over we can still be friends.'

Annie was saved from answering by the waiter speeding over with their drinks. As he poured Annie's wine he turned to Suzy and said bashfully, 'I hope you don't mind me asking, Miss Carrington, but can I have your autograph?'

'Of course.' Suzy reached flirtatiously into his apron pocket, took out his notepad and scribbled something on it. Annie watched as she added a few extravagant kisses and handed it back, reducing the waiter to a mass of quivering hormones.

'I'm trying to break into acting myself,' he babbled, turning his back on Annie. 'I just wondered if you had any advice –'

'Yes. Don't give up the day job.' Annie snatched her glass away as he filled it to the brim. He shot her a mean look, then flounced off towards the kitchen.

Suzy sighed. 'Don't you get tired of that happening?'

'Constantly,' Annie said. The last time she'd signed her autograph was on a Save the Whale petition.

Suzy sipped primly at her orange juice. Finally Annie could stand it no longer. 'So why did you want to meet?'

'I thought it was time we cleared the air.' Suzy toyed with her napkin. 'Max told me – about yesterday.'

Annie nearly took a bite out of her wineglass. 'Oh, yes?'

'Yes.' Suzy's thickly lashed eyes came up to meet hers. 'And I must say I'm very disappointed.'

Disappointed? Annie stared at her. *Disappointed*? Blind fury she could understand. Devastated – well, she'd been there too. But disappointed? That was what you felt when your lottery numbers didn't come up, not when your boy-friend unexpectedly snogged his estranged wife.

But then Suzy had all the depth of a car-park puddle. You only had to watch her act to see that.

'It's not going to work, you know,' she went on. 'Max isn't going to fall for it.'

'What are you talking about?'

'You know.' Suzy sent her an accusing look. 'Actually, I feel rather sorry for you, stooping to that kind of emotional blackmail. I thought you had more self-respect than that –'

'Now hang on a minute!' Annie banged down her glass. 'What exactly has Max been telling you?'

'The truth.' There was a hint of cold steel in her blue eyes. 'That he came round to collect his things and that you got very emotional, as usual.'

'Anything else?'

Suzy's lips tightened. 'He told me you threw yourself at him. He didn't want to say anything at first but I knew something had happened.' She lifted her chin. 'I found your hair on his shirt collar.'

'And did he also tell you he tried to get me into bed?' An unnerving hush fell over the entire restaurant. Even the waiters stopped gossiping and looked round.

Suzy's face lost a little of its doll-like pinkness, but she regained her composure quickly. 'Oh, Annie.' She sighed. 'When are you going to give up?'

'But it's true.'

'You mean you'd like it to be.' Suzy gave her a sorrowful look that wouldn't have shamed a daytime TV agony auntie. 'Max is right. You really won't accept it, will you? Perhaps you should get some help –'

The waiter sidled up with their food. He paused just

long enough to give Suzy a winning smile and Annie a look that said he hoped she'd choke on her radicchio before racing off, elbows out against the other waiters, to schmooze Trevor Nunn on the other side of the room.

Annie poked listlessly about in her salad. Maybe she did need help. She must be mad, letting Max hurt her like that again. She knew she hadn't imagined the way he'd looked at her, the way he'd touched her. She'd been so sure he wanted her back. But now, in the cold light of day, she was beginning to see how things really were. This wasn't about Max wanting her again. This was Max wanting to prove no one else could have her.

Looking back on it, she could see how his attitude had changed when he found out about Nick. Had he tried to seduce her just to prove he still could? That even though there was another man in her life, he was still the one she really wanted?

Annie let her fork fall, her stomach burning with anger. She felt used and humiliated. And yet, deep down, she knew she would do it all again, just for the chance to be in Max's arms, even for a second.

'Look, I'm sorry.' Suzy was back to her relentless pitying mode. 'I didn't mean to upset you. That's not what I came here for at all.'

'Then why did you come?'

'To try and build some bridges. And to let you know we're here for you, Max and I.'

She put out a hand. Annie picked up her fork again hurriedly. Suzy had been watching too much *Oprah*, she decided. Any minute now she'd be suggesting they all got together for a group hug.

'I know it's not what you wanted to hear,' Suzy droned on, 'but your marriage is over. It's left you emotionally shattered, I can understand that. But you've got to face up to reality. You and Max just aren't right for each other. You never were. You've got to move on, rebuild your life –'

Annie jabbed at her salad with tightly controlled agitation. If they hadn't been in a crowded restaurant she would have pinned Suzy to the floor with a fork at her throat by now. 'We were fine until you came along,' she muttered.

'But you weren't, were you?' Suzy speared a cherry tomato. 'You were having problems long before that. Anyone could see you two weren't really happy.' She leaned forward. 'You were stifling him, Annie.'

Annie winced. 'I loved him.'

'Yes, but that wasn't the kind of love he needed, was it?' Suzy leaned over again. Any further and she'd be face down in her salad. 'You never gave him any space –'

Look what happened when I did, Annie thought furiously. 'Spare me the psychology. You wanted him, and that's all there was to it.'

'I fell in love with him.' Suzy looked hurt. 'I couldn't help it. You've got to realise how painful this has been for me.'

'For you?' Annie took a swig of her wine. 'You're not the one who got dumped, remember? You're not the one whose so-called best friend ran off with her husband.'

'Before you blame me, perhaps you should ask yourself why he left.'

Annie's blood froze in her veins. 'What's that supposed to mean?'

'If Max had been happy with you, why did he want me?' There was steely determination in that porcelain-pretty face.

Annie regarded the acres of smooth, honey-skinned bosom rising out of her off-the-shoulder top, her baby-blonde hair piled on top of her head, tendrils falling around her provocatively innocent face. There was absolutely no answer to that, she decided.

'Anyway, I haven't come here to spread doom and gloom.' Suzy went back to her salad, as if she had been chatting about the weather instead of tearing the last six years of Annie's life apart.

Annie stared into the murky green depths of her bowl. After a few minutes she heard a word that made her look up. 'Film? What film?'

'Oh, didn't Max tell you? Uncle Victor's making a film of *The Tenant of Wildfell Hall*. He wants Max and me to star in it.' Suzy smiled. 'I suppose he thought it would be interesting, given our real-life relationship –'

Good old Uncle Victor, Annie thought bitterly. She wondered how much Suzy had had to beg him to give Max a part. Well, that was it. She'd never get him back now. If it was a choice between her and a starring role in a Victor Carrington film, she might as well sign those divorce papers right now. 'Very clever,' she said.

Suzy blinked. 'I don't know what you mean.'

'Oh, come on! You know Max has always wanted to be in films. He won't leave you while you're dangling that little prize in front of him.'

'He won't leave me anyway.' Suzy twirled a piece of lollo rosso around her fork with great concentration.

'Really? And what makes you so sure?'

There was a spark of defiance in Suzy's blue eyes. 'I'm pregnant,' she said.

Chapter 12

'Max wanted to tell you himself.' Suzy broke the stunned silence. 'That's partly why he came round yesterday. But you were so emotional he never got the chance.'

Annie was so numb with shock she let this pass without comment. 'When?' she heard herself whisper. 'How long –'

'Five weeks. The baby's due next March.' Suzy smoothed her flat stomach with her hand. 'It happened on tour. If it's a boy we're going to call him Terence, after Terence Rattigan. You know, *Separate Tables*? Or do you think that's a bit kitsch?'

Annie gripped the table-cloth, her fingers white against the red-checked fabric, fighting the terrible urge to tip up the table and scream with rage. Was Suzy deliberately being cruel, or was she just too stupid to realise what she was saying?

'Max is thrilled, of course,' Suzy went on. 'He's completely ecstatic. You should see him, he's treating me like I'm a piece of priceless Dresden. He won't let me lift a finger. Anyone would think I was the first woman in the world to conceive.' She popped another cherry tomato in her mouth. 'It is a bit awkward, though, what with the film and everything. But we should have finished in a couple of months. And Uncle Victor says if I get too huge he'll just shoot my head.'

Someone bloody well should, Annie thought, focusing on Suzy's pink glossy mouth. If she had a gun she'd do it herself.

'Of course, we'll have to find somewhere else to live,' Suzy was saying. 'We'll probably keep the Cheyne Walk flat on because it's so convenient, but London's hardly the place to bring up a child, is it? And I've seen a fabulous place in *Country Life*. A barn conversion in Hampshire. Way out of our price range, of course, but Daddy says he'll chip in and help us.' She giggled. 'It's got masses of land. Can you imagine, me keeping chickens and gorgeous little lambs and things?'

Annie watched her, sick with jealousy. She'll be asking if I want to be a godmother next, she thought.

Suzy appeared to notice her stunned look. 'I'm sorry if this has all been a shock. I didn't mean it to come out this way. But you never know, perhaps this baby will bring us all closer together.' Her blue eyes gleamed. 'How would you like to be a godmother?'

Annie's unequivocal reply was silenced by the trill of Suzy's mobile phone.

'Hello? Oh, hello, darling.' Annie knew straight away it was Max calling. 'Yes, I'm fine. Yes, yes, I'm sure. Oh, you are so sweet –'

It only took a few seconds of Annie glaring for even Suzy to realise that this wasn't the most tactful thing she could do. Excusing herself, she slid from her seat and headed over to the door to continue her conversation.

Alone at last, Annie finally gave in to her feelings. The

hurt was physical, a terrible crushing pain in her chest. She could hardly breathe.

She couldn't remember a time when she hadn't longed for a baby. Max's baby. They'd only been married a few weeks when she first brought up the subject. Max had just talked her out of signing a contract with the RSC, saying it was no way to start their married life, with her a hundred miles away up the M1. Annie assumed it was because, like her, he wanted to start a family immediately.

But he'd insisted it was too soon. 'Of course I want kids, darling,' he had reassured her. 'But for God's sake, the ink's hardly dry on the marriage certificate. Can't we wait a while?'

So she'd waited. Two years on they'd bought a house, Max had got a bit part in *EastEnders* and she was working in the theatre. It seemed like the perfect time to her. But not to Max.

'Give it time,' he'd said again. 'We're only just getting ourselves established. Do you really want to ditch your career to change nappies and wipe snotty noses all day?'

Actually, she did. And besides, she was only working in Theatre in Education, performing Shakespeare workshops to uninterested sixth formers. Taking a break was hardly going to do her career any serious harm. 'We could work round it,' she suggested. 'Maybe we could get a nanny –'

'No way!' Max was adamant. 'No kid of mine is being brought up by strangers.'

And so it went on. Either they were working and didn't have the time to devote to bringing up a child, or they were out of work and didn't have the money.

'We'll know when it's right,' Max kept saying. But somehow it never was.

In the end Annie had stopped mentioning it, knowing

how much it annoyed him. But that didn't take away the wanting, the physical ache that made her look yearningly at pregnant women in the street.

And now he was 'thrilled' and 'ecstatic' because Suzy was having his baby. This betrayal cut more deeply than their affair ever could.

Suzy hadn't just stolen her husband, she'd stolen her dream. That should have been *her* barn conversion in Hampshire. Those should have been *her* chickens and sheep. Most of all, those should have been *her* children, hers and Max's, romping around in their OshKosh dungarees, shrieking after the chickens and soaking each other with the garden hose while she looked on lovingly.

'The bloody bitch has pinched my life,' she hissed. The couple at the next table shot her a wary glance and edged away their chairs.

Suzy came back as she was refilling her wineglass. 'Everything all right?' she asked brightly.

'Fine,' Annie replied through gritted teeth.

'By the way, no one else knows about the baby, so I'd be grateful if you could keep it to yourself for now,' Suzy said. 'We don't want any fuss for a while. At least not until we've finished filming.'

Annie could already see the soft-focus spread in *Hello!* 'I'm hardly likely to tell the world, am I?'

'And we're going to be away on location most of the time, so you won't have to worry about running into us all over the place.' Suzy reached over and gave her hand a reassuring pat.

Annie snatched it away. How dare she pity me, she thought furiously. 'Actually, I'm going to be out of town myself.'

'Really?' Suzy smiled. 'Taking a little holiday, are you? Good idea.'

'As a matter of fact, I've got a job.' The words seemed to come out of nowhere.

The blue gaze sharpened. 'What kind of job?'

'I'm going back to the theatre.'

'Really? Where?'

Annie racked her brains. What was that name? 'The – er – Phoenix, Middlethorpe.'

'Rep? You're going into rep?' Suzy gave a tight little smile of malice. No wonder, Annie thought. To someone as well-connected as her it was the acting equivalent of joining the Foreign Legion.

'I know, but I just couldn't resist it,' Annie lied airily. 'It was such a tempting offer. And the new Artistic Director is a genius, so I've heard. He's just finished directing Shakespeare in Central Park. The RSC has been after him for months.'

It was an outrageous lie, but at least it brought a gleam of envy to Suzy's eyes. She might have made it on TV playing bosomy heroines, but she still liked to consider herself a serious actress and she'd always wanted to play the real classics.

'What's his name?' she asked. 'Maybe Uncle Victor knows him?' But Annie had decided the time had come for a swift exit.

'Is that the time? I really must go.' She stood up as the waiter swanned past the table.

'Leaving already?' he said, looking at her untouched bowl. 'What do you want me to do with your salad?'

'Let her have it,' Annie glanced at Suzy. 'She seems to enjoy my leftovers.'

Her moment of self-righteous triumph carried her

through the restaurant and out into the street. She was halfway down the Strand before her fragile emotions finally gave way. It was like an anaesthetic wearing off, leaving her with a raw, agonising wound. She stood, sobbing, in front of the baby accessories display in Boots window.

It might have brought her a brief moment of satisfaction, lying to Suzy about the job, but it was going to look pretty hollow in a few weeks when she was still jobless and stuck at home.

Oh, God, she thought. What have I done?

Middlethorpe

Chapter 13

Oh, God, what have I done, Annie thought again two weeks later as she sat at the window, watching rivulets of rain trickle down the glass.

It couldn't even rain properly in this town. There was no drenching downpour, no dramatic storm lighting up the roof-tops. Just the same depressing, half-hearted drizzle that had been falling ever since she had first arrived.

The window overlooked the town square, a grim quandrangle bordered by discount shops offering cut-price toiletries and plastic kitchenware. In the middle of it all stood a statue of a dour-looking Victorian gentleman, his bewhiskered chin held high despite the fact he was ankle deep in discarded Coke cans and old Burger King wrappers. This, she had been told, was Josiah Blanchard, founder of the once prosperous mill town of Middle-thorpe.

He wouldn't have recognised the place now, Annie thought. The Victorian architecture had been swept aside to make way for a soulless landscape of concrete, enlivened here and there by flyposters and graffiti. Litter blew down the pedestrian precinct.

Depressed, she shifted her gaze away from the window and back to the gathering. It was the first time the newly formed Phoenix Theatre Company had met and Nick had organised a get-together in the upstairs room of the local pub, the Millowners' Arms. People filled the room, talking, hugging, laughing.

And probably thinking how much older they all looked since the last time they'd worked together, Annie thought cynically.

Then she caught Nick's eye. He was on the other side of the room talking to Adam Gregory, the actor playing Claudio, but she could feel him watching her. They'd hardly spoken since that humiliating phone call she'd made, begging him for a job. To his credit, he had never asked why, or even said 'I told you so'. He didn't have to. It hung unspoken in the air between them like a great black cloud.

'Everything all right?' Caz appeared, looking chirpy. At least she was enjoying herself. Nick had offered her the part of Margaret, the saucy lady-in-waiting.

'Fine.'

'They seem like a great crowd, don't they?'

Annie glanced around the room. There was Clive Seymour, with his lugubrious, bloodhound face, perfect for the comical Dogberry. And there, helping himself to a sly snifter of whisky from his hip-flask, was Henry Adams, who was to play Beatrice's uncle, Leonato. He came from the old school, before TV taught young actors to mumble their lines. The huge voice that rumbled from his grizzled beard could warn shipping.

'They're okay. I hate all this bonding stuff, though.'

'Come on, it could be a lot worse. At least it's not one of those terrible touchy-feely sessions.' Caz giggled. 'I remember one job where we had to spend three days rolling around on the floor giving each other back rubs. And that was only for a dog food commercial. Mind you –' her gaze strayed across to the far side of the room '– I wouldn't mind rubbing *his* back – or anything else, come to think of it.'

Annie craned her neck. The only person she could see was the lanky Irishman playing Don John. 'Not Brendan O'Brien?'

'No, you idiot. That guy talking to him. The tall blond one.' Caz narrowed her eyes speculatively. 'Who is he, I wonder?'

'No idea. I imagine he's playing Benedick.'

'You mean you get to snog him every night? You lucky thing!'

'I suppose so,' Annie agreed listlessly.

'You could show a bit more interest.' Caz shook her head. 'God, he's wasted on you. The state you're in, you could be kissing Robin Cook every night and not even notice.'

She had a point. Ever since Annie had found out about Suzy's baby it felt as if all her feelings had shut down. Nothing seemed to touch her any more. But there was no point trying to explain that to Caz, whose emotions were like a white-knuckle ride, hurtling from high to low in a matter of seconds.

Just as she was wondering whether she could plead a headache and go home, something happened.

'Oh, God!' Annie stared at the door. 'It can't be.'

Caz swung round. 'Oh shit! No one told me she was going to be here.'

They both watched, transfixed with horror, as Georgia Graham made her noisy entrance. She made sure all eyes

99

were on her before she shrugged off her coat, revealing a figure-hugging black linen shift dress.

Annie's heart plummeted. Georgia was a notoriously difficult actress to work with. In a business where success depended on actors working together, she was famous for upstaging and stealing scenes. And as if that wasn't a good enough reason to hate her, she was also a friend of Suzy Carrington.

'I bet you anything she's playing Hero,' Caz said.

'Just what I need.' Annie groaned. It was like finding herself strapped to the school bully in the three-legged race on sports day.

They watched her sashay across the room to where Nick was standing. Flicking her long, glossy black hair off her face, she moved in for a full-on kiss.

'Nothing like going straight to the top, is there?' Caz remarked. 'I wonder if she's slept with him yet?'

'No!'

'Why not? She's famous for it. How do you think she gets most of her work?' Her lip curled. 'Just look at them. He's hardly fighting her off, is he?'

'I thought he had more taste.'

'He's a man, isn't he? And besides –' Caz suddenly clutched at her arm. 'Oh, God, she's seen us. Quick, look busy!'

But it was too late. Georgia was already homing in on them. 'My God, you two!' Annie nearly choked on a cloud of Arpège as she swept them both into her arms. 'Imagine you being here. I had no idea.'

'Me neither.' If she'd had the faintest hint, she would never have got on that train.

'Well, of course, I don't usually do theatre.' Georgia's deep, breathy voice sounded like it had just crawled out of bed after a heavy night. 'But when Nick asked me to come up here as a favour to him, I simply couldn't refuse. He's such a dear, *close* friend.' Annie felt Caz's 'I told you so' look burning into the side of her head. 'Anyway, it looks as if the poor darling needs all the help he can get. I mean, this lot are hardly the cream of the acting world, are they? Present company excepted, of course,' she added insincerely.

Annie bristled. 'What do you mean?'

'Darling, just look around you.' Georgia's slanted green eyes were full of contempt. 'Poor Henry's hardly ever off the booze these days. And old Edwin's just working his ticket until they find him a place in the Old Actors' Home. And as for Brendan O'Brien –' she leaned forward confidingly '– the rumour is he had to get out of London sharpish. Owed a lot of money to the wrong kind of people, if you know what I mean.'

Annie frowned. No doubt she'd be dishing the dirt to Suzy about her later on.

'What about the blond guy?' Caz did her best to sound casual.

'Him? Oh, that's Dan. Daniel Oliver. He's playing Benedick. You must know him, darling. He's being tipped as the next Ralph Fiennes. Or at least he was, until –'

'Until what? What?'

'Poor Dan.' Georgia sighed. 'He turned down an offer from Hollywood because his wife didn't want to go. But he'd no sooner torn up his contract than she ran off with someone else. A car mechanic from Bushey Heath, can you believe it?'

'God, how awful,' Annie murmured.

'Well, quite. I mean, she could have been sipping martinis in the Beverly Hills Hotel by now, if she'd played her cards right.' Georgia missed the point entirely. 'Dan's devastated, as you can imagine. But I think he's more upset at losing his kids than the Hollywood deal.'

Annie gazed across the room, feeling instant sympathy for him. He was smiling as he chatted to Brendan, but she could see in his eyes the shell-shocked look of a fellow survivor.

Caz gulped back the rest of her wine. 'I'll just get another drink,' she said.

'I'll come with –' Annie started to say, but Caz interrupted her.

'No, I'll get them. You stay and talk to Georgia.'

They watched her drift across the room towards Daniel. 'She'll be lucky,' Georgia commented. 'The poor darling's still hopelessly smitten with his wife.' She turned to Annie. 'Perhaps you should talk to him? I mean, you'll know what he's going through, won't you?' She tilted her head. 'How are you coping, by the way?'

'Fine.'

'So brave of you to try and rebuild your life like this,' Georgia went on. 'It can't be easy for you. Especially with Max and Suzy practically on your doorstep –'

Annie's gaze sharpened. 'What are you talking about?'

'Didn't you know, darling? This film they're making. Apparently they're on location somewhere around here. Well, I suppose they'd have to, it being a Brontë classic. They couldn't very well film it in Torquay, could they?'

But Annie wasn't listening. 'Where?' she demanded.

'Sorry, darling?'

'Where are they filming it?'

Georgia shrugged. 'God knows. Suzy did tell me. Out on some ghastly moors, I think. Why? Are you thinking of paying them a visit?'

At that moment Nick arrived. Annie's head was still reeling so much she barely noticed how Georgia snuggled up to him. Across the room, Caz had accidentally on purpose spilt her drink over Daniel and was helping him wipe down his jeans with rather more enthusiasm than was decent. The whole world seemed to be paired off, except her.

'Excuse me,' she mumbled.

Out in the square, the rain seeped through her sweater as she huddled at the huge stone feet of old Josiah.

Max was here and she didn't know whether to be appalled or excited at the prospect. Part of her didn't want him near her. Why couldn't he be safely in London, far out of temptation's reach? She'd done what everyone wanted her to do, she'd sent herself into exile, made a stab at rebuilding her life. It wasn't fair of him to end up here, where she could bump into him at any time.

But part of her felt it must be A Sign. She'd done her best to get away from him, yet Fate had thrown him in her path again. There must be a reason why it had happened.

Rain dripped off her nose as she looked across the square. It was early evening, the discount shops were putting up their shutters and people were emerging from their offices to begin the weary trek home. As they struggled with their umbrellas and bags, none of them bothered to glance at the other side of the square, to the building that stood empty and forlorn, its face shrouded in a veil of scaffolding and tarpaulin.

This was the Phoenix: the theatre that was to be her home for the next six weeks.

'Not much to look at, is it?' She'd been so deep in thought she hadn't heard Nick approaching.

'I'm sure it'll be very nice when it's finished,' she said.

103

'I don't know about that. I doubt if it'll ever win any prizes for architectural beauty. But as they say, it's what's inside that counts.' He handed her an umbrella. 'I thought you might need this.'

She smiled up at him, wet curls sticking to her neck and dripping down her face. 'It's a bit late now, but thanks anyway.'

Nick nodded back at the theatre. 'Of course, you're not really seeing it at its best. You should see it when the sun's shining. It looks so –' He searched for the word.

'Radiant?' Annie suggested.

'Dull.'

She laughed. Then Nick said, 'What was Georgia saying to you?'

'Sorry?'

'I know she must have said something for you to rush out like that. What was it?'

'It doesn't matter.'

Nick frowned. 'You mustn't take any notice of her. You know what she's like.'

Annie hoped he might go back inside and leave her alone, but he didn't. He sat down next to her. For a long time they sat in silence, staring at the theatre. 'So what changed your mind?' he asked suddenly.

'What do you mean?'

'This job. You never told me why you decided to come.' He glanced at her. 'I take it the reconciliation with Max didn't work out?'

'You could say that.' She thought of telling him about the baby, but the words wouldn't come.

'But now you're not so sure you did the right thing, running away?'

She blinked at him. 'What makes you say that?'

'It's been written all over your face ever since you got here. You look like you've just been handed a life sentence.'

Annie twisted the umbrella in her hands. 'I'm sorry. I didn't mean to seem ungrateful. You were good enough to give me the job –'

'I didn't do it out of the kindness of my heart. I did it because we need you. I need you.' His eyes met hers, honest and direct. 'But I'll understand if you want to go back to London. It won't do either of us any good if your heart's not in this.'

Annie looked up at the theatre. The tattered tarpaulin flapped in the breeze like the sails of a battle-scarred galleon. 'I don't want to leave,' she said.

'Really? But I thought –'

'I've changed my mind. I want to stay.'

'I see. Can I ask why?'

'I just feel it's something I need to do.' No need to tell him about Max being here. She doubted if he'd understand.

He looked at her for a long time. 'Well, I can't promise you won't regret it,' he said finally. 'It'll be hard work. And even then there's no guarantee we'll sell a single ticket –'

'Keep talking and I might change my mind!' she joked.

Nick wiped the rain off his face. 'Tell you what, why don't we go out for a drink tonight?'

'I've already told you I'm staying. You don't have to bribe me with alcohol.'

'Call it a celebration. I'll meet you in the pub at eight, shall I?'

'If you like.'

They watched the throng of early-evening commuters

dispersing across the square. 'I'm glad you're here,' Nick said.

Annie thought about Max, somewhere out on those wind-swept Yorkshire moors. 'So am I,' she said.

Chapter 14

Annie sprinted through the rain to where her ancient Beetle was parked on its own behind the shops, surrounded by a gaggle of adolescents in ski hats and shiny track suits. They eyed her as she flung herself at the door. Then one of them muttered something and they all started laughing.

She edged her way in behind the wheel, stung by their unspoken criticism. She knew what they were thinking. There was no point in stealing the tyres when they were balder than Duncan Goodhew. And anything they could do to the rusting paintwork could only be an improvement.

She turned the key in the ignition, aware that the gang was watching her with interest. 'Please start,' she whispered. 'Please, please start!' Beryl the Beetle cleared her throat, spluttered a little, then died. Gritting her teeth, Annie tried again. This time the car gave an irritable whine. Gingerly she began to lift her foot off the clutch. Everything died.

The youths were sniggering now. Annie wound down the window. 'Haven't you got any phone boxes to smash up?' she yelled. But this convulsed them even more.

'Oh, bog off!' She wiped her face with her sleeve.

'I hope you're not talking to me?' Caz stared through the gap in the window, her dark hair plastered to her face. 'You could have waited,' she accused.

'Sorry.' Annie reached over and yanked at the stubborn lock on the passenger side.

Caz dived in. 'You left a bit sharpish. Why didn't you wait for me?'

'I didn't know if you'd be coming. You and Daniel seemed to be getting on so well –'

'No such luck,' Caz grumbled. 'And why have you got that window open? It's freezing in here.'

Annie wound up the window laboriously. 'The car won't start.'

'What a pile of junk!' Caz snorted. 'When are you going to sell it for scrap and get yourself a nice new one?'

Annie took a deep breath and turned the key in the ignition. This time it coughed into life.

Caz settled back into her seat with a satisfied smile. 'See?' she said. 'You've just got to show it who's boss.'

'I think it already knows.' Annie noticed the youths hanging around on the corner and veered deliberately through a puddle towards them, sending an arc of muddy spray over their white trainers.

'So why were you in such a hurry tonight?' Caz gave her a sly look.

'Sorry?'

'Don't worry, I won't let on.' Caz pulled off her boot and examined the soaked purple suede. 'I just happened to hear him telling Georgia, that's all.'

'What are you talking about?' Annie crunched the gears.

'Come on, don't go all coy. You're seeing Nick tonight, aren't you?'

'Oh, that.'

'You're a quick worker. You've only been here five minutes and you're already dating the boss. Georgia was furious.'

'It's not like that.' Annie peered through the blurred windscreen. The rain was more than a match for her creaking wipers.

'Of course not.' Caz looked knowing. 'Still,' she sighed, 'at least you've got a date tonight. I was that far from getting Daniel to ask me out, until that old drunk Henry Adams butted his big red nose in. Half an hour of flirting and where's it got me? Nowhere!'

'Give him time,' Annie said. 'His wife's just left him, remember?'

'But that was months ago,' Caz protested. 'Anyway, how can he still be pining for her, after the way she's treated him?'

'How indeed?' Annie sighed. No one could have treated her worse than Max, yet she still pined for him. 'He's probably still in shock. I know how he feels.'

'But it hasn't taken you very long to find someone else, has it?'

'I told you, Nick and I are just friends, that's all.' She glimpsed a flash of movement through the streaming windscreen and jammed on the brakes just as a juggernaut rumbled out in front of her.

'If you say so.' There was a pause. 'You don't think he's gay, do you?'

'Who? Nick?'

'No! That man's testosterone on legs.' Caz shook her head. 'I mean Daniel.'

'Caz, he's got two kids.'

'That doesn't mean anything these days. And there's got to be a reason why his wife left him.'

'Maybe she just fell out of love.'

'That's what he says,' Caz muttered darkly. 'But is he telling the truth? I mean, he's hardly likely to admit she walked out because she caught him in bed with a minicab driver called Frank, is he?'

Annie laughed. 'And this is all because he didn't ask you out?'

'Well, can you think of another reason?'

'Maybe you're just not his type?'

Caz swung round, shocked. 'Don't be ridiculous!'

It must be wonderful to have such unshakeable self-esteem, Annie decided.

'So where's he taking you?' Caz asked.

'Who?'

'Nick. Romantic dinner *à deux*, is it?'

'I told you, we're just –'

'Friends. Yes, I know.' Caz raised her eyes heaven-wards. 'I reckon he fancies you.'

'He doesn't,' Annie said firmly. 'And even if he did, I don't fancy him. Okay?'

Caz shot her a shrewd look, but said no more.

Number 19 Bermuda Gardens stood out from all the other neat little post-war semis in the street. It might have been the rose-coloured stone cladding, the Elizabethan lattice windows or the row of mock crenellations along the roof edge, but whatever it was, it sat among its sober neighbours like a drag queen at a WI meeting.

Annie turned into the drive, carefully negotiating her way through the minefield of Grecian urns, stone cherubs and ornamental wheelbarrows overflowing with petunias. A regiment of gnomes glared up at her from their sentry duty around the miniature wishing well. Apparently it played 'Three Coins in the Fountain' when you dropped money into it, so Caz had informed her gleefully.

It was like no theatrical digs Annie had ever known. But then, Jeannie Acaster was like no other landlady she'd ever known, either.

There were no house rules. In fact, Mrs Acaster positively encouraged lewd behaviour after lights out. She seemed disappointed that they'd been there for two days and neither had yet brought home a single decent-looking young actor.

She didn't seem to mind when they used the kitchen, mainly because she seldom ventured in there herself, except to get some ice for her gin and tonic. 'I don't cook and I don't clean up after people,' she told them bluntly. 'I had enough of that when my miserable old sod of a husband was alive.'

In fact, living chez Acaster might have been perfect, except for one thing.

Trixie.

As they got out of the car Caz eyed the front door nervously. 'Do we have to go in?'

'It'll be fine,' Annie reassured her. 'As long as we stick together and remember not to slam the –'

But it was too late. Caz let the car door go with a resounding bang. The next moment there was a volley of frantic yapping and the thud of something flinging itself repeatedly against the other side of the door inside the house.

They hesitated on the step. 'You go first,' Annie pleaded.

'And let that thing rip my new trousers to shreds? No thanks.'

'Then there's only one thing for it.' They looked at each other then, as one, they both made a dash for the back door.

They almost made it. As they got into the kitchen there was a low-flying blur of blonde fluff and pink ribbon, and Trixie launched herself at their ankles.

As a dog, she was a pathetic specimen. Shave off her great bouffant of peroxide fur – which Annie had been sorely tempted to do – and she would be the size of a malnourished hamster. But whether it was her size or the ludicrous ribbon she was forced to wear, something had given Trixie the need to prove to the world she was more than just a powder-puff on legs. Like a canine kamikaze, she would take on anything that moved. Which at that moment was Annie's boot.

'That dog's got a serious attitude problem,' Caz said.

'She'll have a serious dental problem if she even thinks of biting me.'

'Is that you, girls?' Jeannie Acaster called from up the hall.

They went into the living-room, Trixie still snarling around Annie's ankles. The room was decorated in Soho massage parlour chic, with lurid pink satin, scarlet velvet and gold tassles everywhere. In the middle of it all, reclining on her chaise longue watching the Home Shopping Channel, was Jeannie Acaster.

'What do you think of that pendant?' She nodded towards the screen.

'Very nice.'

'Do you think so? Not too flashy?'

Annie glanced at Jeannie's well-upholstered, pink-satin-clad body. Despite it being only six o'clock she was already in full glamour make-up, her bleached hair piled up on top of her head. Her ear-rings could have picked up Sky Sport. 'I think you could carry it off,' she said tactfully.

Jeannie looked pleased. 'Did you remember my fags, by the way?'

'I've got them here.' Caz handed them over.

'Good lass. But I hope you didn't get them from the corner shop. I said I'd never go in there since that tight old bastard stopped my tick.' She beamed at Annie. 'Playing with my little Trixie, are you? That's nice. She's got a real soft spot for you, I can tell.'

I've got one for her, too, Annie thought grimly. Out in the back garden, under the ornamental pond.

'So, did you have a nice time, girls?' Jeannie fluttered her false eyelashes at them. 'Meet any nice men?'

'It's funny you should say that –' Caz plonked herself down on the chaise and launched into a blow-by-blow account of Daniel. Annie managed to escape from Trixie and left them gossiping while she went up to run herself a bath.

Like the rest of the house, their bedroom was a psychedelic nightmare. Animal prints on the walls vied with black satin on the beds. Tarzan meets Lily Savage, Caz called it. It appealed to her sense of retro kitsch. But after two days of living there, Annie had begun to crave Laura Ashley.

While she waited for her bath to run, she pulled her case out from under the bed to finish unpacking. Most of it was already done, but there were still a few bits and pieces to sort out.

Like her self-help books. Annie took out a handful and

glanced through the titles. *Loving a Difficult Man. Women Who Love Too Much. Women Who Need Too Much.*

How about *Women Who Read Too Much*, she thought, tossing them on to the bed. They hadn't done her much good so far.

Perhaps she was going about it all the wrong way? Maybe Caz had the right idea. If one relationship breaks down, just move on to the next. No regrets, no looking back. It seemed to work for her. But then Caz changed her men as often as she changed her shampoo brand. It was easier saying goodbye to someone after six weeks than six years.

As if to prove it, there was their wedding photo, staring up at her from the bottom of the suitcase. Annie picked it up and hid it in her bedside drawer, trying not to meet Max's eye. So much for not looking back. There were some things she could never leave behind, no matter what.

She closed the drawer, then changed her mind and opened it again. A photo wasn't enough. Knowing he was so near, she couldn't resist the chance to see him just one more time.

It only took a couple of phone calls on her mobile to find the information she needed. She pressed the off button, feeling pleased with herself.

'What do you think you're playing at?'

She swung round in alarm. 'Do you have to sneak up on people? You nearly gave me a heart attack.'

'You're the one being sneaky.' Caz stood in the doorway. 'Who were you whispering to on the phone?'

'I wasn't.'

'You were calling Carrington Productions, weren't you? And don't bother to lie, I heard everything.'

'I don't know what you're talking about.' Annie stalked past her into the bathroom. Caz followed.

'Georgia told me about Max being up here.' She folded her arms across her chest. 'Why, Annie? Why do you want to track him down, after everything he's done to you? For God's sake, haven't you got any pride?'

'You wouldn't understand.'

'You're right, I don't. Bloody hell, he couldn't make it any more obvious that he doesn't care. Why don't you just take the hint?'

'I have. I just – I can't explain it. I just have to see him again, okay?' She tested the bathwater with her hand and turned off the taps.

'You realise this is how stalkers start?' Caz persisted. 'Next thing you know you'll have a restraining order slapped on you.'

'Caz –'

'Can't you see how pathetic you're being? Catch me making a fool of myself over some man.'

'That's rich! You were practically cleaning Daniel's boots with your tongue this afternoon.'

'At least he's available,' Caz pointed out coldly. 'Anyway, what about Nick? You were supposed to be meeting him tonight, or had you forgotten?'

She had forgotten. But she wasn't about to admit that when Caz was in such a disapproving mood. 'I'm not seeing him until later. Anyway, he'll understand.'

'So you're determined to go ahead and make a complete prat of yourself?'

'Caz –'

'Fine. I'll expect the call from the police station in a couple of hours, shall I?' Caz turned on her heel and walked out of the room.

Chapter 15

Caz was right, Annie reflected some time later, as she sat shivering behind the steering wheel looking at the Roebuck Hotel. She was crazy. Why else would she be out here, in the middle of nowhere, trying to catch a glimpse of her husband and his new girlfriend?

It had taken her a while to find the place. Several times she had to pull off the narrow country lane to consult the directions the woman at Carrington Productions had given her. And the further she strayed from Middlethorpe, the more her doubts grew. It would be dark in an hour or so, and the rain was coming down more heavily. Beryl the Beetle's lights had never been her most reliable feature. Suppose she ended up stranded out here in the middle of the moors? It all looked pretty bleak.

Then, just when she was beginning to wonder if she should give up and turn back, she found it. An old country inn, nestling in the valley.

Annie pulled her car off the road behind some trees where she could get a good view of the pub and waited. The Roebuck looked warm and welcoming, its lights twinkling invitingly. She crouched behind the wheel, the sound of the rain drumming on the roof, punctuated by the half-hearted squeak of the windscreen wipers.

Now what, she wondered as she sat there, her fingers cramped from gripping the steering wheel. The compulsion that had brought her all the way out here seemed to be ebbing away, leaving her feeling cold and rather foolish.

She was just about to start the engine when the location bus rumbled into the car-park. Annie sank down behind the wheel, pulling up the collar of her jacket. She watched the crew tumbling off the bus, squinting through the rain-blurred windscreen to make out the shapes. And then she saw him.

She knew straight away it was Max. Annie pressed her face closer to the window, straining to catch another glimpse of him. As she did, he turned around suddenly.

She dived down in her seat again, bashing her head against the steering wheel. But she was trembling so much from the adrenalin pumping round her body that she hardly noticed.

What if he saw the car? What if he suddenly appeared at the window and demanded to know what she was doing? What if –

Slowly she edged her way back up to risk another peek. He was still standing there. Then she realised with a shock that he hadn't recognised her. He was too busy looking at Suzy.

Annie watched as he put out a hand to help her off the bus. The rain was soaking him, but he didn't seem to care as he slipped off his jacket and draped it protectively round her shoulders.

How did Suzy describe it? Like a piece of priceless Dresden? Annie hadn't really believed it until now. It was so different from the Max she'd known. This was not a man who would knowingly take all the hot water or make her sleep on the edge of the bed.

He bent his head and whispered something to her. Suzy laughed and lifted her face to his. There they were, the two of them, looking so – in love.

Annie couldn't bear to watch any more. Her hand shaking, she turned the ignition key. The engine whined, then stalled.

Oh, God, not now. Please not now, she prayed, turning the key again. Silence. She turned it again and again, more frantically each time.

'Need any help?' A man was coming towards her across the car-park. Annie spotted the green Carrington Productions logo on his bomber jacket.

'Start, damn you!' Panic-stricken, she wrenched the key in the ignition. Beryl the Beetle coughed, spluttered and sprang to life.

'Thank God.' Annie lifted her foot off the clutch. Beryl strained forward, but didn't move. She listened to the ominous whizzing sound.

'Looks like your back wheel's stuck,' the man yelled. 'Hang on a sec. I'll get some of the lads to give you a push.'

'No!' But he was already ambling back across the car-park.

Annie leaped from the car. The freezing mud sucked at her boots as she scrambled round to the back. She had to shift Beryl before he came back with the others. He might bring Max! Not that she could imagine him turning out on a rainy night to rescue a damsel in distress, but she couldn't take any chances.

She leaned her full weight against Beryl and heaved

hard. Her feet slipped and skidded in the mud, but she kept on pushing.

She'd heard stories of people who developed super-human strength in times of crisis, but she'd never believed it was possible until, incredibly, Beryl began to inch forward.

The men were coming out of the pub. Annie flung open Beryl's door and dived behind the wheel. Crunching the gears in her panic to get away, she'd reached the lane before they got halfway across the car-park.

Luckily there were no other cars on the road that night as she drove, her foot slammed on the accelerator, taking corners recklessly. She didn't even try to read her map and it was only by sheer fluke that she ended up on the road back to Middlethorpe.

She found herself in the town centre, the rain-washed streets empty and desolate, even though it was still only just after nine o'clock. Annie slumped in her seat, feeling wrung-out. Her clothes and shoes were splattered in mud, and cold had seeped right through to her bones. She would just nip into the pub, buy some ciggies and head for home.

Then it dawned on her. The pub. Nick. Oh hell.

Chapter 16

It was Talent Nite in the Millowners' Arms. A middle-aged man with thatched hair and a spangly waistcoat was sweating his way through 'Copacabana' as Annie peered through the dense, smoky haze, looking for Nick.

Of course he wasn't there. How could she expect him to wait over an hour for her? Especially on Talent Nite. It was more than flesh and blood could stand.

Annie came out of the pub into the wet night, feeling guilty. Poor Nick. She'd completely forgotten about him in her desperation to see Max. Now that craving had subsided she felt deeply ashamed of herself.

She was heading back across the square when she spotted the light in one of the upper windows of the theatre. Someone was moving about up there, a dark shape outlined in the light.

It must be Nick. He had become tired of waiting for her and gone back to the theatre to catch up with some work instead. Annie walked towards the building.

The stage door was open. The street lamps outside cast a dim, eerie light down the narrow corridor, which smelled strongly of wet paint and sawdust. Annie's breath made coils in the air as she picked her way towards the door at the end.

After a lot of tripping and cursing in the dark she found herself on the stage, looking out into the empty auditorium. In front of her the rows of seats, swathed in dust-sheets, made eerie shapes in the gloom. A sense of foreboding crept through her veins.

'Nick?' Her voice sounded like a gunshot in the dense silence. The only other sound was her heart, thudding somewhere below her tonsils.

She groped her way to the front of the stage, her hands moving over crumbling patches of ornate plasterwork. Something brushed past her in the darkness, briefly touching her face.

Annie's shriek of terror echoed around the building. She wasn't easily spooked, but this was just too creepy. And there was a strange smell, too, mingling with the wet paint: dark, aromatic and smoky. Annie lifted her chin, sniffing the icy air. It smelled just like –

'Turkish cigarettes. They were her favourites.'

The voice croaked out of the darkness behind her. Annie swung round and found herself trapped in a beam of torchlight as the stooped figure shuffled out of the shadows. He was the oldest man she'd ever seen, so crooked with age his nose was pointing at the bare boards of the stage.

' 'Course, she'd smoke 'owt if she had to, even my Capstans. But them Sobrani things was always her favourite.' He cocked his head to fix her with rheumy, yellowed eyes. His skin hung in wrinkled folds off his bones. 'I suppose you'll be one of them new lot?'

'I'm Annie Mitchell.' She flinched as he aimed the torchbeam straight into her face. She wondered where

Nick had dug him up. 'Dug up' being the operative phrase.

'Aye, she told me you'd be coming.' He nodded approvingly. 'She likes you. Not everyone can sense her, y'know. Only them she trusts.'

'Really?' Annie took a step backwards. 'That's – er – nice.'

He tweaked at his old cardigan with a shaking hand. 'You'll do well here, you will. You'll come to no harm. Jessie Barron takes care of them she likes. Not like some.'

'Oh – good.' He was obviously rambling. Oh well, better humour him. 'So you look after this place, do you? You and your – er – friend Jessie?'

A cackle wheezed up from his thin chest. 'That's right.' He chuckled. 'Me and Jessie look after things now. Been here all my life, I have. Right from a lad. I was here when the place closed down, thirty years back.'

'Really?' Judging from his musty smell, Annie wondered if he'd been stored away in an old props basket somewhere backstage.

' 'Course, there's some as said the place should never be opened up again. Not after all that's happened.' He fixed her with a beady look. 'Told you about the curse, have they?'

'What curse?'

'Didn't think they would. Wouldn't want you running away, would they?'

'All right, Stan. I'm sure Annie doesn't want to hear any of your fairy stories.' Annie nearly collapsed with relief as the house lights went on and Nick emerged from the wings.

'They ain't fairy stories!' Stan looked indignant. 'It's the truth!'

'Whatever you say.'

'And I'll tell you summat else true an' all. It weren't her that started that fire.' He looked them up and down defiantly.

'So you keep telling me, Stan.' Nick put his hand on the old man's shoulder. Next to him, Stan's frail, stooped body was like a child's. 'Now, I think it's time we locked up for the night, don't you?'

Stan touched his cap. 'Right you are, Mr Ryan, sir.'

As he shuffled off, jangling his keys, Annie turned to Nick. 'Thank God you turned up. He was giving me the creeps.'

Nick smiled at her. 'Take no notice of old Stan. He's barking mad, but harmless.'

'Where did you get him from? A youth opportunities scheme?'

'He found me. He heard word the theatre was reopening and came to see me about a week ago. Apparently he's worked here on the stage door all his life. So I took him on as a caretaker.'

'He doesn't look as if he can take care of himself, let alone this place,' Annie said doubtfully.

'I know, but I couldn't just send him away. And it's got to be better than mouldering in a day centre, staring at the walls and waiting to die.'

'What about his wife? Is she as decrepit as he is?'

'I've no idea. I didn't even know he had any family.'

'So who's this Jessie character he's been going on about?'

'Ah, you mean Jessie Barron.' Nick's brows lifted.

'That's right. I hope she's not going to leap out of the woodwork as well?'

'I very much doubt it. She's been dead for nearly sixty years.'

'What? But he said —'

'Stan likes to live in the past. Besides, you wouldn't be bothered by a ghost, would you? Most theatres have them.'

'Yes, I know.' Annie shivered. 'But I never imagined I'd be sharing a dressing-room with one.'

'Don't worry, you won't have to. I've been here nearly two weeks and I haven't seen a thing.'

Annie thought of the strange, cloying smell and the thing that had brushed her face in the dark, but said nothing. 'And what about this curse?' she asked. 'Is that a figment of Stan's imagination too?'

Nick's smile disappeared. 'There is no curse,' he said flatly.

For some reason Annie didn't feel reassured. 'But Stan said —'

'Stan's wrong,' Nick cut her off. 'If there's any ill will towards this place, it's from the living, not the dead.' He noticed her dismayed expression. 'Sorry.' He sighed. 'I didn't mean to snap. I've just had a lot on my mind tonight.'

'Problems?'

'Nothing a couple of thousand extra pounds wouldn't sort out.' Nick rubbed his eyes. 'I've just spent the last hour on the phone to the builders. They reckon they've found some new kind of rot under the stage. Apparently the whole thing's got to be ripped out and replaced.'

'Sounds expensive.'

'It will be. I shouldn't think the trustees will be too happy about it when they find out.'

'The trustees?'

'The people who own the lease on this building.' He explained how a group of local business men and women had got together to buy it. 'The council wanted to redevelop it. If the trustees hadn't stepped in when they did, this place might have been a department store by now.' His face was grim. 'I think they're beginning to wonder if they did the right thing.'

Annie noticed the lines of fatigue etched in his face and felt guilty. Poor Nick. He looked as if he could have done with some cheering up tonight.

'I didn't think you were coming.' He seemed to read her thoughts.

'I know – I'm sorry. I – er – got delayed.'

'Nothing serious, I hope?'

'No.' Her brain raced. 'It was Caz's fault. She – er – wanted me to help her.'

'I see.'

'She's going out, you see, and she needed me to help her find something to wear.'

'For an hour? She must have quite an extensive wardrobe.'

'Well, not for a whole hour, obviously.' She could feel herself squirming. 'She wanted me to do her hair too. And her make-up. She was in a terrible state, poor thing.'

'Funny,' Nick said. 'She sounded quite calm when I phoned earlier.' His eyes raked her. 'It's all right, Annie. You can stop lying. I know you've been to see Max.'

Chapter 17

One look at his face and she knew there was no point in denying it. 'Caz told you?'

He nodded. 'I called your house when you didn't turn up. I was worried about you.'

He was worried about her. And all the time she'd been hanging around on the moors, trying to catch a glimpse of a man who didn't give a damn.

Annie looked at his hurt face and felt even more guilty. She'd behaved appallingly. Nick deserved much better than this. 'I'm really sorry,' she said. 'You must be furious.'

'Only with myself.' His voice was bitter. 'I thought you'd come up here because you wanted this job. I might have known he'd be the reason behind it.'

'But I didn't know Max was going to be here.'

'Don't tell me it's just a coincidence? Come on, I'm not that stupid. Why else would you have taken it? You said yourself, it's hardly a great career move.'

'I had no idea Max was here until Georgia told me. I came because I wanted to get away from him.'

'Which is why you took off across the moors looking for him the minute you found out?'

He had a point, she realised. Why should he believe her? Why should he ever trust her again after the way she'd behaved? 'You're right,' she admitted. 'It was completely stupid. I just wanted to see him again.'

'And did you?'

'Oh, yes. I saw him all right. And her.' Tears stung her eyes. 'They looked so – perfect. Like they were meant to be together.'

'Maybe they are.'

'Maybe.' She took a deep, steadying breath. 'But it's not easy to accept, is it? That the person you love most in all the world wants someone else?'

'No,' Nick said softly. 'No, it's not easy at all.' There was a silence. 'So what are you going to do now?' he asked.

'What else can I do? Start doing what everyone's been telling me and get over him, I suppose.'

'Do you think you can?'

'I don't know.' She swallowed the lump in her throat. 'But I don't think I've got much choice, have I?' She looked at him again. Perhaps he really did care about her, she thought. In spite of everything. She made up her mind that if he gave her another chance, she wasn't going to blow it. She was going to buckle down, work hard and show Nick the best Beatrice he'd ever seen. And maybe, in the process, she would forget about her aching heart.

'I am sorry,' she said again.

'I don't like being lied to.'

'It won't happen again, I promise.' She glanced up at him and crossed her fingers surreptitiously. 'I'll understand, though – if you don't want me around.' She bit her lip, waiting.

At last he spoke. 'I don't know about you, but I need that drink,' he said.

Talent Nite was just reaching its riotous conclusion. They stood outside the Millowners' Arms for a moment, listening to the sounds of crashing furniture and smashing glass.

'Let's go back to my place,' Nick suggested. 'You can leave your car here. I'll drive you back to collect it later.'

He lived just outside town, at the end of a long row of old millworkers' cottages clinging to the hillside overlooking Middlethorpe.

'Sorry about the state of the place,' he said, turning the key in the lock. 'I wasn't expecting any visitors.'

Inside, the house was warm and cosy. Lamps cast soft pools of light over the kelim rugs and bookshelves. The living-room was dominated by two huge squashy sofas, strewn with sections of the *Sunday Times*. It was endearingly untidy, welcoming and the kind of place Annie could have stayed in for ever.

She sighed enviously as she took off her muddy boots on the doormat. 'This is certainly better than our digs.'

'Why? What's your place like?'

'The knocking shop from hell!' She grimaced. 'The landlady's okay, but the place looks like Lily Savage has been let loose on it.'

Nick laughed. 'Sounds delightful. Now, shall I open some wine? Or would you prefer a brandy? I've just got the one bottle. Do you think that will be enough?' He dodged the cushion that Annie hurled at him. 'I'll take that as a no, shall I?'

'Just coffee, thank you,' Annie said primly.

While he was clattering about in the kitchen, she took a look around the room. Like her, Nick appeared to be a compulsive collector of clutter. Books, photos, old news-papers – he didn't seem to throw anything away.

'You know, you can tell a lot about a person from his bookshelves,' she commented, browsing through the titles on the spines.

'So what do mine say?'

Annie frowned at the overloaded shelves, buckling under the weight of Pinter and Shaw, with elderly copies of *Beano* and *Private Eye* piled haphazardly on top for good measure. 'Same as mine. Disorganised and on the point of collapse.'

'Sounds about right.'

She moved across to the photos on the dresser, each with a handful of bills and old letters stuffed behind them. Nick's filing system seemed remarkably like hers too. Then one of the photos caught her eye. It was Georgia, draped over a chair, wearing black stockings, a bowler hat and a come-hither smile. 'To darling Nick. Thanks for everything,' was scrawled across her bosom.

And what exactly was *everything*, Annie wondered. 'So how long have you known Georgia?'

'A couple of years. I directed her in *Cabaret.*'

'That must have been interesting.'

'I know she can be a bit difficult at times, but she's pretty talented,' Nick said. 'She just needs careful hand-ling.'

Annie was about to ask how much handling had gone on when she noticed her reflection in the mirror. 'Oh, my God!' she shrieked. 'Why didn't you tell me?'

'About what?' Nick stuck his head round the door. 'Oh, that. You don't look bad.'

'Not bad?' Annie stared at her dirt-streaked face and

wild hair. She looked as if she'd been mud-wrestling – and the mud had won.

'Your clothes are worse,' Nick pointed out mildly.

'Thanks a lot. May I use your bathroom?'

'Upstairs, first on the left. There are some clean clothes in the wardrobe if you want to change.'

After their bathroom at home, which looked liked stock-taking day at the Boots No. 7 counter, Nick's seemed positively minimal. Annie quickly dragged a brush through her curls and washed her face. The towels smelled of Nick – clean, fresh and lemony.

Then she wandered next door to his bedroom to find something to wear. It felt strange to be there, among his clothes, his books, his most personal things, as if she was somehow intruding on his private space. But at the same time she couldn't resist looking around and taking in the details: the simple, iron-framed bed with its navy quilt; the script, covered in scribbled notes, left carelessly on the pillow ready for tomorrow's rehearsal; the old pine chest of drawers, crowded with yet more photos. Annie crept across the room to look. Nick's parents, his brothers – she'd never met them but she couldn't miss the resemblance. A laughing blonde stretched out on a sun lounger. His sister? Couldn't be. His wife? Annie peered closer, curious to see the woman Nick had fallen in love with.

Then she noticed another photo, of her and the rest of the gang, taken the last time they were on the road. Annie grimaced. God, she was so young! And her hair – it certainly wasn't her most flattering angle. There were Rob and Ian and Claire. And there was Nick, standing beside her, his arm round her shoulders, easily the most handsome of them all.

She heard Nick calling from downstairs and dropped

the photo guiltily. It fell with a clatter, skittering all the others.

'Annie? Are you okay up there?'

'I'm fine.' She set them straight hurriedly, worried Nick would appear and find her snooping. 'I – er – won't be a minute.'

When she came downstairs he was pouring the coffee. 'That's an improvement,' he remarked.

'Thanks.' Annie cinched in the thick leather belt that held up his faded Levis. She'd grabbed the first shirt and jeans she could find. It seemed all wrong to be up there, poking around in his wardrobe. 'I'll let you have them back as soon as I've washed them.'

'Whenever.' He pushed a mug towards her. 'White, no sugar. That's how you like it, isn't it?'

'You still remember after all these years? I'm impressed.' She curled up on the sofa and tucked her bare feet under her.

'So how exactly did you end up covered in mud?' Nick asked.

'My car got stuck so I had to push it.' She explained about the minibus and the man, and how desperate she'd been to get away. 'I don't know how I managed to get it out of the mud, but I knew –' She broke off, seeing Nick's face. 'Are you laughing?'

'No.'

'Yes, you are. It wasn't funny. You should try being face down in mud some time and see how you like it.'

'I did once. Don't you remember, that night Rob managed to put the van into a ditch?'

'And you came up with the brilliant idea of levering it out?' Annie started to laugh. 'Serves you right for being such a know-all. I told you we should have called the AA.'

'Yes, you did. And as I recall, you were still telling me when I was pulling myself out of the mud.'

'Not just mud. There were cows in that field, remember?'

Nick grimaced. 'Don't remind me. I can't think why we decided to leave it all behind and head for the bright lights of Broadway, can you?'

There was an awkward silence. Annie thought about the photo upstairs, of her grinning lopsidedly into the camera, Nick's arm casually round her shoulders. It all seemed such a long time ago. 'So what was it like in America?' she asked.

'Pretty tough, at first. I think I must have gone to every audition in town when I first arrived there.' Nick poured himself more coffee. 'I nearly caught the next plane back to England. But I promised I'd give myself a year to make it, so I decided to stick it out.'

'What happened then?'

'I was so desperate for cash I signed up to teach some acting classes. That's where I met this other guy, Mark Ellis. He was in the same boat as me, so we decided to get together and put on *A Streetcar Named Desire* off-Broadway.' He sipped his coffee. 'Neither of us really expected much to come of it. We just did it to make the rent, really. But we struck lucky. Someone from the *New York Times* happened to see the show, wrote an incredible review and by the following week we were suddenly the hottest ticket in town.' He stretched out on the rug. 'Funny how things work out, isn't it? It could all have been so different.'

Indeed it could. Annie's hands tightened around her mug. 'So is that where you met your wife? In the theatre?'

'Kind of. She came along to the opening when we transferred to Broadway.'

'So she's not an actress?'

'Elizabeth? God, no.' He laughed. 'Her father would have had a fit. He was furious enough about her marrying me. I think he was hoping for a doctor or a lawyer as a son-in-law, not an impoverished theatrical. Lizzie came from an old Boston family, you see. Her father made it sound as if I was practically marrying into royalty.'

Annie thought of the smiling blonde in the photo. 'Is that what split you up?'

Nick shook his head. 'Things just fizzled out. There were no big bust-ups, or anything like that. We simply agreed to go our separate ways. Elizabeth packed her stuff, moved back in with her parents and a year later married a heart surgeon from Connecticut. Daddy whole-heartedly approves, so I'm told.' His mouth twisted wryly.

'And it doesn't hurt you to see her with someone else?'

'Not really. I think Lizzie only married me to annoy her folks and I was – well, let's just say my heart wasn't in it.' He put down his mug. 'I'm truly glad we both realised our mistake before it was too late. It would have been more difficult if there'd been kids involved.'

Annie felt a shaft of pain. Was that why Max had never wanted a baby? Because he knew he would leave her one day? 'I wonder if things would have been different if we'd had children?' she mused.

'I doubt it. Marriages break up even when there are kids involved. Look at Daniel Oliver. It's just more compli-cated and painful when they do.'

'You're probably right.' She'd never know now, anyway.

'What about you?' Nick asked. 'What made you fall for Max?'

Annie smiled mistily. 'He swept me off my feet.'

'Love at first sight, you mean?'

'Something like that.' Except in her case it had been stomach-melting lust at first sight. And in Max's – well, she didn't know how long it had taken him to notice her.

Nick yawned and stretched out his legs. 'I don't know if I've ever believed in all that stuff.'

'You mean you've never seen someone and realised they were the one?'

'I wish I had. By the time I'm aware of it, they've usually gone off with someone else.' His eyes met hers fleetingly over the rim of his mug.

Annie looked away. 'I just wish I could get over him as quickly as I fell for him.'

'You will,' Nick promised. 'Wait and see. In a few months' time you'll be able to listen to all your CDs without bursting into tears. And in a year or so you'll probably be able to look at your old photos and feel only mildly suicidal.'

'Now there's something to look forward to.' Annie sighed. 'Is that how long it took you to get over your wife?'

His eyes held hers. 'No,' he said. 'That's how long it took me to get over you.'

At first she thought he was joking, then realised with a shock that he wasn't. She knew some kind of response was called for, but what the hell did he expect her to say?

'Don't look so shocked.' Nick grinned. 'Surely you must have known how I felt about you?'

'I – I knew we were friends, but –' Yes, of course she knew. In her heart of hearts she'd always known. Why else would she have felt so terrible about dumping him?

'It's all ancient history now, of course.' Nick seemed to read her thoughts. 'A lot's happened since then. We've both grown up. And it's never a good idea to try and turn back the clock, is it?'

'No.'

'Maybe I shouldn't have said anything.' He watched her carefully. 'I'd hate you to feel awkward about it.'

It was a bit late for that now. Annie experimented with a carefree laugh. It didn't work. 'Me? Awkward? Don't be silly.'

'That's okay, then. More coffee?' Nick picked up the pot. 'I can make some fresh, if you like?'

'God, is that the time?' Annie looked at her watch. 'I really should be going.' She headed over to the door where she'd left her boots.

'But it's only eleven.'

'I know, but we start rehearsals tomorrow, don't forget.' She knew she was gibbering as she found her boots and pulled them on. 'We don't want to be late on the first day.'

'I can't be late. I'm the director.' She could feel Nick watching her with amusement. 'Hang on, I'll fetch my car keys.'

'There's no need –'

'Your car's still in town, remember?' He smiled, his eyes crinkling. 'You can't walk all the way back to Middle-thorpe on your own.'

Oh, I don't know, Annie thought as she followed him reluctantly to the car. After what she'd heard tonight, some fresh air might be just what she needed.

Chapter 18

'I told you he fancied you!'

Caz sat on the end of the bed in her bra and knickers, drying her hair. Even with her head upside down, Annie could see her triumphant expression.

'I don't know what you're grinning about,' she grumbled.

'Oh, come on.' Caz switched off the hairdryer and fluffed up her spiky crop. 'It's not every day some gorgeous man tells you he's in love with you. Admit it, you must feel just a teeny bit flattered?'

'Not really,' Annie lied. 'And anyway, he doesn't feel that way about me any more. He said so.'

'So what are you panicking about?' Caz picked her way across to the wardrobe, threw it open and began hurling things out. 'He doesn't fancy you, you don't fancy him. What's the problem?'

'Don't you see? This makes things very awkward.' Annie dodged sideways to avoid a pair of low-flying pedal pushers. 'How can I face him after this? It's embarrassing.' She hadn't been able to sleep all night thinking about it.

'I know what's wrong with you.' Caz pulled out a flimsy scrap of black fabric and began to shake out the creases. 'You do like him. And you're terrified you might do something about it.'

'Don't talk rubbish,' Annie snapped. 'I'm not ready for a relationship. I'm still coming to terms with being alone –'

'Oh, yes? And which self-help book did you get that out of? *Learning To Love Celibacy*, or *How To Be a Boring Old Fart for the Rest of Your Life*?'

'You're not taking this seriously.'

'You're right, I'm not. Look, all I can see is you're single, he's single, you obviously like each other –'

'As friends,' Annie put in quickly.

'So why don't you forget about your horrible ex-husband and just get on with it?' Caz held up the shirt. 'Bugger, it's still all creased. I'll have to find something else.'

'You're making a lot of effort just for a read-through.' Annie remarked. 'This wouldn't have anything to do with Daniel, would it?'

'Ten out of ten.' Caz retrieved a skimpy-looking T-shirt from one of the assorted piles around the room. 'And you'd better get a move on too. Have you seen the time?'

'I don't know if I can face it. My throat feels a bit sore –'

'Liar. Come on, we'll be late.'

She was right. By the time Caz had finished slapping on her make-up and Beryl had creaked to life, it was already ten o'clock. It was nearly half past when they hurtled into the church hall they'd borrowed as a rehearsal room. Everyone else was already there, sitting in a circle. There was a noisy scraping of chairs as people turned round to look at them. Georgia consulted her watch ostentatiously.

Of course there were only two chairs left. And, of

course, one of them was right next to Nick. There was a moment of comic shuffling as Annie and Caz raced each other to the only other available seat. Caz got there first. Shooting her a mutinous look, Annie retreated to sit between Nick and Fliss, the Deputy Stage Manager she'd met at that fateful audition.

'Nick's been showing us the set,' Fliss explained.

Annie looked at the model box, the miniature mock-up of the stage with its tiny cardboard pillars and plinths. This was the working model that the designer produced for the director's approval, before work started on the real thing.

'The way I see it, there's really two love stories,' Nick was explaining. 'First there's Hero and Claudio. The golden couple. They've fallen in love for the first time and everything's incredibly idealistic and romantic.'

Just like Max and Suzy. Annie remembered the way they'd been together, bathed in the glow of love: a perfect pair.

'And then at the other end of the scale there's Beatrice and Benedick,' Nick went on. 'She's been through it all before, she's been hurt and now she's wary of getting involved again.' Annie looked up sharply. He could have been talking about her. 'Benedick's in the same boat. He's seen his friends lose their heads over women and he's not going to let it happen to him. Yet in spite of it all, there's an attraction between them they can't hide away from.' Their eyes met. 'No matter how much they try to fight it, in the end they know what's going to happen.'

Annie felt her mouth go dry. Then Georgia piped up, breaking the tension. 'I see your point, Nick darling, but I always think of their story as being subordinate to that of Hero and Claudio. I don't feel we should fall into the trap of making too much of it.'

'Not if it keeps you off the stage, anyway.' Adam Gregory, who played Claudio, raised his eyebrows at Annie.

'I agree. Which is why I plan to highlight the differences.' Nick reached down beside his chair and pulled out a portfolio of sketches. 'I got these costume ideas from the designer yesterday. As you can see, I want to emphasise the fact that Hero is young, fresh and idealistic, and Beatrice is –'

'A raddled old hag, by the sound of it.' Annie frowned.

'Representing the darker, more cynical side of love.' Nick grinned at her. Annie felt her stomach do a back flip. 'Do you think you can do that?' he asked.

'After the month I've had? On my head, I should imagine,' she replied.

They began the morning's work with a read-through. As everyone opened their texts, there was an immediate gasp of protest from Georgia. 'But shouldn't we spend some time on our characters first?' she asked. Like Caz, she'd dressed up for the occasion in a scarlet top and skin-tight black capri pants. Her glossy black hair was pinned on top of her head, showing off her bone structure. 'When I did *Cymbeline* at the National we spent a week exploring our inner depths –'

'Or inner shallows, in your case,' Henry Adams snorted through his beard. His eyes were suspiciously bloodshot this morning, Annie noticed.

'I'm sure it would be useful, but we don't have time,' Nick said tactfully. 'We open in less than four weeks.'

'Yes, but –'

'And I've never thought there was much to be gained by talking. Surely you can find out more by doing something than by sitting around discussing it?'

'Hear, hear,' muttered Cecily Taylor, the elderly actress playing Ursula. She had put down her text and was busy knitting.

'You're the director.' Georgia stuck out her lip.

'Thank you.'

'But don't expect me to give of my best. I don't work well under this kind of pressure.'

'I'll bear that in mind,' Nick said levelly. 'Now, if we could just get on with the read-through?'

They all picked up their texts again. Georgia gave a stifled moan. She continued to whimper through Act One, Scene One, between Annie, Henry – who played Beatrice's uncle Leonato – and a messenger, played by Clive Seymour.

Georgia had one line: 'My cousin means Signor Benedick of Padua.' She delivered it, then burst into noisy tears. 'It's no good, I can't do it.' She sobbed. 'I know nothing about my character.'

'Perhaps you should have read the play?' Adam pointed out kindly.

In the end, much to everyone else's disgust, Nick gave in. 'Okay,' he said. 'We'll do some character exercises. Get into pairs, everyone.'

There was another unseemly dash across the room, as Caz and Georgia raced each other to Daniel. Georgia won by a neck and a well-aimed elbow.

Caz retreated sulkily back to the empty seat beside Annie. 'Look at her.' She shot Georgia an evil look. 'If she sits any closer she'll be kissing him!'

'Let's just get on with it, shall we?' Annie had done this exercise a million times. Actors got into pairs and took it in turn to ask questions, which the other had to answer in character. 'What do you want to ask me?'

'I bet I know what she's asking *him*. Bloody harpy!'

Nobody except Georgia seemed to be taking it seriously. As they swopped partners around the room, Annie discussed Adam's pregnant wife's heartburn, the best bet for the two forty-five at Haydock with Brendan O'Brien and cooed over photos of Cecily's new grandchild. And all the time she could feel Nick watching her.

'Right, is everyone happy now?' he asked half an hour later. 'If we could just get on with the read-through?'

They did. They might have been sitting in a circle reading from their scripts, but it didn't take Annie long to forget her troubles and get caught up in the story that was unfolding. She began to feel herself taking on the character of feisty Beatrice. She understood her dilemmas. She had been let down in love and was reluctant to offer her wounded heart again. And there was Benedick – a friend, a soul mate, but a lover?

She glanced across at Nick. His head was bent over his script, following each line. The trouble was, he was extremely fanciable in a dark, rugged kind of way. Caz was right, she could easily go for him. But it was too soon. She should still be mourning her marriage, not looking around for someone new. Beatrice might be falling in love, but she couldn't. In her current state she needed a new man like she needed wider hips.

She was suddenly aware that all eyes were turned in her direction. 'Oh, God, sorry. Is it my line?' Blushing, she thumbed through her script.

'"Is Claudio thine enemy?"' Daniel came to her rescue. 'Line two ninety.'

'Thanks.' Annie didn't dare look up as she scrabbled for her place. What a great start. Her most important scene and she'd day-dreamed her way through it.

'I'm really sorry,' she said to Daniel as they broke for lunch later. 'I hope I didn't put you off too much, missing my cue like that?'

'Don't worry.' Daniel grinned. He had wicked green eyes, Annie noticed. No wonder Caz fancied him. 'We're all going down to the Millowners' for lunch. Are you coming?'

'We'd love to, wouldn't we?' Right on cue, Caz appeared.

'You go on. I'll join you later,' Annie looked across at Nick, who was deep in conversation with Fliss. She knew she should talk to him, maybe apologise for making such a hasty exit last night. After all, it was quite an ego boost to be told that someone had once secretly fancied you. Maybe she should ask him out to lunch? Just as friends, of course . . .

He looked up and smiled as she approached.

She wetted her lips nervously. 'I was just wondering if you'd like to –'

'Ready, Nick darling?' Georgia appeared and threaded her arm possessively through his. 'I thought we'd try that Italian in the High Street? It looks pretty dire but at least there's a chance the food will be edible.'

'Coming.' Nick looked back at Annie. 'Sorry. What was it you wanted?'

'It can wait.' So much for her fears about him fancying her, she thought. Like the man said, it was ancient history now.

Chapter 19

After lunch they began the blocking rehearsal. Fliss had marked out an area with tape to represent the stage, with different coloured markings to show any pillars, steps or props that would appear on the final set. She was sitting next to Nick, making technical notes in The Book.

This was the period in which the actors began to move around, trying to put movement to their speech. For Annie, it was the most exciting time as she looked for outward ways of expressing her character's inner feelings. She felt a familiar tingle, something she hadn't felt in a very long time. She was back where she belonged, doing something she loved. And she was enjoying herself.

But this didn't stop Georgia breaking everyone's concentration and offering unhelpful advice.

'Do you really think Beatrice would be that flirtatious?' she queried, as they stood on the sidelines, watching a scene between Benedick and Claudio. 'I mean, she's a bit of a social embarrassment, isn't she? Over the hill and still not married off.'

'How come you're not playing her, if you know so much about it?' Caz muttered.

'Too young, darling,' Georgia flashed back.

Annie skimmed her lines and tried to ignore their bickering. Then suddenly everything stopped.

'Wow!' Georgia whispered. 'Who's that?'

'No idea. But he's bloody gorgeous, whoever he is.'

Annie looked up and her heart shot like a high-speed lift into her throat. He was just like Max. Tall, fair-haired, in an immaculately tailored grey suit that obviously didn't come from Middlethorpe High Street. His cool gaze searched the room until it found Nick.

'My guess is he's one of the trustees.' Georgia ran the tip of her tongue over her lips. 'Maybe I should go over and introduce myself.'

But Nick beat her to it. Annie watched him talking to the stranger. From the agitated way his hand went through his dark hair she could tell they weren't exchanging pleasantries.

Finally he came over. 'I'm afraid we're going to have to end rehearsals for the day. Something's come up at the theatre.'

'Nothing serious, I hope?' Adam asked.

Annie noticed Nick's shoulders slump. 'So do I.'

There was an end-of-term feeling among the actors at the unexpected holiday.

As usual, on the drive home Caz could only talk about Daniel. 'I feel so sorry for him,' she said. 'Do you know, his wife wouldn't even let him take the kids for a holiday?'

'Maybe she doesn't want them upset.'

'Or maybe she's just being vindictive. She knows how much he adores those girls. She's just doing it to hurt him.' Caz put her feet up on the dashboard. 'And yet he still talks about her as if she's some kind of saint. He really

144

needs to find someone new. A person who'll really appreciate him.'

'Someone like you, you mean?'

'Why not? I'd be perfect for him.' Caz's chin lifted. 'The trouble is, how do I get him to realise it?'

'Perhaps it's just not meant to be.'

'Oh, spare me! I haven't let a man slip through my fingers since Matthew Hargreaves in my fourth year at school. And that was only because his family moved to Australia before I'd had a chance to snog him.' Her eyes flashed with the light of battle. 'No, I'm going to get Daniel if it's the last thing I do.'

'Why don't you just get him drunk and seduce him?' Annie had meant it as a joke, but she should have known better with Caz.

'That's it! That's the answer! Annie, you're a bloody genius.'

'Am I?' Annie looked blank. 'What did I say?'

'We'll have a dinner party.'

I don't remember saying that, she thought.

But Caz was already lost in her own fantasies. 'It's a brilliant idea. We can have soft lights, music, delicious food ... He won't be able to keep his hands off me!'

'Aren't you forgetting something?'

'What? You mean the drink? Don't worry, we'll have loads.'

'You'll need it,' Annie said grimly. 'You can't cook, remember?'

'Of course I can.' Caz looked scornful. 'I cook all the time. I cooked the other night. My speciality.'

'Caz, this is a proper, grown-up dinner party we're talking about. Somehow I don't think a boil-in-the-bag curry is going to impress anyone.'

145

Caz looked crestfallen for about three seconds. 'You're right,' she said. 'I don't know how to cook. But you do.'

'Me? Oh, no, count me out.'

'Come on, Annie. What about all those posh dinners you used to cook for Max?'

'That was different. Dinner parties take planning, preparation –'

'You've got a couple of days, haven't you? Blimey, you're only planning a meal, not the D-Day landings.' She settled back in her seat. 'I suppose we'll have to invite quite a few people, just so it doesn't look like a set-up. We've got to be subtle about this.'

Annie glanced at Caz's glittery green nails and flimsy frock, and wondered if she understood the meaning of the word. She gritted her teeth. 'So how many were you thinking of inviting?'

'Oh, I don't know. Maybe eight or nine.'

'What?' Annie jammed on the brakes just in time to avoid skidding into a Volvo's rear end. 'And where were you thinking of holding this – this extravanganza? Will you be hiring a marquee?'

'At home, of course. I'm sure Jeannie will be cool about it.'

As predicted, Jeannie Acaster was extremely cool about it. Especially after Caz had primed her with a packet of Benson and Hedges.

'So you see?' Caz said brightly. 'There's really no problem, is there?'

None at all, Annie thought. Except that she had been saddled with cooking for a dinner party she didn't even want.

But there was worse to come. She was enjoying a

leisurely soak in the bath half an hour later when Caz came in and plonked herself on the furry leopardskin-covered toilet seat. 'I've been thinking,' she said, 'about this dinner party. Maybe entertaining eight people would be a bit ambitious.'

'Hurray.' Annie adjusted the gold dolphin taps with her toe. She'd been having a waking nightmare in which she had been trying to stretch a Lean Cuisine eight ways.

'I think we should stick to a nice round six, don't you? I've made a list.' Caz produced a scrap of paper and a pencil stub.

'Why bother?' Annie sank beneath the bubbles. 'Why not invite the whole bloody company and have done with it? Or ask Jeannie Acaster if she wants to bring a few friends home from Bingo –'

'Do you want to hear this list or not?' Without waiting for an answer, Caz went on, 'I thought we'd invite Daniel, of course, and Adam and his wife –'

'What about Georgia?'

'And watch her trying to get off with Daniel all night? No, thanks.' Caz chewed her pencil end. 'But we do need a spare man, so I thought we'd ask Nick.'

Chapter 20

Thankfully, Nick didn't turn up to rehearsal the following morning so Caz had no time to put her plan into action.

They were greeted by Mel, the Assistant Director. 'Nick's busy so I'll be looking after things for today,' she told them.

'A director too busy to direct his own play? Whatever next?' Henry Adams remarked, not looking up from his text.

'There's no problem, is there?' Adam Gregory asked.

'Nothing serious. Just bit a bit of a crisis at the theatre, that's all.'

'Crisis? What kind of crisis?'

Mel shrugged. 'A burst pipe or something. Nick just needs to be there to sort it out. Now, shall we get started?'

But Annie knew it would take something more drastic than a burst pipe to keep Nick away from rehearsal. So after they finished for the day she made her way to the theatre to see for herself.

And she was right. As soon as she walked in through the stage door she stepped up to her ankles in cold, greasy water. The smell of damp filled the air. This was a small flood the way the Black Death was a nasty bug.

From the other end of the corridor came the sound of blaring pop music. She took off her boots, rolled up the legs of her jeans and followed the noise. There she found a couple of builders propped against the wall, smoking.

'Have you seen Nick?' she shouted over the din.

They looked up, dull-eyed.

'Eh?'

'Nick Ryan? The director?'

'Who?'

'Oh, forget it. I'll look for him myself.'

'I'd put your armbands on first, love.' As she walked away she heard them sniggering like schoolboys.

Someone had laid a makeshift path of boards over the puddles. Annie picked her way cautiously through it, her boots in her hand. The smell of damp and decay filled the air. Water dripped eerily from the ceiling. Every so often an icy drop would catch her and run down the back of her neck.

Then she heard it. Faint but unmistakable, the sound of music coming from upstairs. Scratchy, like an old gramophone. She strained her ears, trying to pick out the tune.

Annie followed the sound. Stumbling in the gloom, she made her way up the narrow staircase.

There it was again. More clearly this time. Annie stopped to listen. She remembered the tune now. From an old film, or was it a musical? *I'll see you again, whenever spring breaks through again.*

As she reached the upstairs landing, the music grew louder. It was coming from behind one of those doors. Annie made her way towards it. 'Nick?' she whispered. But when she opened the door, the music died away.

She fumbled for the light switch. Nothing.

'There's water in the electrics.'

Annie screamed and swung round. Even in the half-light she couldn't mistake the stooped figure in the doorway. 'My God, Stan, do you always creep up on people?' She put a hand to her thudding chest.

'Sorry, Miss. Thought you were intruders snooping around.' She noticed he was armed with a heavy-duty staple gun.

'And what were you going to do? Staple me to the wall until the police arrived?'

He grinned, displaying a sparse array of yellow stumpy teeth. 'Can't be too careful. Been all kinds of goings-on around here lately.'

'Maybe it's Jessie up to her old tricks?'

Stan stiffened defensively. 'Don't try to pin the blame on Jessie. She wouldn't do nowt to hurt this place, no matter what anyone says.' His beady eyes gleamed. 'No, Miss, it ain't the ghosts that bear this place any malice and that's a fact.'

Annie remembered what Nick had said about ill will coming from the living, not the dead. 'What do you mean?'

'It ain't really my place to say, Miss. But I'll tell you this.' He wagged a crooked finger. 'There were a lot of people in Middlethorpe didn't want this theatre to reopen. And there's a lot stands to gain if it doesn't.'

'What kind of people?'

Stan looked around him, then he leaned forward confidingly. 'Ever heard of Bob Stone, Miss?'

'No.'

'Well, I dare say he knows you. Ain't nothing goes on in this place that Bob Stone don't know about.' His eyes darted around. 'He's got eyes and ears everywhere, has Bob.'

Annie backed away from his graveyard breath.

'He was the one wanted to put a stop to this place. He's on the council, see.'

Frankly, she didn't. 'But why would he want to do that? Surely the council would be pleased to see the theatre reopen?'

'Not Bob.' Stan shook his head. 'His old friend Blanchard was after the land. He wanted to tear the old building down and put up some big shop thing here instead.'

'Blanchard? As in that bloke out in the square? The one with the pigeons on his head?' Oh, dear. Looked like old Stan had got stuck in his parallel reality again.

'No, not him. He's been dead donkey's years.' Stan sent her a withering look. 'His great-great-grandson or sum-mat. He wanted hold of this land, and Bob Stone as good as promised it him. Until the trustees snatched it out from under his nose. Bob weren't pleased about it, I can tell you. He tried all ways to put a stop to it.' He clutched at her sleeve, pulling her closer. Annie held her breath and tried not to gag. 'Might still be trying, for all we know.'

'You think Bob Stone might be behind all this?' Annie touched the damp plasterwork.

'I don't think nothing, Miss. It ain't my business to think.' Stan's face was closed. 'All I know is there's a few people round here I wouldn't trust further than I could throw 'em!' He broke into a toothless smile. 'Still, Mr Ryan will sort it all out. I reckon he's got his head screwed on right.'

'Where is Nick? Have you seen him?'

'He was here earlier, Miss. With that Mr Brookfield.'

Annie couldn't help noticing his distaste when he said the name. 'Mr Brookfield?'

'One of them trustees. You must have seen him? Tall, fair-haired fella, very full of himself? Always hanging around here he is, making a bloody nuisance of himself, poking and prying into things that don't concern him.'

'Sounds as if you don't like him.'

'I don't! And he don't like me, neither. He tried to get rid of me, but Mr Ryan wouldn't hear of it. I'll give him old and useless.' He shook with fury. 'Jessie don't like him, either. She told me.'

Here we go again, Annie thought. She began to edge away. 'Will you be all right here on your own, Stan?'

'I'm not on my own, am I?'

Annie smiled nervously. 'I suppose Jessie's with you?'

'No, Miss. But the builders are.'

I suppose I asked for that one, she thought. 'By the way, how did you get your music to work without the electricity?'

'Music, Miss? I ain't been playing no music. But if you mean that racket downstairs –'

'No, this was more old-fashioned. Sort of like a –'

'A gramophone? Playing "I'll See You Again", I suppose?'

'That's right.' A cold trickle ran down her spine. 'Oh, God, don't tell me.'

'It were Jessie's favourite, Miss. She were always playing it in her dressing-room.' He cackled. 'I told you she liked you.'

Annie made her way back downstairs. As she reached the corridor the two builders were still leaning against the wall, still smoking.

She stopped. 'Shouldn't you be doing something?'

'We are. We're having a fag.' The bigger of the two spoke up. 'We're on our break.'

'But you were on your break half an hour ago.'

'That were a different break.' His mate chortled at this startling piece of wit. 'Besides, we can't do nowt till t'blow heaters arrive.'

'You could make a start clearing up this mess.'

'Oh, no, we couldn't do that. That's ancillary work, that is.'

'So?'

'So we're skilled labour. Ancillary work ain't in our contract.'

It was like arguing with a brick wall with learning difficulties. 'Couldn't you do it anyway?' she pleaded. 'Just to help out?'

They looked at each other, deeply affronted. 'Are you asking us to break the terms of our labour agreement? That's harassment, that is. We could down tools over that.'

'You'd have to pick them up first.' Annie was exasperated. No wonder Nick looked so exhausted all the time. Dealing with prima donnas like Georgia must seem like a breeze after tiptoeing round these sensitive egos.

'Besides,' he went on, 'we're on –'

'Your break. Yes, I know.' She gritted her teeth. 'You call this a break? I've known shorter retirements.'

'She's right.' Annie swung round. The man who'd interrupted yesterday's rehearsal was standing behind her. His fair hair glinted in the half-light, his immaculate suit out of place amid the chaos.

The workmen straightened their shoulders, instantly humble. 'But we were told –'

'Never mind what you were told.' He cut through their protests with impressive authority. 'I want this mess cleared up before you go home, or you won't have a job in the morning.'

Grumbling, the men threw their cigarette stubs into the nearest puddle with a sizzle.

Annie smiled at him. 'How did you do that?'

'Years of practice.' The man held out his hand. 'I'm James Brookfield.'

'Annie Mitchell.'

'Ah, yes. Our Beatrice.' Was it her imagination, or did he hold her hand a fraction longer than necessary? 'So what brings you here?'

'I was just curious. And I was looking for Nick.'

'I'm afraid you've missed him. He went home half an hour ago. Won't I do?'

She shook her head. 'I need to see Nick.'

'Lucky Nick.' This time she knew she hadn't imagined the gleam in his blue eyes.

Annie went home, but she was restless and worried. The flood was worse than she'd imagined and she wondered how Nick was taking the set-back. She longed to see him, but she didn't feel she could just turn up on his doorstep.

Then inspiration struck. The clothes she'd borrowed. Surely he wouldn't think it was strange if she returned them?

It took a moment for him to answer the door. He looked slightly flustered to see her. 'Annie! What are you doing here?'

'I brought these back.' She thrust the shirt and jeans through the narrow gap in the door.

'Oh, right. Thanks.'

'I would have left them until tomorrow but if Caz gets hold of them there's no knowing if you'd ever see them again.' She waited to be invited in. 'I've – er – been to see the flood.'

He grimaced. 'Not good, is it?'

'Put it this way, the builders were constructing an ark.'

'At least they were constructing something. All I've seen them do is smoke cigarettes and read the paper.' There was an awkward pause. 'Look, I'd invite you in, but –'

'Red or white, Nick?' Annie's mouth fell open as Georgia appeared behind him, bearing a bottle in each hand.

'Georgia's here.'

'So I see.' And very cosy she looked, too, her hair loose around her catlike face.

Georgia sidled up to the doorway. 'Nick's very kindly helping me with my character,' she said.

'I'm sure he is. Well, I won't keep you. I expect you two have a lot to get on with.'

As she turned to go, Nick called her back. 'Actually, I've been meaning to ask you. Caz phoned and invited me to dinner on Saturday.'

'Oh yes?'

'I forgot to ask her at the time, but is it okay with you if I bring someone?'

You can bring the whole of the Dagenham Girl Pipers if you want, she thought silently. 'Why not? The more the merrier.' Her face muscles ached.

'What's this about a dinner party?' Georgia interrupted. 'Sounds like fun. When is it?'

'Saturday night.' If she'd had any kind of backbone at all, she told herself later, she would have left it at that. But Georgia fixed her expectantly with those cool green eyes and, as usual, she felt herself crumble. 'You're – er – welcome to come, of course.'

'Really? Who else is going to be there?'

Annie felt herself redden as she reeled off the guest list. Why did Georgia always make her feel like a schoolgirl?

'Is that all?' Georgia looked disappointed. 'I'll have to check my diary and get back to you. Okay if I tell you tomorrow?'

Annie nodded, wondering how Georgia had managed to turn it round so she sounded as if she was doing them a favour.

She scurried back to her car, burning with curiosity. Whoever Nick was planning to bring, it certainly wasn't Georgia. So who the hell was it?

Chapter 21

Annie stood at the sink with a potato peeler in her hand and murder in her heart. So much for Caz's dinner party. For the past two hours she had chopped onions, julienned carrots – and most of her finger-nails – and ribboned courgettes. All Caz had done was languish in the bath humming Spice Girls songs.

She listened in a fury to the sounds of splashing coming from upstairs. The guests would be arriving in half an hour. She was red-faced and sweating, her hair had frizzled in the steamy heat of the kitchen and she had potato dirt ingrained in her cuticles. She hadn't prepared the starters. And she was still smarting from the conversation they'd had earlier that afternoon.

'What difference does it make who Nick brings?' Caz had asked as she watched her chopping the onions. 'Unless you're jealous?'

'Don't be stupid!' Annie cursed in frustration as the knife slipped. 'I told you, I'm not interested in Nick. I love Max.'

'Really? Then how come you haven't mentioned his name for days?'

'What do you mean?'

'When we first got here, all you ever talked about was Max. Now it's Nick. What does that mean, do you suppose?'

Annie opened her mouth to protest, then closed it again. 'I'm not even going to have this conversation.'

'Suit yourself. Anyway who cares who Nick brings, as long as it's not Georgia bloody Graham. I don't think I could stand seeing her across the dinner table all night.' She shuddered.

Annie looked anxious. 'Actually, I've been meaning to talk to you about that . . .' She began to explain what had happened.

Caz listened in unnerving silence. 'Oh, God, you didn't!' she whispered. 'Please tell me you didn't invite her.'

'I had no choice –'

'You could have said no! I bloody well would have.' Caz paced the kitchen furiously. 'She'll be all over Daniel. I won't stand a chance. And now that Nick's bringing someone, it means we're two spare men down. I'm going to have to do some phoning around.'

'But you're meant to be helping me.'

'I can't now, can I?' Caz shot her an accusing look. 'You do realise this dinner party's going to be a disaster, thanks to you?' She'd grabbed her address book, disappeared upstairs and hadn't been seen since.

Annie plunged her hands into the sinkful of muddy water, searching around for more potatoes. They were supposed to be grated and shaped into rosti, but she was buggered if she was going to do it. Life was too short and so was her temper.

She dried her hands, lit a ciggie and puffed mutinously.

She had a good mind to go down to the pub and leave Caz to stuff her own mushrooms.

And as for all that nonsense about Max – how could Caz even think she was getting over him? Okay, so she hadn't mentioned him for a while, but that didn't mean he wasn't on her mind constantly. Or at least when she wasn't rehearsing, or learning her lines. Or thinking about Nick . . .

She inhaled deeply. She was just curious about him, that was all. All right, if truth be told, she did fancy him a bit. But not enough to do anything about it. And besides, whatever Nick had once felt for her, it was obviously over and forgotten now. He seemed to have women swarming round him like flies these days. And he wasn't exactly fighting them off, either.

Jeannie came down in a cloud of cerise chiffon as Annie was making a start on the garlic-stuffed mushrooms. 'Right lovie, I'm off to Bingo,' she announced, looking suspiciously overdressed for a night out at the local Mecca. 'I've locked Trixie in the bedroom so she won't make a nuisance of herself.' She watched Annie struggling with the gooey breadcrumbs. 'What's that you're doing?'

'I'm stuffing these mushrooms.'

'And what's the point of that, then?'

What indeed, Annie thought, blowing a damp curl out of her eyes.

'Smells nice, anyway.' Jeannie sniffed appreciatively. 'What is it you're having?'

'Roast lamb with a rosemary and sun-dried-tomato stuffing.' She hadn't dared open the oven to check it yet, but the herby aroma filling the kitchen seemed hopeful.

Jeannie's nose wrinkled. 'I don't hold with all this fancy foreign stuff myself. They do say the way to a man's heart is through his stomach, but personally I've always found the other way's a lot more fun.' She roared with laughter. 'Take a tip from me, love. Put on a nice low-cut top and he won't even notice what he's eating.'

Jeannie left and Annie lit up another cigarette to calm her temper. It was Saturday night and she should have been curled up in front of the TV watching *Blind Date*, not feeding the five thousand.

Caz swanned into the room just as she was finishing the last mushroom. 'How do I look?' she asked, doing a quick twirl.

'Wonderful.' Annie didn't look up.

'You don't think it's a bit too much?'

Annie glanced up. 'Bloody hell!' she breathed.

Even by Caz's eccentric standards it was over the top. The black lycra catsuit clung like a second skin, finished off by vampish thigh-length boots with lethal spiked heels. All she needed was a whip and a studded dog collar, and she could have had her own exposé in the *News of the World*.

'I don't know how I'm going to wee in it, but who cares?' Caz shrugged. 'By the way, shouldn't you be getting ready? They'll be here in ten minutes.'

'Ten minutes!' Annie dropped the mushroom. 'Oh, my God, I've barely got enough time for a bath –'

'You've barely got enough water, either.' Caz looked sheepish. 'I used it all. Sorry.'

'Thanks a lot.' Annie's grip tightened on the palette knife. She thought about beating Caz around the head with it, but that would only waste more time.

Shouting instructions about taking the carrots off the heat, she rushed upstairs to get ready. She had a lightning bath and washed her hair in four inches of tepid water, rinsing it under the cold tap.

She was still in her tatty dressing-gown drying her hair when she heard the tinny sound of 'Que Sera Sera' on the doorbell, closely followed by Trixie's frenzied yapping as she hurled herself at Jeannie's bedroom door.

'Don't worry, I'll get it.' Caz's heels clattered up the hall, followed moments later by the sound of voices. Annie strained to listen. There were Adam and his wife Becky, Brendan O'Brien – was he really Caz's idea of a spare man? – and Daniel.

She could hear everyone in the sitting-room, getting stuck into the wine. The soulful voice of Lauryn Hill drifted up the stairs, mingling with the sound of laughter and the strangely acrid smell of –

'The carrots!'

Still in her dressing-gown, Annie flung herself downstairs. But she was too late. The carrots had not only boiled dry, they'd welded themselves to the blackened bottom of the pan. Cursing Caz, she thrust it under the cold tap, where it sent up a huge hiss and a cloud of evil-smelling steam.

Just then the doorbell rang. 'Door!' she yelled, but everyone ignored her. 'Can someone get the door?' The sound of laughter in the sitting-room grew louder.

'Bloody hell, do I have to do everything around here?' Still clutching the pan, Annie stomped to open it.

'God, I hope that's not our dinner?' Georgia's arched brows rose in mild disgust. She swept into the hall and threw off her white cashmere pashmina to reveal a strappy cream dress that showed off acres of tan. She looked Annie up and down. 'I didn't know it was a come as you are, darling.'

But Annie barely noticed her cutting comment. She was too busy watching Nick and his mystery guest getting out of their car. It couldn't be. Surely not . . .

'I know. Amazing, isn't it?' Georgia followed her gaze. 'Close your mouth, sweetie. You'll catch flies.'

But Annie's jaw seemed glued to the doorstep as she watched Nick and his companion coming up the path.

Chapter 22

'Thanks ever so much for inviting me.' Fliss's grey eyes shone behind her owlish specs.

'Any time.' Annie's mind raced. Nick and *Fliss*? It didn't make sense. She was much too young for him for a start. What on earth did he see in her?

'I hope we're not too early?' Nick said.

'No, it's fine. We're just –' She looked down in horror at her tatty towelling dressing-gown and realised what he meant. 'Oh, hell! Excuse me.' She dashed upstairs, blitzed her wardrobe and finally decided on a flowing black skirt and white lace top. She slapped on some make-up and raced back to join the party.

They were all in the living-room, getting stuck into the wine. Adam and Becky, who was heavily pregnant, were squashed together on the chaise longue. Daniel was in the armchair, with Caz draped over the arm. So much for subtlety, Annie thought. Brendan and Georgia were having hysterics over the musical mini bar in the corner. Brendan kept topping up his whisky just to hear it play 'Begin the Beguine'.

And there, on the red velvet sofa, were Nick and Fliss. She was fiddling with her mousy hair, her drab beige sweater and trousers a bizarre contrast to Caz's outrageous bondage queen outfit. Annie couldn't take her eyes off them. It was too unbelievable to be true.

'More drink, anyone?' she asked and everyone started talking at once.

'Could I have a mineral water?' Becky patted her bump. 'Sorry to be boring. I'll pretend it's a gin and tonic.'

'Could I have a mineral water as well?' Fliss asked.

'Don't tell me you're pregnant too?' Georgia smiled slyly. 'Or are you just boring?'

Annie noticed Fliss's embarrassed flush and felt a twinge of pity for her. Then she saw Nick's arm go round her shoulders and her sympathy vanished.

'Fliss is driving me home,' he explained.

Annie was uncorking the wine when Caz came into the kitchen. 'So, what do you think about Nick's mystery girl-friend? I would never have believed it, would you?'

'Why not?' Annie's voice was tight. 'Fliss is a nice girl –'

'I know, but she's hardly his type, is she?' Caz giggled. 'I feel a bit sorry for her, actually. Georgia's taking the piss out of her endlessly, but she's either too nice or too dim to realise it.'

'And what about Nick?' Annie couldn't stop herself asking.

'He's spitting, but he daren't show it because he doesn't want to embarrass Fliss.' Caz helped herself to a handful of peanuts. 'You should go in and have a look. It's hilarious.'

'No, thanks. I hate blood sports.' Annie glugged some wine into her glass and downed it so quickly it made her head spin.

'Careful with that! You'll be plastered before we start eating.'

'Good.' She refilled her glass defiantly. 'Anyway, what

are you watching me for? Shouldn't you be keeping your eye on Dan? Georgia could have him pinned to the sofa by now.'

'Oh, God, you're right!' Caz grabbed a handful of drinks and dashed off.

Annie found the oven gloves and took the leg of lamb out of the oven. At least something was going right. Now all she had to do was put the mushrooms under the grill, finish off the vegetables and she could enjoy the rest of the evening.

Who was she kidding? When it came to enjoyment, this dinner party was right up there with having a wisdom tooth out.

As she refilled her glass, she sensed someone come into the kitchen behind her. 'Yes, I am having another drink,' she said loudly, thinking it was Caz. 'And no, I don't care if I am under the table by the time the starters arrive.'

'Sounds like fun.'

Annie swung round. Standing in the doorway, holding a bottle of Pinot Noir, was James Brookfield. 'I rang the bell, but no one answered.' He handed her the bottle. 'Seems as if I've got a bit of catching up to do.'

They stood there, appraising each other. He reminded her of Max, with his flopping blond hair and lazy, sexy smile that lit up his deep-blue eyes. It was a smile that made her want to rush upstairs and check her make-up.

'Sorry about the greeting,' she said. 'Things are getting a bit frazzled, as you can see.'

'Really? You look perfectly in control to me.'

'Yeah, right.'

'You do. Serene, in fact.'

'The others are in the sitting-room if you want to join them.' Her mouth was dry suddenly.

'Couldn't I just stay here with you?' Annie realised with a shock that he really was flirting with her this time.

Caz appeared in the doorway. 'When are we going to eat? Brendan's already half cut, and –' She caught sight of James. 'Oh, hi. I'm Caz Wilde. We spoke on the phone.'

'Of course.'

'Sorry the invite was at such short notice. I hope you didn't mind me ringing you out of the blue?'

'Not at all. I'm delighted you asked me.' James gave Annie a look that made her toes curl.

'Just go through and introduce yourself. I'll be with you in a minute.' As he disappeared off into the hall, Caz turned to Annie. 'What do you think?' she said gleefully. 'Did I come up trumps with a spare man or what?'

'He seems – very nice.'

'Nice? He's gorgeous. And he's rich, too. He's a lawyer. They earn pots of money, don't they?' She grinned. 'I tell you, Georgia owes me one for this.'

'Sorry?'

'For fixing her up with James. He's just her type, isn't he? And it'll help keep her sticky paws off Dan.' She stuffed a handful of peanuts into her mouth. 'Now tell me I'm a genius.'

Annie sighed. 'You're a genius,' she agreed wearily.

To her embarrassment, Annie found herself seated next to James, with Georgia on his other side. She picked at her stuffed mushrooms. Why did everyone always seem to be paired off but her, she wondered, not for the first time. Caz had attached herself to Dan. Adam and Becky were feeding each other. And there, across the table, were Nick and Fliss. He was whispering something to her, making her laugh. She was staring up at him with those doe eyes, hanging on to his every word.

'Look at them. Love's young dream,' Brendan whispered beside her.

'Hardly.' Annie took a vicious stab at a mushroom.

'I suppose that just leaves you and me.' He sighed. 'I don't suppose you fancy a quick snog, do you?'

'Brendan!'

'Well, it sometimes works.' He looked injured.

She tried not to laugh. 'You amaze me.'

'Mind you, it helps that they're usually half cut when I ask them.' He reached for the bottle and topped up her glass. 'So there's not much point in me wasting my second chat-up line on you, then?'

'Ask me again when this bottle's empty.' She took a sip of her wine. Brendan cracked a few jokes and for the first time that evening she began to feel more cheerful. So what if Nick and Fliss were a couple? So what if the dinner party had about as much atmosphere as the surface of Mars? She could still have a laugh, even if it was only at Georgia's heavy-handed flirting with James.

'I'm just slipping upstairs to freshen up.' Georgia glided out of her seat, making sure James got a good look down her cleavage as she did so. 'See you in a moment.' With a final meaningful flash of her green eyes she was gone.

Annie watched her leave. 'I think you're meant to follow her,' she pointed out.

'Why? I don't want to freshen up. Besides, I'd rather stay here with you. I've been longing to talk to you all evening.'

Of course, Annie thought. That's why you've been staring at Georgia's cleavage. She wondered how she could have fancied him, however fleetingly. The guy's charm could cause a North Sea oil slick.

'So what do you think of our little theatre?' he asked.

'I'm looking forward to working there.'

'And you're not worried about the curse? I thought you actors were meant to be such a superstitious bunch.'

His comment was like an electric cattle prod, startling the others to attention.

'Curse? What curse?' Caz looked panic-stricken.

'Oh, fock, I knew it,' Brendan groaned. 'No wonder the bloody nags have been letting me down.'

Annie looked round at their shocked faces. James was right. Actors were notoriously superstitious. She knew some who would refuse to go on if they heard whistling backstage.

'Of course, it's probably nonsense,' James went on. 'But the locals reckon the place is built on the same spot they used to burn witches back in the seventeenth century. They believe the site's been cursed ever since.'

A heavy silence followed his words.

'Rubbish,' Nick said flatly.

'A lot of people believe it.'

'A lot of people believe they've been abducted by aliens, but that doesn't make it true.'

Annie looked from one to the other. There was no love lost between them, that was for sure.

'So how do you explain the strange things that have been going on lately?' James asked. 'That flood, the rot under the stage, the problems with the builders – it's got to be more than a coincidence, hasn't it?'

'I agree. But you know as well I do it's got nothing to do with the supernatural.'

James broke the tense silence. 'More wine anyone?' He picked up the bottle and everyone started talking again.

'I don't think your boss likes me,' he whispered to Annie.

'What did he mean, "you know as well as I do"?'

'No idea. Maybe he thinks there's someone out to get us.'

'You mean like Councillor Bob Stone?'

James's smile dropped. 'What do you know about him?'

Not as much as you, obviously, she thought, noticing how pale he'd gone. 'Just something I'd heard,' she said. 'Do you think he's got anything to do with all the things that have been going wrong at the theatre?'

'If I did, I wouldn't go around telling other people. Not if I wanted to keep my kneecaps.'

Annie laughed. 'Come on, he can't be that bad.'

'No?' James looked troubled. 'Let's just say I've had a few dealings with Councillor Stone in the past. I know what he's capable of.'

Annie was about to ask more. But before she could say anything, Georgia came back. 'I don't know if this is important,' she said, 'but there's some kind of rodenty thing eating your joint.'

'What?' Annie shot out of her chair, sending it clattering backwards.

'I was on my way back from the bathroom when I heard this yapping, so I just opened the door and this horrid little thing shot past me.' Georgia looked at the faces around the table. 'Don't look at me like that. It's not my fault. Anyway, I've probably saved you from a social faux-pas. No one eats red meat these days.'

'Oh, my God! Trixie!' Annie ran into the kitchen, but

it was too late. Trixie was gone and so was most of the lamb. All that remained was a mangled bone.

'I'm going to kill you.' Fired up with fury, she grabbed a skewer off the draining board. 'Come out, you little –'

'What are you planning to do with that?' Nick stood in the doorway, his arms folded.

'Kebab that bloody dog, when I find it.'

Nick touched her shoulder. 'Have a drink,' he advised. 'You'll see things differently.'

She didn't. Half a glass of Cabernet Sauvignon later, she could still see a thoroughly chewed leg of lamb on a plate in front of her. If anything, it looked even worse.

She bit her lip. 'I wonder if I could disguise it with some kind of sauce –'

'Annie, a witness protection scheme couldn't disguise that.'

Tears spilled down her cheeks. She rubbed them away with her fists. 'What am I going to do?' she wailed.

'Can I help?' Fliss's earnest face appeared around the door. Then she saw the lamb remains. 'Oops!'

Annie glared. 'If that's all you can say –'

'Thanks, Fliss, but I think the situation's beyond help.' Nick cut her off.

Fliss inspected the joint. 'Couldn't you cook something else?'

'Of course. Why didn't I think of that? I'll just whip up a quick Beef Wellington, shall I?'

'I think that might take a bit too long.' The dart of sarcasm seemed to go over Fliss's head. 'Why don't we see what else we've got?' Annie watched as she delved in the fridge. 'There are a couple of big bags of prawns, and some – oh, well, that's it really.' Her face brightened. 'Prawns it will have to be, then.'

'Terrific.' Annie felt even more gloomy. 'So it's prawn sandwiches all round?'

'I think we can do better than that.' Fliss rolled up her sleeves. 'Now, I'm going to need a few extra things. I don't suppose there's a late-night grocer anywhere?'

'Only Patel's, on the corner.'

'That'll do. Nick, if I give you a list, can you go down there and fetch a couple of bits and pieces? Just some extra vegetables and some spices and things. They shouldn't be too hard to find.'

'No problem,' Nick said.

'Tell you what.' Annie refilled her glass. 'Why don't you pick up a couple of loaves and fishes while you're down there? Because I reckon we're going to need a bloody miracle.'

It was like watching an alchemist turning lead into gold. Fliss moved around the kitchen, grinding pepper here, adding a touch of spice there and filling the air with delicious aromas. Within what seemed like minutes she had produced a dish of fragrant stir-fried prawns, served with rice and spiced vegetables.

'I hope it's okay,' she said modestly. 'By the way, I don't know if you've noticed but your dog has just thrown up behind the dresser.'

By the time dinner was served, everyone had heard the sorry tale. Fliss almost received a standing ovation when she brought her culinary masterpiece to the table.

Annie sat among the rapturous congratulations, feeling depressed. She knew she should be grateful to her for saving the day and she was, but she couldn't help feeling a little resentful. Why was it everything she did seemed to go so terribly wrong?

'I'm sure your meal would have been wonderful,' James whispered.

'I doubt it. Even the wretched dog couldn't keep it down.'

'Maybe your talents lie elsewhere?'

She flinched as his hand came to rest on her knee. Carefully she shifted her leg away. 'So how did you become a trustee?' she asked. 'Are you interested in the theatre?'

'To be honest, I don't know my Aristophanes from my elbow.' James grinned. 'I only took on the job because my firm handled the lease transfer.'

'And is that how you met Bob Stone?'

'You're very interested in him, aren't you?' His smile didn't quite reach his eyes. 'If you must know, Councillor Stone and I had some disagreements over the terms of the lease.'

'You mean he didn't want us to have it?'

'Let's just say he didn't make it easy.' He moved closer. 'Look, do we have to talk about the theatre? I'd much rather talk about you.'

Annie felt the warm, firm pressure of his hand on her leg again. She started to move away, then thought better of it. James obviously knew more about the notorious Mr Stone than he was letting on. And if flirting with him was the only way to find out, it was worth a try.

Trouble was, after all these years she'd forgotten how.

'So, are you married?' James asked.

Annie felt herself sobering up at the question. 'Not so you'd notice.'

'Annie's husband ran off with her best friend,' Georgia chimed in. 'She's broken-hearted, aren't you, darling?'

'Really? I'll have to do something about that.' James

picked a prawn off his plate and offered it to her. 'Broken hearts are my speciality.'

Mending them or causing them, Annie wondered.

'So what exactly does a trustee do?' Georgia fluttered her eyelashes. 'Do you have a lot of power? I've never been able to resist a powerful man.'

As Annie reached for the bottle, she caught Nick staring at her across the table, his eyes like flint. Why was he in such a bad mood, she wondered. He wasn't presiding over the worst dinner party since the Last Supper.

'I suppose you could call it power, in a way. The ten of us jointly own the lease on the building. It's our job to make sure the theatre opens on schedule and within budget. Neither of which looks likely at the moment, I have to say.' He glanced at Nick.

'It'll be fine,' Caz said. 'Everything always looks like chaos until we get to the first night.'

'*If* we get there.' James's words hung in the air for a moment, then everyone started talking at once.

'Are you saying there's a chance we won't?' Brendan asked.

'I certainly hope we will. But to be honest, things are beginning to look doubtful.' James shrugged apologetically. 'We're way behind schedule and the building costs are rocketing. There comes a point where you start to wonder if you might be better off cutting your losses –'

'Can we talk about this later?' A muscle moved in Nick's jaw.

'But they can't pull the plug.' Adam looked worried. 'I turned down a sitcom to come up here.'

'The Phoenix will open.' Nick looked around the table, his steady gaze taking them all in one by one. 'Your jobs are safe. You can count on it.'

173

'I don't know if you can make those kind of promises,' James said. 'I've been looking at the figures. The trustees –'

'I'll talk to them.'

'Look, I know you think you're invincible, but even you can't magic money out of thin air.'

'I said I'll talk to them.' Nick's eyes were dark and forbidding.

Annie stood up quickly, rattling plates to distract him. 'Let's have pudding, shall we?'

Alone in the kitchen, she dumped the plates in the sink, forgetting to scrape them clean first. She ran the taps full blast, watching as a few remaining prawns bobbed one by one to the surface.

Wearily, she took the chocolate roulade out of the fridge and was searching around in the drawer for a suitable cutting implement when she felt a pair of hands cupping her bottom.

'That looks good.' James's breath was warm against her ear.

'Thanks.' She felt the hardness of his hips grinding into her back. 'I – er – take it you haven't come to help with the washing up?'

'Hardly!' James's arms twined around her, pulling her into him. 'You don't know how much I've wanted to touch you all night.'

'Look, James –' She turned around to disentangle herself and, instead, found herself locked in his arms, her back pressing against the work top. She felt her hips sink into something unpleasantly squidgy. 'Oh, no – the roulade!'

'Fuck the roulade,' James groaned. A second later, his mouth was on hers.

As Annie finally struggled up for air, she realised Nick was standing in the doorway watching them.

Chapter 23

'Am I interrupting something?' he asked coldly.

Annie pushed James away and smoothed down her skirt guiltily.

James, meanwhile, seemed unruffled. 'Yes, as a matter of fact.' He straightened his tie.

Nick looked as if he wanted to punch him. 'I need to talk to Annie.'

'Can't it wait?'

'No.'

James gave in with a shrug. 'Fine, I'll leave you to it, then.' Annie winced as he planted a kiss on the top of her head. 'See you later, sweetheart,' he said and sauntered off.

As the door closed, Annie let out a sigh of relief. 'Thank God you came in.' She picked up a cloth and started dabbing cream off her skirt. 'It was like wrestling with an octopus.'

'What did you expect?'

She stopped dabbing and looked up. 'What's that supposed to mean?'

'Oh, come on! You've been flirting with the guy all night. You didn't think he was going to end the evening with a handshake, did you?'

'I wasn't flirting with him.' Annie's face grew hot with indignation. 'If you must know, we were talking about the theatre –'

'How intellectual. Was that before or after he put his hand on your leg?' Nick's mouth curled. 'What are you playing at, Annie? One minute you're moaning you'll never love anyone again, the next you've got your tongue down someone's throat.'

'I was fighting him off!'

'Not too hard, I noticed. Didn't take you long to get over Max, did it?'

That hurt. Any ideas she'd had of telling him what she'd discovered about Bob Stone and the theatre disappeared instantly in a rush of white-hot anger. 'Don't you get all self-righteous with me! I'm not the one with the bloody harem.'

Nick's eyes narrowed. 'What?'

'You and all your women. First I come round and there's Georgia looking very cosy at your place. The next minute you're turning up here with Fliss Burrows.'

'You don't know what you're talking about.'

'Oh, so it's okay for you to lecture me about my love life, but yours is out of bounds, is that it?'

'If you must know, I invited Fliss because it was her birthday and she had no one to spend it with. And as for Georgia,' he went on, as Annie opened her mouth to interrupt, 'I told you she came round to work and that's all it was. Work.'

She ignored the flutter of relief in the pit of her stomach. 'I couldn't care less what you get up to in your private life.' She turned away and stared at the squashed remains of the roulade. 'Just stay out of my life and I'll stay out of yours, okay?'

'My pleasure,' Nick growled. He stalked out, slamming the door after him.

Annie continued to stare at the roulade, too rigid with fury to move. How dare he condemn her, especially when she was only trying to help. Did he really think she'd seriously be interested in someone like James Brookfield? And he hadn't even had the good grace to listen to what she had to say. She picked up a ladle and slammed it on the work top. Well, sod him! In future he could sort out his own problems.

She was still seething when she got back to the dining-room. She banged what was left of the roulade down on the table, making the cutlery tremble.

'Don't ask!' She shot a furious look around the table. 'I sat in it, okay?' No one said a word. Even Georgia could only manage a faint smirk.

'Not hungry?' James whispered, as she pushed her pudding around her plate ten minutes later.

'I've lost my appetite.'

'Been giving you a hard time, has he? Take no notice of him.' Annie felt his hand on her knee and jerked her leg away. She didn't feel like playing that game any more.

'Oops, it must have been serious.' James grinned. 'Don't tell me, he told you I was a big bad wolf and you were to keep away from me?'

'Something like that.'

'He's probably right.' James sent her a challenging look. 'Still, it's a pity. I was going to ask you to come out to dinner with me.'

Annie glanced at Nick from under her lashes. He was still watching them, his mouth a narrow line of disapproval. How dare he try to dictate what she did with her life?

She lifted her chin and met his gaze with defiance. 'I'd love to,' she said.

Two hours later, Annie was already regretting it.

'I don't know what you're moaning about.' Caz sat at the dressing-table, creaming off her make-up before bed. 'He's gorgeous. And he's loaded. I never thought he'd be interested in you.'

'Thanks a lot.'

'You know what I mean.' Caz was in a good mood because Dan had finally asked her out.

'But I haven't been on a date since Duran Duran were in the charts,' Annie wailed. 'How will I know what to do?'

'Just do what you used to do, I suppose.'

'I used to go to the Odeon and pretend to be old enough to get into an X film.' Somehow she couldn't imagine James being too impressed by that idea.

She didn't even want to go out with him. Now her defiance had worn off, she could see what a mistake she'd made.

'You'll be fine,' Caz reassured her. 'Just make sure you've sussed out the four Ss, that's all.'

'The what?'

'The four Ss. Don't tell me you haven't heard of them? Single, Straight, Solvent and Sexually Compatible?'

Annie stared at her. 'You mean he might not be?'

'You can't be too careful,' Caz said wisely. 'I mean, he could have a girlfriend locked away somewhere – or even a boyfriend. And you don't want to end up in the bedroom and find out he's got some kind of weird fetish.'

'We won't get that far.'

'You never know.' Caz waggled her brows. 'Still, at least you can be sure he's solvent.'

'As if that matters.'

'There speaks someone who's never been on a date to the local Burger King.' Caz smiled pityingly. 'I can see you've got a lot to learn.'

But I don't want to learn, Annie thought. I don't want to be single and out there picking my way through the dating minefield. I want to be happily attached and never have to worry about whether men are married or commitment phobic or fetishistically addicted to vinyl handbags. 'I want to be married,' she wailed.

'Don't we all?' Caz sighed. 'But let's see if you can get through the first date, shall we?'

But before that she had to get through Monday's blocking rehearsal. And it wasn't going to be easy. Nick was in a foul mood. He sat at one end of the hall, his script bunched in his fist, watching them from under lowered brows.

The atmosphere was leaden. Aware of his black mood, the actors tiptoed around, giving each other wary looks and following Nick's suggestions, which were beginning to sound more like orders.

The mutterings began when he finally called a lunch break. 'About bloody time,' Brendan moaned. 'I've already missed the one thirty at Sedgefield.'

'Why don't you complain to the boss?' Adam suggested.

'And get my ear chewed off? No focking thanks!'

'I can't understand what's got into him. He's always been so courteous and professional,' Henry grumbled.

Annie was just glad to escape. Perhaps it was paranoia, but Nick seemed to be picking on her more than anyone else. She couldn't say a line without him pouncing on this inflection or that, making her repeat the scene over and over again, changing his mind until she neither knew nor cared which was the right way. Then he'd snapped at her for not knowing her lines, even though everyone knew actors seldom let go of their scripts until much later in rehearsal.

Henry was right. Nick was usually so calm and in control. He listened to everyone's ideas and made them feel as if they were really contributing something. But not today. Even Fliss looked near to tears as he shouted at her yet again.

'Bugger this,' Caz whispered. 'Let's go shopping.'

'Do you think we should?' Annie had planned to spend her lunch break going over her lines, determined Nick shouldn't find fault with her again.

'Look, we're not called again until three. And I'm not going to sit around here waiting for him to start bellowing at me again.'

'You're right.' Annie agreed. She had the feeling she could have been word perfect and Nick would still have picked on her.

Middlethorpe wasn't exactly the fashion capital of the north. There were precisely two clothes shop in the whole town, if you included the one that sold nothing but crimplene trouser-suits for the fuller figure. But it still took Caz ages to make up her mind what to buy. They crossed the precinct again and again while she dithered between the red leather miniskirt or the leopardskin sling-backs.

'Just buy them both!' Annie glanced at her watch. 'Come on, it's ten to three. We don't want to be late back, do we?'

Everyone looked up as they stumbled through the door twelve minutes later. The only one smiling was Georgia.

In the middle of them all sat Nick, his fingers steepled together in front of his face. His expression was blank. He seemed to be gathering all his strength to speak. 'Where the fuck have you been?' His voice was filled with icy menace.

'We're only two minutes late.' Caz protested.

'Not you – her.' He pointed at Annie. 'You were called at two thirty.'

'No, I wasn't. It was three o'clock.'

'Two thirty. It's there on your call sheet, if you'd cared to look.'

'But –' Annie was about to get out her call sheet and show him, then she saw Fliss's stricken face and it all became clear. The poor girl had given her the wrong time. Now she was trembling, waiting for her terrible mistake to be exposed. 'You're right,' Annie said. 'I should have checked. I'm sorry.'

'Sorry!' Nick's jaw tightened. 'That's all you can say, is it? So it's okay to keep the rest of us waiting here for half an hour, just because you can't be bothered to read your bloody call sheet properly.'

Annie looked at Fliss again. Her eyes were swimming with tears.

'But I suppose the normal rules of courtesy don't apply to you, do they?' Nick stood up and walked towards her, measuring out the distance between them with his long strides. 'Perhaps it doesn't matter to you that the rest of us have been standing around like idiots for the past half-hour, waiting for you to grace us with your presence?'

His words bit deep. She was transported back to the third form, being carpeted by a sadistic form mistress over her lost maths homework. She felt a dull flush of embarrassment creep up her face, aware of everyone's pity.

Fliss stepped forward. 'Nick –'

He didn't even flicker. 'Well?' he snapped.

'I said I'm sorry.' Annie stared at a crack in the floorboards.

'Look, it's no big deal.' Adam tried to lighten the atmosphere. 'Everyone's late once in a while –' Nick swung round, making him flinch. He was a big man, but even he cowered under the director's steely gaze.

'I'll decide if it's a big deal. And this isn't just about being late. It's about attitude.' He turned back to Annie. 'I think yours leaves a lot to be desired. I realise you think it's all a bit beneath you, but the rest of us are working bloody hard to make a success of this place. And I'd appreciate it if you showed a little more commitment.'

As he turned away, Annie found herself retaliating. 'I'm working just as hard as everyone else.'

'Are you? It seems to me if you spent as much time worrying about your work as you do about your love life, we might start to see some results.'

Annie gasped. 'That's not fair.'

'No, you're right. It isn't. It isn't fair on me and it isn't fair on anyone else. I think we've all made more than enough allowances for your fragile emotional state. From now on, I want one hundred per cent commitment. If you're not prepared to give me that then you might as well leave now.'

A shocked silence followed his words. Even Georgia stood rigid.

Annie took a deep breath to stop herself trembling. 'Fine,' she said. 'I will.' With the weight of everyone's gaze on her she picked up her bag and walked out.

Chapter 24

Annie yelped as she jabbed the mascara wand in her eye for the third time. She rubbed at the black streaks on her cheek, then gave up and tossed the brush down in frustration. It was no good. After the day she'd had, her brain just wasn't up to putting on make-up.

How could he have fired her! Never mind that she'd chosen to walk out. He hadn't given her much choice. And he certainly hadn't tried to talk her out of it. She'd spent most of the afternoon seething by the phone, willing him to ring so she could tell him exactly what she thought of him. But he hadn't.

Instead, she'd had to wait for Caz to come home. 'What a bastard!' she'd declared, throwing off her leather jacket. 'He had no right to talk to you like that. You did the right thing, walking out.'

'What happened after I left?'

'Well, Nick couldn't believe it. He went a bit quiet and stared at the door like this.' Caz made a face like a dazed haddock. 'Serves him right, the high-handed sod.' She looked around. 'Where's Jeannie?'

'Having a bath. She's got a big date tonight, apparently.'

'She's not the only one. I hope she doesn't take all the hot water.'

Annie ignored her. 'So what happened then?'

'What? Oh, you mean Nick? Well, he sort of sat there with his head in his hands for a while. Then he started bitching about your lack of professionalism. He said it was a good thing you'd gone and if the rest of us had a problem with the way he'd treated you we were welcome to go too. Of course, no one did.'

'Thanks.'

'Not that we're not all totally behind you, of course. But we need the work.' Caz shrugged apologetically.

'He'll be sorry,' Annie fumed. 'How's he going to cope with no Beatrice?'

Caz blushed. It was a rare sight. 'He's – um – asked Georgia if she'll read it.'

'What?'

'You said yourself, he's got to find someone to do it. And since you're not coming back –'

Who said I'm not coming back, Annie was about to say. Up until now, she'd thought of her walk-out as a kind of token protest, to show Nick she wouldn't be pushed around. Suddenly it occurred to her he might not actually want her back.

'Maybe James could help get your job back?' Caz suggested. 'He's one of the trustees, isn't he? Perhaps he could put in a good word with Nick?'

Yes, and she could imagine what that would do. Nick hated James even more than he hated her. Which was really saying something at the moment.

'I'm not sure I want the stupid job anyway.' She sniffed.

Caz shook her head. 'You and Nick Ryan are as

stubborn as each other. You know, I'm sure he'd love to have you back, if only you'd –'

'Go crawling to him? Forget it. I'm not that desperate.'

'Suit yourself.' Caz stood in front of her wardrobe, tossing clothes on to the floor as she rejected them. 'This needs a wash, this is too boring, he's seen me in this –' She turned away in disgust. 'What are you wearing tonight?'

'You're looking at it.'

'That?' Caz wrinkled her nose.

'What's wrong with it?' Annie glanced down at her ankle-skimming black skirt and little grey twinset.

'Nothing – if you're a librarian. Why don't you dress up a bit?'

'This *is* dressed up.'

Caz plunged her hand into her wardrobe and dragged out a sliver of dark-red satin that looked like a hankie on a coat hanger. 'No, *this* is dressed up.' She pulled it off the hanger and tossed it at Annie. 'Try it on. You'll look sensational.'

'Sensational is right. I'd get arrested wearing this.' It would have looked indecent on a Barbie.

'Go on. Just see what it looks like.'

Ten minutes later Annie stood gawping at her reflection in the full-length mirror. Caz stood beside her, surveying her creation proudly. 'Well? What do you think?'

'It's a bit short, isn't it?' Annie yanked at the hem. The satin fabric slithered through her fingers.

'It's supposed to be. Besides, you've got amazing legs. You should show them off, instead of hiding them under those frumpy skirts.'

'I like to be comfortable.' She took a step closer to the mirror and nearly fell off the spiked heels Caz had bullied her into wearing. 'Can I take these things off now, before I break my neck?'

'No. They go with the dress. Besides, your Doc Martens will look stupid with sheer black tights.' Caz tweaked at a stray curl. 'Perfect.' She sighed. 'You should wear your hair loose more often. You look like a Pre-Raphaelite painting.'

'I feel like a hooker on her night off.' But she had to admit Caz had done wonders with her hair. Set free from its restraining pony-tail, it flowed like a copper river over her bare shoulders. 'Can I put my clothes back on now?' she begged.

'No. You're going out like that and that's final.' Caz grinned. 'James won't be able to keep his hands off you.'

That's what I'm worried about. Annie's amber eyes stared back at her from the mirror. She'd agreed to have dinner with him out of a mixture of spite and curiosity. He obviously knew more about the sinister happenings at the theatre than he was letting on. She had hoped to charm him into telling her more about Bob Stone. But now that the Phoenix was nothing to do with her any more it seemed pointless going on with the charade. Why should she help Nick, when he so obviously didn't give a damn about her?

She'd tried to call James to tell him dinner was off, but he was out of the office all day and no one could get a message to him. Annie sighed. It was too much to hope he'd stand her up.

On the dot of eight, James's sleek silver Mercedes convertible turned the corner into Bermuda Gardens.

'Right on time,' Caz said gleefully, peering through the net curtains. 'He must be keen. Where's he taking you?'

'I'm not sure. Some Italian place, I think.'

Caz sighed. 'God, I envy you. We're going to the Millowners' Arms. I might get a packet of cheese and onion crisps if I'm lucky.'

James leaned back in the driver's seat, the slight breeze ruffling his fair hair. He looked like something out of a glossy car ad, in his immaculately pressed chinos and white Versace shirt that showed off his tan.

'My God, you look gorgeous.' His eyes devoured her as she got into car. 'What do you say we skip dinner and I'll eat you instead?'

Annie smiled feebly and pulled at her hem. Why had she ever let Caz talk her into wearing this obscene dress? Now she was going to have to spend the whole evening fighting him off.

But perhaps she shouldn't? After all, she was virtually a single woman and he was an attractive man, if a bit too slick and charming for her liking. Perhaps she should just do what everyone had been telling her to do – get on with her life and enjoy herself. But as he leaned across to kiss her, she couldn't help averting her face so he only caught the corner of her mouth.

Luckily he didn't seem to notice, as he started up the engine with a macho burst of revs. 'So how are things at the Phoenix?' he shouted over the roar.

Annie swung round to face him. 'Why? What have you heard?'

'Nothing.' He sent her a sideways look. 'Don't tell me there are more problems?'

'Just a few – artistic differences, that's all.' She certainly wasn't going to ruin her appetite talking about Nick. 'I'm not Mr Ryan's favourite person at the moment.'

'Join the club.' James laughed. 'I'm afraid I'm permanently in his bad books. Especially now.' He glanced at her.

'Why?'

'He's pissed off I'm going out with you.' His mouth twisted. 'Come on, you must know he's got the hots for you?'

'No.'

'It's true. You saw the steam coming out of his ears when he caught us together the other night. He's jealous because I got to you first.' Annie squirmed uncomfortably as his gaze travelled the exposed length of her thighs.

'I gathered you two weren't the best of friends.' She changed the subject quickly.

'You could say that. Nick doesn't understand about money. He doesn't like it that I have to keep hold of the purse strings. He can't seem to realise we aren't a bottomless pit for his artistic whims.' He pulled up at the traffic lights and drummed impatiently on the steering wheel. 'The only reason he hasn't been hauled over the coals before now is that half the trustees are too senile to take in how much money he's spending. And he's got the head of them on his side. Lady Carlton won't hear a word said against him. I reckon the old trout fancies him.' The lights changed and he roared off, casually cutting in front of an elderly couple in a Metro. 'Bloody idiots! Shouldn't be allowed on the road.' He grinned at her frozen expression. 'Why are we talking about Nick, anyway? I want to forget about him tonight.'

'Me too,' Annie replied with feeling.

But after a moment or two she realised they didn't actually have anything else to talk about. 'It's – um – a very nice car,' she commented at last.

James beamed with pride. 'Mercedes CLK coupé. There's a three-year waiting list for these at the Stuttgart factory. But I pulled a few strings and got mine in two months.'

Annie tried to look impressed as he went into great detail about his car-getting coup. It all sounded terribly complicated. She was about to ask why he didn't just go to a dealer and buy a car like everyone else, but something told her that wasn't the point.

Thankfully, they had arrived at the smart Italian restaurant on the outskirts of town. Annie expected the usual trattoria décor, but there wasn't a chianti bottle or a faded poster of Firenze in sight. It was all very white and minimalist with splashy modern art on the walls and black marble tables. From the way the maître d' fluttered up to James, he was obviously a valued customer.

'Very exclusive, this place,' he whispered as they were shown to their table. 'People kill to get a table here. Luckily I've got a few contacts –'

'It looks wonderful,' Annie said quickly before he got started on another story of how many strings he'd pulled.

She glanced around, conscious of the knowing smiles the waiters were giving her. 'Why do they keep staring at me?'

'Because you're the most beautiful woman in the room.' James reached across to stroke her bare arm. 'And they're crazy with jealousy because you're coming home with me.' Annie tried not to flinch as his fingers brushed her breast. God, how embarrassing, she thought. Not to mention presumptuous.

The same thought crossed her mind a few minutes later when the waiter arrived to take their order. Annie was still making up her mind between the lemon sole and the chicken cacciatore, but James insisted on ordering for her.

'They do a marvellous pasta arrabiata here,' he said. 'Take it from me, it's the best thing on the menu.'

Annie controlled her irritation. You're supposed to be enjoying this, she reminded herself firmly. She couldn't help feeling that she would have enjoyed herself far more in the Millowners' Arms with Caz and the others.

But she was there to winkle out information and that was what she was going to do. 'So,' she said, when they'd finished ordering. 'You were going to tell me all about Bob Stone.'

'Was I? I don't remember that.'

'How well do you know him?' she persisted.

'Everyone knows Bob Stone. He's one of our most eminent local councillors, he runs several businesses in the area, his wife's a stalwart of the WI. He's a real pillar of the community.'

'Then why is everyone so afraid of him?'

'Shall we order some wine?' James picked up the wine list. 'Which do you prefer, red or white?'

'Everyone I speak to clams up whenever his name's mentioned. What is he – some kind of gangster?'

'Red's probably best. They do a very good Pinot Noir here –'

'I've also heard he wanted to sell the Phoenix site to his friends the Blanchards for their department store.'

That worked. James's eyes flicked to hers. 'Who told you that?'

'It's true, then? That's why Bob Stone wants the theatre to fail.'

'They're your words, not mine.'

'But you said yourself, all those things going wrong at the theatre aren't an accident.'

James went back to the wine list. Annie looked at him in exasperation. 'You promised you'd tell me.'

'I didn't promise you anything.' James slammed the menu shut, startling her. 'Look, you don't know what you're getting into. The Blanchards have owned most of this town for years. Their reputation is whiter than white. And they like to make sure it stays that way.' His mouth tightened.

'And what about Bob Stone?'

'Bob Stone is a dangerous enemy to have. I should know.'

'Why? What's he ever done to you?'

'So it's a bottle of the Pinot Noir, then.' James lifted his finger to summon the waiter.

Annie waited impatiently until he'd finished ordering. All kinds of thoughts were going through her mind. 'What did he do, James?' she asked. 'Why are you so afraid of him?'

James stared at her, his blue gaze steady. 'If you must know, he threatened to ruin me.'

The waiter arrived, bearing their wine with a Latin flourish. Ignored by both of them, he filled their glasses and retreated.

'Are you saying he tried to blackmail you?' Annie whispered.

'Not at first. When we met initially he couldn't have been more charming. He even offered me money to mess up some paperwork over the lease. It was only when I said no that he turned nasty.'

'So what did he do?'

James leaned across the table and took her hands in his. 'Can you keep a secret?'

'Of course.'

'Promise to tell no one? Not even Nick?' Annie nodded. James took a deep breath. 'He threatened to tell everyone I was – illegitimate.'

For a moment she sat in stunned silence, wondering if she'd heard him properly. 'But that's nothing to be ashamed of, surely?' she said. Where she came from, it was positively trendy.

James looked affronted. 'It may not seem like a lot to you, but in a little place like Middlethorpe it could be enough to finish me,' he said. 'This place is a social time warp. I've spent years building up my reputation, trying to forget who I am and where I came from. This could ruin my professional reputation.'

But everyone knows all lawyers are bastards. Annie bit back the joke. 'Why didn't you go to the police?'

'And tell them everything? What good would it do? Bob Stone's brother-in-law just happens to be the Chief Constable.' He shook his head. 'As it turned out, Stone never went through with his threat.'

'He changed his mind?'

'Or had it changed for him. You see, exposing me would have meant exposing my father too.' James's eyes met hers. 'And my father is Philip Blanchard.'

Chapter 25

He smiled cynically at her stunned expression. 'I know, I had very much the same reaction when I found out.'

'But wha—? How?'

'My mother worked for them when she was a teenager. I suppose she must have caught the boss's eye. When she found out she was pregnant the family closed ranks and tried to force her into an abortion. The Blanchards didn't want a hint of scandal attached to their great name.' He looked bitter. 'She refused, so they offered her a pay-off. A huge sum of money to sign a contract saying she would never make a claim against the Blanchard name, or tell anyone the identity of her baby's father. Not even me.'

'So how did you find out?'

'Well, she told me in the end. She felt she had to. Besides, I was entitled to know.' There was a touch of defiance in his hard blue eyes. 'Everyone has a right to be acknowledged by their own father.'

'And were you?'

'No.' He sipped his wine broodingly. 'Once I'd qualified as a lawyer the first thing I did was to check over that contract my mother had signed. It was watertight. There was no way either of us could make any claim on them. Those bastards robbed me of my birthright.' He caught her looking at him in dismay and his face relaxed. 'So, now you know why I got involved with the Phoenix,' he said. 'As soon as I found out the trustees were trying to stop the Blanchards getting hold of the site I was determined to help them. That's why I got myself voted on to the board. I may not have your friend Nick's artistic vision, but I've got a damn good reason for wanting to see the theatre succeed.'

No one could argue with that, Annie thought. She felt an unexpected surge of pity for him. Under that slick exterior lurked a sad, scared man.

Their food arrived and she stared in horror at her plate. Oh, God. Who in their right mind ordered spaghetti on a first date? Spaghetti was for that stage in your relationship when you'd given up wearing make-up for bed. It was impossible to eat impressively. Either you shovelled it in and risked disgusting your new partner, or you twirled it decorously around your fork all night and slowly starved to death.

Annie opted for twirling. James, she noticed, ploughed through it like a JCB. 'What I don't understand', she said, 'is what Bob Stone has to gain by trying to stop the theatre opening? I mean, the lease is ours now, isn't it? There's nothing anyone can do.'

'Don't you believe it.' James slurped a few stray pasta strands noisily. 'It's not as simple as that. Our friend Mr Stone still has one more trump card up his sleeve. He made sure our lease was conditional. We have to prove the project is viable within a certain time. If we fail, the council has the right to close us down and renegotiate the lease.'

'Sell it to Blanchards, in other words.' She fought the

urge to dab sauce off his chin. 'So how long have they given us?'

'Until this time next year.'

Annie dropped her fork with a clatter. 'A year? But that's ridiculous!' No wonder Nick was so stressed. Annie knew even a potentially successful theatre needed a couple of seasons to settle down before it started making money. Bob Stone had set them an impossible task.

'So you see what he's doing? The more delays and problems we have, the less time we'll have to make a profit. You've got to hand it to him, he's a clever swine.'

'And Nick knows about all this?'

'Of course he does. But he won't let us tell anyone, especially you lot. He keeps saying it's his problem and he'll deal with it. Talk about sticking your head in the sand.' He nodded towards her untouched plate. 'Aren't you going to eat that?'

'I'm not hungry.' Annie pushed it away. Poor Nick. No wonder he was under so much pressure. And now she'd just added to his problems by walking out.

The rest of the meal seemed to drag by. She did her best to keep the conversation going, but her heart wasn't in it. She couldn't stop thinking about Nick and his doomed task at the theatre.

Not that James seemed to notice. He was quite happy to talk about himself, needing only the minimum of nods and vague smiles from her to keep going. It was a relief when the evening ended and they left the restaurant for the warm air outside.

'So,' James said, as they walked back towards his car, 'are you coming back to my place?'

'I'd rather go home, if you don't mind.' She was about

to launch into a complicated litany of excuses, but James cut her off.

'Fine.' He shrugged. 'Your place it is, then.'

He'd taken her refusal well, Annie thought as she sat beside him in the car, the soothing sounds of the Lighthouse Family washing over her. Too well, in fact. She was beginning to wonder whether he'd got the message. She looked at him sideways. She could hardly ask, could she?

'Are you okay?'

She jumped at the question. 'Of course. Any reason why I shouldn't be?'

'No. You've just gone very quiet, that's all.' He reached over and stroked her thigh. Annie edged out of his reach until she was right up against the door.

As they drove through the town square, Annie found herself gazing longingly at the Millowners' Arms. It was a lively night, as usual. Three men were brawling around the fountain, egged on by a couple of women waving handbags.

James sighed. 'And Nick thinks these people need cultural entertainment.'

Annie smiled back. But deep down she was thinking what fun it would be to drop in for last orders.

'I see the Ghost of Theatre Past is still hanging around.' James nodded towards the stage door, where the slight, stooped figure of Stan the Stage Door Man was fumbling shakily with his keys. 'Look at him. How can Nick call him a caretaker?'

'He's harmless.'

'Exactly. We need someone with a bit more muscle. Especially with Bob Stone's heavies hanging around. But as usual Mr Ryan knows best. I told him, you can give the old sod a job, but there's no way we're paying him.'

'You mean Stan works for nothing?'

'He would if I had my way.' James frowned. 'No. Nick pays him directly out of his own wages. Talk about a soft touch!'

Annie felt a twinge. 'What does Stan say about it?'

'He doesn't know. That's what's so pathetic about the whole thing.' 'Nick insists we have to go through this great sham of sending him a payslip like everyone else. He reckons it's something to do with his pride. As if an old crock like that had any.'

'I suppose he'd be better off watching game shows all day at the local OAP centre,' she suggested, remembering what Nick had said to her.

'Absolutely.' James didn't notice the ironic tone in her voice. 'There are enough people on the payroll as it is.'

'There'll be one less after today.' Annie sighed deeply. 'I suppose I'd better tell you, as you'll probably find out anyway. I've resigned.'

James nearly swerved off the road. 'You're joking! Christ, when did that happen?'

'This afternoon.' She explained about their bust-up. 'It was partly my fault. I had no idea Nick was under so much pressure —'

'That's no excuse to take it out on you. Bloody hell, I bet he's panicking now.'

'I feel terrible. The last thing I wanted to do was add to his problems.' Annie knotted her fingers in her lap. 'I suppose I'd better apologise, try to get things straightened out —'

'No way! After the way he's treated you? If anyone apologises, it should be him.'

'Yes, but –'

'I mean it, Annie. Don't you dare go crawling to him. If I were you I'd pack my bags and go straight back to London. You were always too good for this place anyway.'

Annie frowned. James might have the best interests of the theatre at heart, but he couldn't resist having a jibe at Nick.

When they got back to Bermuda Gardens, Annie thanked him quickly and got out of the car. But by the time she reached the front gate he was there ahead of her, opening it for her. 'Don't I even get a coffee?'

'Well, I –' Annie hesitated. 'I suppose so.'

The house was in darkness. Annie cursed silently. She was hoping Caz or Jeannie would be at home. But it seemed that even Trixie wasn't there to protect her. As she slid her key into the lock all she could hear were frustrated yaps coming from upstairs.

'So – coffee, then?'

'I'd rather have you.'

He had pinned her against the wall before she had time to put away her key. Annie disentangled herself firmly. 'I'll put the kettle on,' she said, heading for the kitchen.

By the time she came back with the tray, James was sprawled out on the chaise longue. He'd helped himself to whisky, Annie noticed.

'Be careful, you're driving,' she warned.

'I could always stay the night.'

She forced a smile. 'What about Caz?'

'I don't fancy Caz.'

'We share a bedroom.' She put down the tray and picked up his cup.

'Really? Sounds very cosy.' He caught her wrist as she

put down his coffee, pulling her gently towards him. 'She's not into threesomes, is she?'

Whether it was deliberate or not she wasn't sure, but as their mouths were about to collide, her hand holding the cup jerked downwards, splashing hot coffee everywhere. There was a howl of agony as James danced round the room, clutching his groin.

'Oh, God, I'm sorry!' Annie put her hands to her mouth. 'Here, let me help you –'

'Get off me,' James managed to gasp. 'You've already done enough damage.'

'There's a cloth in the kitchen –'

'I don't need a cloth. I need bloody surgery.' He was doubled up with pain. 'Where's your bathroom?'

'Upstairs on the left.'

Annie listened to him hobbling up the stairs, then quickly reached for the phone.

It took her several minutes to get through to Caz at the Millowners' Arms. Annie crouched behind the sofa, listening to the background of noisy drunkeness at the other end and praying James wouldn't come downstairs.

'Hello?' Caz shouted at last.

Relief flooded through her. Caz would know what to do. 'You've got to help me!'

'Who is this?' Her voice was slurred.

'It's Annie.'

'Annie? Where the bloody hell are you? Listen. I'm having the most pig awful time. You'll never guess –'

'Never mind that. James is here and he wants to sleep with me.'

'But why are you calling me? Sounds as if you're doing all right on your own.' Caz cackled down the phone.

'That's just it, I'm not.' Annie glanced nervously

towards the door. 'He seems to think I want to sleep with him, but I don't. And now I can't—' She broke off, aware that Caz was no longer listening to her. 'Caz? Are you still there?'

'Speak up! It's a bad line.'

'I can't, he might hear me.'

Speaking as slowly as her thudding heart would allow, Annie told her the whole story.

'You're kidding! You mean he's in the bathroom nursing third-degree burns and you're hiding behind the sofa phoning me?' Caz spluttered.

'It's not funny!'

'So what do you expect me to do about it?'

'I don't know.' She chewed her thumbnail. 'Couldn't you come home early and save me?'

'Forget it,' Caz said. 'Georgia's circling Daniel like a shark. I daren't leave them alone. Which reminds me —'

There was silence at the other end of the phone. Annie listened to a few agonising minutes of static before Caroline's voice came crackling down the line again. 'Sorry about that.' She chuckled. 'Brendan's just been telling me the most hilarious joke. There was this Irishman in a bacon factory —'

'Caz!'

'Oh, God. Sorry, I forgot. Now, what did you want to ask me again?'

'What am I going to do about James?' Annie pleaded.

'I don't know.' A burst of music exploded on the other end of the phone. 'Why don't you just sleep with him?'

Annie lowered her voice. 'Look, I don't fancy him. I don't even like him that much. How do I tell him I don't want to sleep with him?'

'How about to his face?' She looked up sharply. There, leaning in the doorway, was James.

Chapter 26

He would have made an amusing picture in shirt-tails and damp underpants, if he hadn't been so furious. 'I've had some disastrous dates in my time, but no one's ever actually rung the Samaritans before.'

Annie slammed down the phone. 'Look, I can explain –' she started to say, but James held up his hand.

'I can work it out for myself, thanks.' He winced painfully. 'I think it's best if I go home, don't you?'

'Are you all right?' She knew instantly it was the wrong thing to say.

'I may need a skin graft, but apart from that –' He moved gingerly towards the door. 'I'll put my trousers on again.'

He was still limping when she saw him to the door. 'I'm sorry,' she apologised for the fiftieth time.

He didn't smile. 'A word of advice. If you want a man to get the message there are easier ways than scalding off his private parts.'

Annie bit her lip. 'One day you'll look back on this and laugh.'

'I doubt it.' James sent her an icy look. 'As a matter of fact I've a good mind to sue you for loss of amenity.'

She went back into the living-room and sank wearily on to the chaise longue. It had been a hell of a day, even by her chaotic standards. And it had started to rain again. Annie closed her eyes and listened to it pattering against the glass. Didn't it ever stop? At least she wouldn't miss the dismal weather when she went back to London.

Back to London. She shuddered at the thought of packing all her things and returning to her empty house. Not to mention telling Julia what had happened. Annie could already imagine what her reaction would be.

Unbelievable as it seemed, she would miss Middle-thorpe. She was just beginning to realise how much the place meant to her. She'd miss Caz and Adam and Daniel, and even Brendan. She'd miss Jeannie and the Millowners' Arms. She'd even miss Trixie trying to take chunks out of her ankle every time she set foot inside the front door.

And she'd miss Nick. Talking to James tonight had made her see him in an entirely new light. She'd never understood how much pressure he was under, with the future of the theatre and everyone who worked there riding on his shoulders. Yet in spite of it, until today he'd always been good to her. He took time to listen to her. He'd shown superhuman patience even when she was droning on about her marriage break-up. He was kind, warm, funny . . .

And now she'd blown it. Annie swallowed hard. The thought of not being there with the others on opening night filled her with misery.

She was just summoning up the energy to go to bed when there was a knock on the door. She looked at the clock. It was nearly eleven. No doubt Caz had stumbled home too drunk to find her key.

But it wasn't Caz.

'Where is he?' Nick stood on the doorstep, rain flattening his dark hair and dripping down his face. He was breathing hard as if he'd been running.

'Who?'

'That sod Brookfield.' He shouldered past her into the hall.

'Halfway home, I should think. Why?'

Nick swung round, his eyes narrowed to black slits. 'Did he touch you?'

'Sorry?'

'Did he force himself on you?' His mouth tightened with suppressed rage. 'If he laid a finger on you I swear I'll kill the bastard.'

Annie stared at him for a moment. Then slowly it dawned on her. 'You were in the pub. When I phoned Caz –'

'She made it sound like you were being date raped, or something.'

Annie sighed. Trust Caz. She could just imagine her broadcasting it to the whole pub. It was a wonder the landlord of the Millowners' Arms hadn't sent a lynch mob over. Thank heavens James had gone, she thought, looking at Nick's angry face. 'It was nothing, really.'

'Are you sure?'

She nodded. 'Just a misunderstanding, that's all.'

They stood in the hall, like strangers caught in the same bus queue.

'Well, I'll be off then.'

'Thanks for coming over.'

He was halfway out of the door when suddenly he turned back, his eyes blazing. 'Look, I can't stand this! I've got to know. Are you going back to London or not?'

She was taken aback. 'Is that — what you want me to do?'

'Of course it bloody well isn't.' He raked his hand through his wet hair. 'Do you think I'd have come all the way over here if it were? Do you really think I'd care?' His shoulders slumped. 'Look, Fliss told me it was her fault you were late today. I know I've said some unforgivable things to you and I'm sorry. I wouldn't blame you if you did decide to go.' His eyes met hers. 'But I want you to stay. I need you here.'

She could hardly breathe for the lump in her throat. 'Do you?' she whispered.

'I don't think I can do this without you.' For a moment they looked at each other. Then he dragged his gaze away, breaking the spell. 'We open in three weeks,' he said gruffly. 'The last thing I need right now is to have to find a new leading lady.'

'Yes, I can see that.' Annie wondered at the plummeting feeling in the pit of her stomach.

'Do you think we could discuss this inside?' Nick turned up his collar against the drenching downpour.

'Oh, God, yes — I'm sorry.' She stood back to let him in. He shrugged off his dripping coat. His wet hair was plastered to his head. 'Come into the kitchen and get warmed up.'

She fetched a towel so that he could dry his hair, then put on the kettle. As she concentrated on spooning coffee into the mugs she tried hard not to notice how the damp fabric of his shirt clung to his broad shoulders and the flat, tapering planes of his stomach.

He idled in the doorway. She could feel him watching her.

'That dress you're wearing —'

'It's Caz's.' She yanked self-consciously at the hem. 'I know. Awful, isn't it? I don't know how she talked me into putting it on.'

'I was going to say it looks great.'

'Thanks.' She could feel herself blushing like a school-girl. 'I – I think it's me that owes you the apology actually,' she stammered. 'You're right, I have been a bit selfish lately. I didn't think of the pressure you might be under.' She glanced over her shoulder at him. 'I know about Bob Stone and the lease.'

Nick's face hardened. 'I suppose James has been whining to you? I told him not to say anything.'

'Why didn't you tell us what was happening?'

'And worry you all even more? You know how much everyone's invested in this place. They're anxious enough as it is, without me making it worse. This is my problem and I'll deal with it. That's what I'm being paid for, after all.'

Annie felt a twinge of sympathy. How could she not have noticed those shadows etched under his eyes, or the grim lines of tension around his mouth?

She knotted her hands in her lap, resisting the sudden, urge to reach out and massage those rigid shoulders. 'So do you think we'll be able to pull it off?'

'I don't know. But I'm damned if I'm going to give up without a fight.'

As they talked about the theatre, the atmosphere between them seemed to thaw.

'Caz told me you'd asked Georgia to read my part.' Annie said.

'Only to shut her up,' Nick groaned. 'I'd already spent two hours listening to her telling me why she should do it.'

'So – um – how was she?'

'Okay, I suppose. But nothing like you. The whole time she was reading I just kept imagining you standing there.'

Annie looked into his crinkly, laughing eyes. Suddenly her mouth went dry and she felt a jolt in the pit of her stomach.

Whatever had just happened to her seemed to hit him at the same moment. His eyes moved from hers to linger on her mouth and back again.

She knew what was going to happen and it filled her with panic. She turned away and focused on the kitchen clock instead. She could feel Nick's stare still fixed on her.

'Annie?' Slowly she turned to face him. They were so close she only had to breathe to touch him –

'Cooee! Anyone home?'

The crashing of the front door was like a bucket of icy water. They sprang apart as the kitchen door flew open. There was Jeannie, her cerise lips smudged and her blonde beehive slightly askew.

'You go on up, Bobby love, I'll be there in a minute,' she called up the stairs. 'Don't start without me, will you?' She gave a shriek of laughter, which nearly toppled her as she collapsed into the room.

'Oops, sorry love, I didn't know you had company.' Jeannie's appraising gaze fell on Nick. 'This is James, is it?'

'Actually, it's Nick.' Annie felt herself going red.

'Two in one night?' Jeannie grinned, oblivious to the sexual tension that crackled around the room. 'Bloody hell, lass, and I thought I was a fast worker.' She peered flirtatiously at Nick from under her false lashes. 'I was just about to have a little drinkie,' she slurred. 'Can I get you something? Gin? Whisky? You look like a Jack Daniels man to me.'

'I'm just leaving.'

'Surely not? Don't go on my account, love. I'll just get those drinks.'

'Sorry about that.' Annie grimaced, as Jeannie tottered off towards the sitting-room.

'She's scary.'

'I think she quite likes you.'

'That's what frightens me.'

'Do you have to go?'

His eyes met hers. 'I think I should.'

Annie followed him into the hall. Suddenly they were back to being polite strangers again.

'So I'll see you tomorrow? At rehearsal?'

'Fine.' She stared at the carpet.

There was a long pause. She could feel his eyes on her. 'Annie?' he said softly.

'Yes?'

He's going to kiss me, she thought. Her heart did a lambada in her chest – and nearly stopped when he planted a light peck on top of her head. 'I'll see you tomorrow.'

And then he was gone. Fighting off an unexpected feeling of frustration and disappointment, Annie watched him striding down the path.

Jeannie was reclining on the chaise longue, one sling-back dangling seductively, when Annie came in alone. Her heavily made-up face fell. 'Oh,' she said. 'Your friend Dick gone, has he?'

'Nick. Yes, he's gone.'

'Pity.' Jeannie sighed. 'He's gorgeous, isn't he? Married?'

'No.'

'Good.' A thought struck her. 'He doesn't – you know, travel on the other bus?'

Annie smiled in spite of herself. 'No.'

'I thought not. I can usually tell.' Jeannie smiled back. 'You want to snap him up, love, before someone else beats you to it.'

I think I'm already too late, Annie thought. Six years too late. 'I'm going to bed.'

'Goodnight, love. Oh, and watch yourself up there, won't you? I've brought a friend home.' Jeannie looked coy.

At least someone's got her love life sorted out, Annie thought, trailing up the stairs.

As she reached the landing the bathroom door suddenly flew open and a stranger appeared. He was short, stocky and wearing nothing but a plastic shower cap jauntily over his private parts. 'Come on, my little Yorkshire pudding! Naughty Bobby's ready for his bed bath.' He lunged at Annie, then stopped and peered at her. 'You're not Jeannie,' he accused.

'No.' Thank God, Annie thought, averting her eyes. This was the second near-naked man she'd seen in as many hours. Poor Caz, and she had to go out for her entertainment.

'Oh, bloody hell! Sorry lass, I can't see a thing without my glasses.'

She watched him hurry into Jeannie's bedroom and slam the door. A second later it opened again and a small, yapping scrap of fur flew out. 'Bugger off, Trixie,' he grunted, as the door closed again.

Annie smiled ruefully. 'Well, Trixie old pal, it looks like we're both alone tonight.'

Chapter 27

A week later the renovations were nearly finished and rehearsals moved to the theatre.

Even on a sunny morning, the building echoing with gossip and laughter, a chill crept through Annie's veins as she stood on the bare stage, looking out over the empty auditorium. The smell of sawdust and paint still hung in the air.

'God, this place gives me the creeps.' Georgia sat on an upturned box at the side of the stage, huddled under several layers of sweaters. 'Is anyone else freezing? I hope there's central heating in the dressing-rooms.'

'I hate to break this to you, but at the moment there aren't even any dressing-rooms.' Caz didn't look up from *The Stage*.

'You're kidding? What are they expecting us to do, then? Get changed in a phone box like Superman or something?'

'Nick says it'll all be sorted out by opening night,' Cecily Taylor said soothingly over the frantic click of her knitting needles.

'Nick? Where the bloody hell is he while all this is

going on?' Georgia grumbled. 'He should have been here half an hour ago.'

'Fliss says he's stuck in a meeting with the set builders.'

Georgia tutted. 'It was never like this at the National.'

Why don't you go back there, then, Annie thought. Everyone was very tense. There were just over two weeks to go until the show opened and Nick was looking more exhausted every day. He spent all his time running from rehearsals to meetings and overseeing the last of the building work. They hadn't been alone together since that night at her place. Annie was beginning to wonder if he was avoiding her.

Someone who wasn't avoiding her, unfortunately, was James Brookfield. He'd taken to appearing at rehearsals, watching over them.

He was hanging around them now as they sat in a circle, warming their hands on their lighted cigarettes. He still moved very cautiously, Annie couldn't help noticing.

'Of course, you know this place is haunted?' he said casually.

'I knew it,' Georgia said. 'My aura's been disturbed all morning.'

'All theatres are haunted.' Cecily didn't look up from her knitting. 'It's a tradition.'

'Ah, but not all of them have a ghost like Jessica Barron.'

'What's so special about Jessica Barron, whoever she is?' Caz asked.

'She hates this theatre and everyone in it.'

'Oh, great. You mean she sits in the audience and heckles?' Brendan said.

'Worse than that.' James's face was sombre. 'If I were

213

you I'd be very worried. Jessica's been known to do some rather sinister things.'

'So who is she?' Georgia asked. They were waiting for him to tell his story. Only Annie tried to ignore him as she carried on skimming her lines.

'She and her husband Leonard starred in the original Phoenix repertory company, nearly seventy years ago. But Leonard had an eye for the ladies. He had an affair with one of the chorus girls – Sara something, I think her name was. Anyway, she wanted Leonard to leave Jessica and marry her, but he wouldn't. He was worried about what the scandal might do to his career.'

'Typical,' Caz muttered.

'So they decided to kill Jessica,' James went on. 'They reckoned once Leonard was a grieving widower there'd be nothing to stop them marrying. The plan was that Sara would start a fire in Jessie's dressing-room just before the curtain came down. Jessie ended up getting trapped.'

'And that's how she died?'

James shook his head. 'The plan went wrong. The fire swept out of control through the building and several other people were killed. Sara managed to escape and so did Leonard. But instead of saving himself, he had a fit of remorse and went back for Jessica. He died saving her.' James looked round at the circle of rapt faces. 'Jessica lived although, as it turned out, it might have been kinder if she had perished. The fire left her badly disfigured.'

'So what happened then?'

'She became a recluse. After she finally died, they found all the mirrors in her house smashed to pieces. But not only that, for years everyone blamed her for starting the fire. The rumour was she'd left a cigarette burning in her dressing-room. She went to her grave a broken woman, shunned by the theatrical world she had once loved.'

'So when did they find out the truth?' Caz asked.

'Not until Sara died many years later. She left a note attached to her will confessing everything. But of course by then it was too late for Jessica.' He paused, letting the full effect of his words sink in. 'They rebuilt the place, but they reckon she still walks the dressing-rooms and corridors, wreaking havoc on the theatre that turned its back on her. Some people say if you listen you can hear her gramophone playing and smell her cigarettes to this day –'

'Not to mention the unmistakable whiff of bullshit.' They all turned round. Nick was watching them with lazy amusement. 'What is this? Stories round the camp fire?'

'I was just filling them in with a bit of local history.' James looked defensive.

'Filling them with crap, you mean.' Nick smiled, but his eyes were cold. 'Thanks for the entertainment,' he said. 'But if you don't mind we've got work to do.'

James shot him a look of barely veiled dislike. Relations between them were even worse than usual, it seemed.

'Nobody told me I'd be working in a bloody psychic minefield,' Georgia grumbled, as they settled down to rehearsal.

'Oh, come on, you don't really believe that stuff, do you?' Caz teased.

'Why not? I told you my aura had been disturbed. And what about that curse? And all the things that have been going wrong with this place? You've got to admit it's weird.' She turned to Annie. 'What do you think?'

Annie thought about Stan and the cigarettes, and the distant scratchy sound of the gramophone. *I'll see you again, whenever spring breaks through again* . . . 'I think we've got better things to worry about than a ghost,' she said.

'Well, I don't.' Georgia shuddered. 'In fact, I'm thinking of phoning my agent.'

'Me too,' Brendan agreed. 'I've always had a bad feeling about this place.'

Annie glanced around. They were all shuffling their feet and looking awkward. James had obviously got to them. She thought of telling them about Bob Stone, but that would only make them more paranoid. And she'd promised Nick she wouldn't breathe a word.

'But if we give up now, what have we got left?' She turned to Brendan. 'Do you really want to go back to London still owing money to all those people? And you –' She swung round to face Caz. 'You do realise if this falls through you'll be doing those kids' parties again?'

'Oh God, anything but that.' Caz recoiled.

There was a general mumbling of discontent. Then, to her relief, they picked up their scripts and went back to work.

'Thanks.' Annie jumped as Nick whispered in her ear. 'I think you've averted a mutiny.'

Were the four layers of jumpers and thermals finally doing the trick, or was it being so close to him that made her feel so much warmer?

'James seems to get a kick out of causing trouble.' His mouth thinned.

'Everyone's a bit jumpy, that's all. They'll calm down.'

'I know. Look, I'm sorry I haven't been here much.'

'You've been busy.' She looked around. 'This place is great, by the way.'

'It's taking shape at last. Who knows, if we carry on like this we might even end up with a theatre on opening night.' They both laughed. This is crazy, Annie thought. Why did she suddenly find it so hard to meet his eye?

'I was thinking,' Nick said. 'Why don't we go out one night? We deserve a break, after all our hard work.'

'That sounds like a good idea,' Annie agreed. 'I'm sure the others will appreciate it.'

'I wasn't thinking of the others. I was thinking about us.'

'You and me?' Annie looked blank. 'You mean, like a date?'

'You make us sound like a couple of sixteen-year-olds.' Nick grinned. 'Don't look so terrified. I was only asking you out to dinner.'

'That would be very nice,' Annie said stiffly.

'Great.'

She stood there, her tongue glued to the roof of her mouth, wondering what to say next.

In the end, Nick saved her the trouble. 'I suppose we'd better get back to this rehearsal, shall we?'

As the morning went on, she found it increasingly difficult to take her eyes off him. She watched the way his dark eyes crinkled when he smiled; how he raked his hand through his hair whenever he was thinking. To her dismay, she even found herself remembering what his body was like under his faded denim shirt.

He glanced round suddenly and caught her. He winked. Annie blushed and buried her face in her script, forcing herself to concentrate on her scene with Daniel. It was near the end of the play and Beatrice and Benedick were still indulging in their favourite sparring.

'I can't seem to get this right,' Daniel's brows knitted in frustration. 'I mean, what's Benedick actually saying here?

217

If they're so crazy about each other, why don't they just come out and admit it?'

'Because they're scared.' Nick came over and took the script from him. 'You're right, they've both realised how much they love each other, but they're hiding behind their usual war of words.' He turned to Annie. 'Benedick's feelings have overtaken him, whether he likes it or not. Or maybe he knows falling for someone like Beatrice isn't going to be easy. Look, he says here – "I do suffer love indeed for I do love thee against my will."'

His eyes met hers, honest and direct. '"Thou and I are too wise to woo peaceably,"' he said softly. Annie held her breath.

'And what about Beatrice?' Daniel asked.

'Beatrice is too scared to let her guard down and make herself vulnerable.' With a last quick look at Annie he handed the script back to Daniel.

'What's going on between you two?' Caz whispered, as they sat in the wings sharing a bag of wine gums half an hour later. On-stage, the villains Don John and Borachio were plotting how to discredit the virtuous Hero in the eyes of her husband-to-be.

'What do you mean?'

'Oh, come on! My God, you two can hardly keep your eyes off each other.'

'That's not true.'

'Oh, well, if you don't want to tell me what's going on –' Caz delved into the bag.

'There's nothing going on.'

'But you'd like there to be, is that it?'

Annie was saved from answering as Caz jumped up, sending the wine gums flying. 'What the hell –'

'Look out!' Adam suddenly leaped at Brendan with a flying tackle that sent them both skidding across the stage, just as one of the lights fell from the overhead gantry and landed with a splintering crash.

For a moment no one moved. Then everyone started talking at once.

'Jesus, how did that happen?'

'I thought the bloody roof was coming in for a minute.'

'Someone could have been killed.'

Slowly, still dazed, Brendan sat up and began to pick off the shards of glass. His long, pale face was even whiter than usual as he stared up at the gantry, then at the smashed remains of light where he'd been standing moments earlier. 'Focking hell,' was all he could say.

'Brendan, are you okay?' Nick ran over to him.

'I – I think so.' Brendan rubbed his eyes with a shaking hand. 'Focking hell.'

As everyone gathered around him, James looked on cynically. 'What did I tell you?' he murmured. 'Jessica Barron strikes again.'

'Shut the fuck up!' Nick swung round, grabbed him savagely by the collar and shook him like a rat. 'This is no time for your stupid bloody jokes. If you haven't got anything constructive to say, why don't you just bugger off and shuffle some papers, or whatever it is you do.' He released him, sending him staggering backwards.

They held their breath, waiting for a fight.

James straightened his tie with as much dignity as he could muster. 'I'll be in the office if anyone wants me.' He stalked off, scattering people in his path. But he left a lot of discontent behind him. Everyone ignored Fliss as she tried to marshal them all back to rehearsal.

'That's it, I'm definitely going to call my agent.'

Georgia shuddered. 'There's no way I'm going to work here.'

'Why don't you just shut up?' Annie glanced at Nick. He didn't seem to be aware of what was going on. He stared at the shattered light in his hand, like a man in a trance. 'It was an accident, that's all.'

'Some bloody accident,' Georgia hissed. 'I could have been killed.'

'We should be so lucky.' Caz raised her eyes heavenwards.

'Look, why don't we all try to calm down?' Adam said reasonably. 'We've all had a shock, but luckily no one was hurt –'

'Until the next time.' Georgia snorted.

Suddenly there was a lot of shouting. Georgia and Caz were sniping at each other; Brendan was still shaking; Adam was trying to calm everyone down and Henry was taking a sly swig from his hip-flask.

In the middle of it all, Fliss was desperately trying to make herself heard. 'If we could all just get back to work?' she pleaded.

'I am definitely not staying here.' Georgia tossed her dark hair petulantly. 'I'm not setting foot inside this building again until there's been a proper health and safety inspection.'

'But –'

'Georgia's right.' They all turned as Nick spoke quietly. 'It's going to take a while to clear this lot up. There's no point trying to carry on. Everyone take the rest of the day off.'

No one needed telling twice. As they hurried off to get their bags, Annie turned to Nick. He was sitting on an upturned box, looking utterly defeated.

'Is there anything I can do?' she asked.

He looked up at her, his face etched with lines of fatigue. 'Take me away from all this.'

Chapter 28

They ended up in York, partly because it was a beautiful and ancient city, which Annie had always wanted to visit, and partly because it was the furthest Beryl could go without needing a spell in intensive care.

But as they explored the narrow streets and trawled the museums and shops, Annie could have been there alone for all Nick noticed of his surroundings. He might have been by her side, but she could tell his thoughts were back in Middlethorpe.

Finally they visited the Minster. Inside, it was dark, cool and full of shadows, an oasis of peace after the bright, busy streets. Annie went on ahead, quoting from the guide-book. She halted in front of the famous rose window.

'Shall we go up the tower? There's meant to be a brilliant view.'

'If you like.'

'And then I thought we could take off all our clothes and throw ourselves off the parapet?'

'Whatever.'

Annie sighed. 'Or we could just go home, if you'd prefer?'

'Is it that obvious?' Nick smiled ruefully. 'Sorry I'm not very good company. I've got a lot on my mind.'

'I know. But try not to dwell on it. At least no one was hurt.'

'It's not just that.' The shadows cast harsh dark planes across his worried face.

'You're not telling me you've started to believe all that stuff about Jessie Barron, have you?'

'I wish I did. But ghosts don't cut through cables, do they? That light coming down was no accident. Someone deliberately tampered with it.'

Annie gasped. 'How do you know that?'

'I checked the cable. Besides, I was there when they were putting up the lighting. There was no way that fitting was loose when it went up.'

Fear crackled down Annie's spine. 'But who could have done it?'

'Someone who doesn't want the theatre to open, I suppose.'

'Bob Stone.' She frowned. 'I still can't believe anyone would go that far. I mean, what does he stand to gain?'

'Quite a lot, from what I've been told.' Nick looked weary. 'Apparently Blanchards promised him a sizeable backhander if the deal went through. It looks like he's got his way, doesn't it? Even if we do make it to opening night, we may not have a cast.'

'Don't take any notice of Georgia. She's always having a tantrum about something. She'll calm down eventually.'

'And what about the others? You saw their faces. They're terrified of what's going to happen next. And frankly, I don't blame them.' His hand rasped over the stubble on his chin. 'How can I put them through this when there's so much danger around? Someone could be seriously hurt next time.'

'Yes, and I could go up that tower and fall off,' Annie said. 'Look, none of us knows what's around the corner. Look at me. If you'd told me a month ago I'd be here, I'd have said you needed certifying. And now –'

'Now you're wondering if you're the one who should be certified.' Nick smiled. 'Thanks for the pep talk, but I think you're too late. Everyone's given up on the Phoenix.'

'No, they haven't. But they might if they think you have.' Annie grabbed his hand impulsively. 'Don't give up, Nick. Not when we're so close.'

She felt his long fingers tightening around hers. He lifted her hand to his lips, his eyes lingering on her face. 'What would I do without you?' he whispered.

Annie pulled her hand away, worried that he might notice how clammy her palm was. 'Come on,' she said. 'I'll race you to the top of the tower.'

From then on they talked and laughed, and he was more like the Nick she knew. But she could still see the tell-tale shadows in his eyes. He was trying to keep it from her, but she knew he was troubled.

They stopped for dinner in a country hotel on the way home. It was a former monastery – an old, ivy-clad building set amid acres of rambling grounds.

'It says they've got four-poster beds.' Annie flipped idly through the brochure as they waited for their table. 'I've always wanted to try one.'

Nick's eyes glinted. 'Is that an invitation?'

'Absolutely not!' Annie stuffed the brochure back into the rack, blushing furiously.

They ate on a moonlit terrace overlooking the lake. The scent of honeysuckle and roses hung in the warm, still air. It was a perfect evening. Or it would have been, if the waitress hadn't taken such an obvious shine to Nick. Much to Annie's irritation, she flirted with him shamelessly.

When she'd flashed her cleavage at him again over the coffee, Annie finally snapped. 'Where's the manager? I'm going to complain.'

'Why? I don't mind.' Nick gave the waitress a devastating smile, which sent her cannoning haphazardly into the wall with the dessert trolley. 'She's quite pretty, actually.'

'That's not the point. You're supposed to be with me.'

His eyes glinted mockingly. 'Don't tell me you're jealous?'

'No.'

'Just like you weren't jealous when I brought Fliss to your dinner party?'

'Certainly not!'

'Or when you found Georgia at my place that night?'

'Georgia Graham makes a point of sleeping with all her directors.' Annie's chin lifted. 'It was only a matter of time before she made a play for you.'

'And it doesn't bother you?'

'Why should it?' she lied. Then she ruined it all by adding, 'So – did Georgia get what she wanted?'

'Oh, yes.' He grinned at her outraged expression. 'She told me she wanted to work on her scenes and that's exactly what we did.'

'Especially her love scenes, I'll bet.' Her voice had a bitter edge.

'You *are* jealous.' Nick looked triumphant. 'Look, if

you're asking did I go to bed with her the answer is no. You're right, she did try a few approaches, but I made it clear I wasn't interested.'

'Why not? She's a very attractive woman.'

'I know. But the only woman I want to take to bed is you.'

There was a silence. Annie picked up an after-dinner mint and started unwrapping it.

'Not that I haven't made it pretty obvious already,' Nick went on ruefully. 'You must have noticed how mad I get when another man goes near you. Christ, I even find myself watching Daniel like a hawk during rehearsals in case he goes too far.

'And as for James Brookfield –' His face was brooding. 'I know I shouldn't have lost my temper with you the way I did. But I couldn't stand watching him flirt with you. And then when you agreed to go out with him –'

'I only did that to find out more about Bob Stone. I thought I could help.'

'I wish you'd told me. It might have stopped me behaving like a jealous maniac.' He smiled. 'Although, on second thoughts, I'd probably still have wanted to kill him.'

There was a silence. Annie abandoned the mint and started unwrapping another.

'It's okay. You can relax.' Nick looked rueful. 'I'm not going to try to seduce you, if that's what you're worried about. I know I'd be wasting my time.'

'Oh?'

'I realise you're still getting over Max. The last thing you need is me coming on to you. But I thought I should tell you how I feel. Just in case it ever entered your head to take a chance.' He reached for her hand. 'I've probably got this all wrong, but that night round at your place, after James left. There was a moment when I thought you might – you know, feel the same?'

She did know and that was what frightened her. It wasn't just that she fancied Nick. If she wasn't careful she could even imagine herself falling in love with him. But she was still in love with Max. At least that's what she kept telling herself, although as the days went by she was finding it harder and harder to believe it. Instead of being a solid, constant presence, Max now floated through her thoughts like an insubstantial wraith. If she got involved with Nick she might forget him completely. And the idea of letting go frightened her.

Just in case it occurred to you to take a chance, Nick had said. But she didn't think her heart could withstand another bruising.

They drove home in silence. Annie tried hard to quell the ridiculous feelings of disappointment that swamped her. If she'd done the right thing, why did it feel so wrong? Why couldn't she stop thinking about her and Nick together?

'I hate to tell you this, but I think you've got a puncture.'

'Sorry?' She glanced across at him, shaken out of her troubled thoughts.

'A flat tyre. Don't tell me you haven't noticed?' Nick frowned. 'Pull over. I'll take a look at it.'

Annie drew in to the verge and he got out. A moment later he stuck his head through the window. 'Flat as a pancake,' he declared. 'I'm going to have to change the wheel.'

'What, now?'

'It would seem to be a sensible idea. Unless you think

227

we should sit here and wait for the wheel fairy to come along and replace it for us?' His brows lifted.

'Do you – er – want me to help?' Annie inspected what was left of her nails.

'Have you ever changed a wheel before?'

'Well no, but –'

'Then I suggest you don't.'

Annie snuggled down in her seat as Nick got to work. It was so nice, she thought, having a practical man around. Max would have thrown a tantrum and called for the AA. They would have been shivering on the verge for hours.

She checked herself for such disloyal thoughts. Not everyone could be practically minded. Max more than made up for it in other ways, she was certain.

It was just that she couldn't think of any, at that precise moment.

Then she thought of something else. Her eyes flicked open and she jerked upright in her seat just as Nick flung open the door and said, 'You don't appear to have a spare wheel.'

'Um – no.'

Nick sighed. 'Don't you think you should have mentioned it earlier?'

'Sorry.'

'So what do you suggest we do?'

She picked his mobile off the passenger seat. 'Do you know the wheel fairy's number?'

He smiled reluctantly. 'We might be better off phoning the local garage and getting a tow.'

'Do you know where it is, or what it's called, let alone the phone number? No, I've got an even better idea.' She wetted her lips nervously. It was now or never. 'The name and number of that hotel are on the bill. Why don't we ring and get them to have us towed back there?'

'Are you sure about this?' Nick asked for the tenth time. Annie nodded, but when they finally reached the reception desk her legs were trembling so much she wasn't sure how long they would hold her up.

She let Nick do all the talking. But she couldn't help seeing the receptionist's disapproving gaze when she noticed they had no luggage.

'Did you see that look she gave me?' Annie hissed as they made their way up to their room. 'I feel really guilty.'

'Why? You haven't done anything – yet.' Nick's eyes glinted wickedly.

By the time they were in their room she was so excited she nearly forgot to breathe. It was heavenly, very olde worlde, with stone walls and narrow lattice windows looking out over the grounds. But it was a long way from the monastic cell it had once been, dominated as it was by a huge canopied bed.

'A four-poster!'

'You did say you wanted to try one.'

Annie smiled up at him. 'You are aware we don't have a toothbrush between us?'

'Who's got time to brush their teeth?' Nick kicked the door closed and pulled her to him.

Annie was shocked to realise how often she'd fantasised about the moment he would kiss her. She gave herself up to the dizzying sensation as his tongue plundered her mouth, gentle, persuasive and lethally expert.

But as they approached the bed she was seized with panic. She'd never been to bed with anyone who wasn't

Max. What if she did it all wrong? What if she took off all her clothes and Nick suddenly didn't fancy her any more?

'Are you sure you're okay?' He read the apprehension in her eyes. 'We don't have to do this, you know – not if you don't want to.'

'I do. I do.' Shakily she began to unbutton her shirt, her fingers fumbling.

'Let me.' Nick gently took over. Annie closed her eyes, praying she was wearing a decent bra.

But he didn't seem to care about the state of her underwear, and neither did she as he unfastened her jeans and traced a flickering line with his tongue over her breasts and down the flat plane of her stomach. Annie groaned, her body arched convulsively, feeling the urgent, pulsing beat of desire. She tore at his clothes, her shyness forgotten, pulling at the buttons of his shirt, desperate to touch him. His skin felt warm, his muscles hard under her fingers.

They fell on the bed, their clothes discarded, exploring each other with hands, tongues, eyes and fingertips, discovering each other for the first time, their desire spiralling until they couldn't stand it any more and their bodies cried out for the inevitable release.

She'd always thought sex with Max was wonderful, but never in her wildest dreams had she ever imagined it could be like this. Max made love like he was giving a virtuoso performance, with her the appreciative audience. There was none of the raw, explosive pleasure she felt now, as she and Nick clung together, their sated bodies drenched in sweat.

Afterwards she lay on the warm, creased sheets, happiness enveloping her like a tight hug.

'Well?' Nick whispered. 'Was the four-poster all you'd hoped it would be?'

'Better.' She curled up against him, her hot skin sticking to his, feeling the rough hair of his chest under her fingers. 'Much, much better.'

She gazed up at the canopy of apricot chintz, trying to imprint every detail in her memory. Outside, the birds were beginning to herald the first chilly light of dawn. She was afraid Nick would say they had to leave. She wanted to hold on to every precious moment for as long as she could.

She listened to the rise and fall of his breathing. 'What are you thinking?' he asked at last.

A chill ran over her skin as the cold wind of reality blew in.

He turned his head to look at her. 'Well?' he whispered.

How could she answer him? How could she tell him she was falling in love with him, but was terrified of the way she felt? She'd given herself body and soul to Max and he'd nearly destroyed her. Her heart told her Nick would never hurt her like that, but her head told her it was better not to take the chance.

' "I do suffer love indeed, for I love thee against my will," ' Annie quoted under her breath. Now she knew how Benedick felt.

'I'm scared about the future,' she whispered. 'About how things will change.'

For a moment he was silent. 'So don't think about it,' he said softly. 'Let's enjoy what we've got now.'

Then his arms went round her, and suddenly the here and now was all she could think about.

They said goodbye outside Nick's cottage. It was after

eight, and the sun was already shining over the town below. Thanks to the hotel organising a mechanic to come and change the wheel, Beryl was now on the road again.

'Are you sure you won't come in?' he said, as they came up for air after another long, lingering kiss. 'There aren't any rehearsals today. We could go back to bed.'

'Don't!' The idea was all too tempting. 'I haven't got used to being a scarlet woman yet.'

'Maybe you need more practice?' Nick kissed her again.

She still had a grin plastered on her face as she drove back to Bermuda Gardens. She was so happy she could barely summon up more than an irritated sigh as Trixie flung herself at her ankles the moment she opened the door.

She tiptoed up the stairs, her shoes in her hand, and nearly fainted with shock when Caz appeared on the landing in her dressing-gown.

'There you are.' Her cropped hair stuck up in spikes around her accusing face. 'Where the hell have you been? I've been ringing round everywhere looking for you.'

Annie thought about telling her, then decided it could wait. 'Why? What's happened?' She was expecting the latest tragic instalment of Caz's love life.

'Prepare yourself for a shock.' Caz took a deep breath. 'Max is here.'

Chapter 29

'He arrived last night,' Caz said. 'I told him you weren't here, but he insisted on waiting for you.'

Annie looked down at the sleeping figure, bundled under a quilt on the chaise longue. 'What does he want?'

'You'd better ask him that.' Caz yawned. 'I'm going to make some coffee.'

Annie couldn't take her eyes off Max. She used to love to watch him sleeping. Sometimes she'd lie awake, just gazing at his beautiful face, the perfect curve of his mouth, the way his long lashes brushed his cheek-bones.

His eyes flicked open and Annie found herself pinned by that oh-so-familiar blue gaze. 'Annie?' He looked around him, disorientated. 'What time is it?'

'Half past eight.'

He struggled to sit up, wincing as he stretched his limbs. 'God, I ache all over. I feel like I've spent the night on the hard shoulder of the M1.' He gave her his most disarming smile. 'I don't suppose you could be an angel and make me some coffee?'

Damn right I couldn't. 'Caz is doing it.' She looked away from his bare chest.

'Caz!' Max groaned. 'She wasn't too pleased to see me

last night. I'd have got a warmer welcome at an Eskimo convention.'

Annie didn't return his smile. 'What are you doing here, Max?'

'Ah, well, that's a long story.' He flung the quilt aside and stood up. He was wearing nothing but a snugly fitting pair of Calvin Kleins.

'Perhaps you'd better start telling it, then.'

He opened his mouth to speak, but shut it again as Caz came in with two steaming mugs. She gave one to Annie, then curled up in the armchair with the other one.

'Nothing for me?' Max made a mock-sorrowful face.

'I didn't think you'd be staying long enough to drink it.'

'You'd probably try to poison me, anyway.'

'Poison you? You'll be lucky.' Caz glared at him. 'Nothing so painless for you, you conniving bastard!'

Annie left them sniping at each other and trudged off to the kitchen to find another mug. Obviously she wasn't going to hear what Max had to say until she did.

She stood at the sink, staring out over the garden, and waited for her emotions to kick in. Where was the excitement, the panic? Where was the sexual meltdown that happened whenever she was in the same room as him? All she felt was numb. Perhaps she was too tired, she told herself, as she poured water into the mug.

Back in the sitting-room, Max and Caz had retreated into glaring silence. Annie sensed Caz's accusing eyes on her back as she handed him his coffee.

'Thanks, angel.' He gave her a smile that once would have sent her pulse into orbit. To her surprise, she felt nothing more than a flicker.

'So.' She seated herself well out of his flirting range. 'Are you going to tell me why you're here?'

'Can you call off your pet Rottweiler first? She's making me nervous.'

They both looked at Caz, who slammed down her mug. 'I'm going to have a shower,' she grumbled. 'I'll be upstairs if you need me.'

'Don't worry, I'm not going to ravish her while your back's turned,' Max drawled.

Caz shot him a look of dislike. 'Just don't take any crap from him, okay?' she warned, before stomping off upstairs.

'I don't think your little friend likes me.' Max stretched out on the sofa. 'Don't tell me she's a lesbian who thinks all men should be castrated?'

'Only you.' Annie eyed him bleakly. Max ignored her pointed remark.

'What are you doing here, Annie? This place is a dump.' He looked around him. 'And as for those oddballs you live with, Christ, I know you've been a bit down on your luck lately, but shacking up with Lily Savage and the Man Hater from Hell –'

'What do you want, Max?' She felt edgy and impatient. 'I'm sure you haven't come all this way because you were worried about my domestic arrangements.'

'You're right, I haven't.' She detected a trace of unease in those faded-denim eyes. 'It's about me and Suzy.'

'Now what? You're getting married? Expecting triplets?' Nothing could shock her any more.

'We've split up.'

Except that. 'When?' she heard herself ask.

'Two days ago.'

'You mean she threw you out?'

'No, I left. I walked out on the film. I've given up everything.' His eyes met hers in direct challenge. 'Call her yourself and ask her if you don't believe me.'

Annie groped in her bag for her cigarettes, playing for time. 'What brought this on?'

'It's been building up for a while. We had a big row on set a couple of days ago and I left. I wanted to tell you myself, before the press got hold of the story.'

Strange that he hadn't shown that much concern when he and Suzy ran off together. 'So what are you going to do now?' she asked, flicking at her lighter. For some reason her hand wouldn't stay steady enough to make the damn thing catch.

'Well, that depends on you, doesn't it?' Smiling, he took the lighter and lit her cigarette for her. His eyes met hers. 'I want you back.'

Upstairs she could hear the rushing water of the shower. Everything was so normal and yet she seemed to be trapped in a bubble of unreality. She felt as if all the breath had been kicked out of her.

'Well, say something.'

'What do you want me to say?'

'Welcome home would be nice.' He laughed. 'I thought you'd be delighted. I mean, it's what you wanted, isn't it?'

Annie took a deep drag on her cigarette and considered it. Once she would have been organising a street party to celebrate. But now – she felt nothing. Maybe it still hadn't sunk in?

Meanwhile, Max was still talking: 'I knew as soon as Suzy and I came up here I'd made a terrible mistake. She's nothing like you. She's self-centred, egotistical –'

'What about the baby?' Annie interrupted him.

'Sorry?'

'Your child. The one Suzy's carrying. Are you walking out on that too?'

He looked genuinely surprised. 'Why should you care?'

Even she didn't know the answer to that one, but she did. Whatever Max and Suzy had done, the baby was an innocent victim.

'Actually, Suzy and I have discussed it,' Max admitted. 'We're going to share the upbringing. Suzy will have custody, of course, but we'll do our share – you know, at weekends and so on.'

'We?'

'Of course. You don't think I'd leave you out, do you, angel?' Max smiled compassionately at her. 'I've learned my lesson. From now on we do everything together.'

'Including taking responsibility for your love child?'

Max looked perplexed. 'I thought you'd be pleased. You were always on about having kids.'

'Yes, but not someone else's.'

'We can have one of our own too. A whole bloody house full, if it'll make you happy.' He put down his mug and leaned forward. 'All I want is for us to be together. That's what you want too, isn't it?'

Annie was silent. Three weeks ago she would have said yes without hesitation. She would have taken Suzy's baby into her home and loved it like her own, if it meant not losing Max. But a lot had happened since then. 'It's not that simple,' she said.

'Why not? Don't tell me you've found someone else?'

Annie thought of Nick. 'Maybe.'

'Yeah, right. Another one of your make-believe lovers, I suppose?'

She felt the terrible urge to wipe the smirk off his face. 'Where do you think I was last night?'

That shook him. His smile wavered slightly. 'I don't believe you.'

'I can show you the hotel bill, if you like?'

Max stood up and paced over to the window. 'So who is it?'

'I'm not telling you.'

'Is it someone from the theatre?' She kept her lips pressed together but her rising blush gave her away. 'I knew it. It is, isn't it?' He shook his head. 'My God, I would never have believed it. You – having a one-night stand!'

She glanced at him. He looked more intrigued than angry.

'I can hardly blame you, can I?' He shrugged. 'After everything I've done –'

'It wasn't a one-night stand.'

He frowned. 'What?'

'It wasn't a one-night stand.' Her chin lifted. 'I love him. And I want to spend the rest of my life with him.'

The words shocked her as much as they did Max. But in a flash she realised they were true. All this time she had been holding on to a dream, trying to compare Nick with a man who didn't exist except in her imagination. Max didn't love her. It wasn't his fault, or hers. He was too vain, shallow and self-centred to love anyone.

And she'd never loved him, either. She had idolised him, like a teenager with a crush on a pop star, grateful for any crumbs of attention he'd thrown her way. But Nick was real. He could make her laugh, make her cry, make her feel cherished one minute and infuriated the next. She could talk to him about anything and know he'd listen. She could argue with him and know he wouldn't leave her. With Nick she could finally be herself.

'You're lying,' Max said flatly. 'You're only saying it because you're angry with me. You want to hurt me –'

'No, I don't. I don't care enough to want to hurt you, not any more.' She shook her head wearily. 'Max, this isn't about you. It's about me. I don't want you any more. I'm in love with someone else.'

He looked uncertain for a moment. Then he shook his head. 'Not you,' he said. 'You know you love me. I'm not saying I've done anything to deserve it, but that's just the way you are.'

He smiled indulgently. 'You'll see. You'll take me back. You always have and you always will.'

Chapter 30

'Lift up your arm for me, would you, darling?' Silence. 'Sweetie?' Vince tutted through a mouthful of pins. 'Look, do you want to go on stage looking like Quasimodo, or what?'

'Hmm?' Annie looked up vaguely.

'Lift. Your. Arm.' He jerked her into position. 'Thank you.' He sighed. 'God, you're in another world, aren't you?'

No, but I wish I were, Annie thought. She wasn't looking forward to this morning's rehearsal.

Maybe she should have phoned Nick last night. Or better still, gone round to his place. A busy rehearsal room was hardly the place to tell someone she loved him. Or to break the news that her ex-husband was back on the scene. She didn't know which she was dreading most.

She reached for her cigarettes. Vince slapped her hand. 'Not until I've finished pinning. You knows those things bring on my chest.'

She put them back.

'You are in a state, aren't you? Don't tell me – man trouble?'

'How did you guess?'

'Just call me Mystic Meg, love.' It certainly suited him better than Vince. 'If I had a fiver for every lovesick lady I've had in here I wouldn't be pinning frocks for a living, I can tell you. So what is it this time? Boyfriend dumped you?'

I wish, Annie thought. A day had passed since Max had arrived and, despite her efforts to get him to go back to London, he had insisted on checking into a local hotel outside Middlethorpe. She had a nasty feeling he wasn't going to give up on her that easily. With Max hanging around, she knew it was only a matter of time before he and Nick came face to face. Which was why it was so important that she told him how she felt first.

On stage, Georgia was pacing around, miming a scene, her rehearsal skirt swishing over the bare boards. Dan and Adam were lying on the ground doing their voice warm-up exercises. Nick and Fliss were at the side of the stage, going over the notes for the day's rehearsal. As Annie approached them, he looked up and smiled.

'Can I talk to you?' she whispered.

'Of course.' Nick gave a final instruction to Fliss, took Annie's arm and guided her towards the darkness of the wings.

'It's about –'

'Shh. Hang on a sec.' Pulling the curtain around them, he bent over and gave her a long, lingering kiss. 'Sorry about that.' He grinned, pulling away. 'I just wanted to make sure I wasn't dreaming yesterday.' He reached out and pushed a stray curl off her face. 'I haven't stopped thinking about you.'

'Me neither.'

'I nearly drove over to see you last night.'

'I wish you had.' She stared at the buttons on his shirt. 'Look, Nick, there's something I've got to tell you –'

'Nick, the musicians have arrived. They want to know what you want for the wedding – oops!' Fliss flung back the curtain and turned red.

'Tell them I'll be right there.' Nick turned back to Annie. 'You were saying?'

'It can wait.' She couldn't just gabble it out in two minutes flat.

He planted a quick kiss on the top of her head. 'We'll talk later,' he promised. And then he was gone.

There wasn't much chance to talk for the rest of the day. Every time she managed to get close to Nick, someone was always there before her, demanding his attention. Then, when they broke for lunch, he was side-tracked by a meeting with the lighting men.

Just as they were wrapping up for the evening Stan appeared in a state of high agitation. 'I tried to stop him, Mr Ryan. I told him he couldn't come in, but he wouldn't listen.' His palsied limbs shook so much he seemed in a state of perpetual motion.

'Told who, Stan?' But before Nick could get an answer, a man appeared from the wings, wearing a shiny suit and an affable expression.

'Sorry to trouble you all like this. I was looking for Annie Mitchell?'

'I'm Annie.' She regarded him warily. She knew that smile. She'd seen dozens like it through her windows on the day Max left.

'Annie. Wonderful to meet you.' He stretched out his hand. 'Dennis Webster, *Goss* magazine. I'm here about the interview.'

'What interview?'

'The exclusive you promised us. About your reconciliation?' His smile dropped. 'Oh, dear, hasn't your husband spoken to you? He said it would be okay when we talked on the phone earlier.'

Annie glanced at Nick. His face was taut, his eyes watchful. 'I – I don't know what you're talking about,' she stammered.

'Don't you? Oh, well, not to worry.' Dennis rallied quickly. 'We've already got Max's side of the story. Now we just need some quotes from you – you know, how delighted you are to be back together, looking forward to the future, etc. Our readers love a happy ending.' He took out his notebook. 'Then later, we'll get some nice romantic shots of the two of you together.'

Annie could feel her face growing hot as everyone stared at her. 'I've got nothing to say to you.'

'But your husband said –'

'You heard her. She's got nothing to say.' Nick stepped between them. 'Now, if you don't mind, we're trying to work.'

'But there must be some mistake. We've already drawn up the contract –' His voice faded as Nick propelled him forcibly back into the wings. 'I'll have to speak to the editor about this,' Annie heard him shout as the stage door slammed.

'Well, well.' Georgia's brows rose. 'This is a surprise. Suzy called last night and told me she'd kicked Max out. I didn't realise he'd come crawling back to you.'

An uneasy silence fell as Nick returned. Annie tried to catch his eye but he didn't glance in her direction as he grabbed his script from Fliss. She could tell from the rigid lines of his body that he was angry. And she knew it wouldn't be long before she felt the full force of it.

She was right.

As everyone drifted off he took her arm and held her back. 'So when were you going to tell me?' he asked. 'Or were you just going to send me a wedding invitation like last time?'

'I – I tried.' She flinched at the harshness in his voice. 'I've been trying to talk to you all day.'

'Shame you didn't try harder, isn't it?' He released her abruptly and turned his back on her. 'So when did all this happen?'

'Yesterday morning.'

'Yesterday?' He swung round. 'And it didn't occur to you to pick up the phone and tell me? I suppose you were too busy enjoying your romantic reconciliation.' His mouth twisted. 'So what did he do? Turn up with a big bunch of flowers? Promise to be a good boy? I don't suppose I even entered your head, did I?'

Annie looked at him sharply. How could he even think that? Did he really believe she could forget about him or their night together that easily? But the warm, gentle man who'd made love to her seemed a million miles away from the harsh, accusing figure who faced her now. He was the one who'd forgotten, not her. 'It wasn't like that,' she said. 'There is no romantic reconciliation. Max and I are not together.'

He frowned. 'That's not what that journalist said.'

'Well, he didn't get the story from me.' Tears of frustration pricked her eyes. 'I told you, Max and I aren't back together. How do you think I could go back to him after what happened between us?'

He looked at her for a moment. 'Because it's what you

want,' he said finally. 'It's what you've always wanted. My God, you've told me so yourself often enough, remember?'

'That's not true.'

'Of course it's true.' Nick's eyes blazed. 'Christ, don't you think I've had long enough to get used to the idea? It's always been him. No matter what I said, no matter what we did, he's always been there.'

'He wasn't there in the hotel,' Annie said quietly.

'That night in the hotel was a mistake.'

His words hit her like a blow. 'You can't mean that.' She reached for him, but he jerked away.

'Can't I? We both got carried away, that's all. I was depressed about the theatre, and you were feeling low over Max. I told you we should enjoy what we had and that's what we did. But now it's over.'

She stared at his cold implacable face in disbelief. This wasn't how it was meant to be. She wanted to tell him how she felt, how things had changed. And he was implying that they hadn't changed at all.

'So what are you saying?' she asked. He didn't answer. 'Nick?'

He couldn't even bring himself to look at her. 'I'm saying,' he said, 'that it might have been better for both of us if that night had never happened.'

Chapter 31

Max came out to greet Annie as she screeched into the hotel car-park amid a hail of skittering gravel and an ominous smell of scorched brake linings.

'Bloody hell, you're in a bit of a hurry,' he observed. 'Couldn't wait to see me, is that it?'

'You bastard!' She slammed the door so hard that Beryl's wing mirror fell off. 'What's this about an interview?'

'Oh, that.' Max smirked. 'I was going to ring you. It was quite a brainwave, wasn't it? A nice pre-emptive strike before the Carrington PR machine grinds into action. I'd like to see them put a positive spin on that one.'

'But it's not true,' Annie shouted. 'We're not together!'

'But that's only a matter of time, isn't it?' He went to put his arm round her, but she shrugged him off.

'I want you to tell them not to print it.'

'I can't do that. How do you think it would make me look?'

'I don't care. You should have consulted me first.'

'I didn't think you'd mind.'

'Mind? *Mind*? Have you any idea how much trouble you've caused me?'

'You're really angry, aren't you?' Amazingly, he clicked. 'Come and have a drink and we'll talk about it.'

As it turned out, Max did most of the talking. Annie sat in the hotel bar, nursing a glass of dry white wine and listening to his litany of complaints, mostly about Suzy and the miserable time he'd had with her.

'Do you know, she wouldn't even introduce me to her family?' he grumbled. 'Apparently her darling daddy didn't like the idea of his daughter getting involved with a married man. As if that randy old sod doesn't have a few skeletons in his closet. Just because he's got a good press agent –'

Annie crunched on a lemon pip and thought about Nick. If only that wretched reporter hadn't turned up. If only he'd let her explain how she felt . . .

'And then there's the film,' Max droned on. 'Of course, I knew it was going to be a fiasco right from the start. We were supposed to have equal billing, but you wouldn't have believed it from the way I was treated. Do you know, I even had to share a trailer with one of the supporting cast?'

Although she was probably wasting her time, she reflected. After what Nick had said about wishing they had never made love, it was pretty obvious he didn't feel the same way.

'Meanwhile, of course, she got treated like a bloody megastar.' Max's mouth tightened. 'I'm telling you, it was sickening the way everyone flocked around her.'

How could Nick say those things, she wondered. Their night together had turned her life around and she had been sure that it had changed things for Nick too. But now he seemed to think it was all pretty unimportant.

'But then, what can you expect when her uncle's the

director? Not that he's any good, of course. That man couldn't direct traffic.'

Annie watched Max's mouth moving. Well, it had been important for her. And with Max's help, she had managed to ruin everything.

She banged down her glass. 'Max, I want you to call that reporter and tell him the truth.'

'I told you, angel, I can't.' He shrugged helplessly. 'Besides, it *is* the truth. I love you. Why else would I be hanging around this dump? My God, they can't even chill a bottle of Chardonnay properly.' He picked up the bottle and peered critically at the label.

'But I don't love you.'

'Of course you do.' He smiled indulgently. 'You're just not admitting it because you want to punish me.'

Annie stared at him, open-mouthed. Why had she never noticed what a self-centred berk he was before?

'You'll see,' Max went on. 'Once we get back to London –'

'London? I'm not going back to London.'

'You've got to go back some time, darling. You can't stay in this hell-hole for the rest of your life.'

'I'm staying for the next four weeks. I've got a job here.'

'So you keep saying.' He patted her hand. 'But don't worry, I expect Julia can work some magic and get you out of the contract. After all, it's her fault for sending you here in the first place.'

'But I don't want to get out of it.' Annie's voice rose stubbornly. 'I like it here.'

Max looked blank. 'Don't you want us to be together? I don't think we should be apart, you know. It's very bad for a marriage.'

Her hands clenched in frustration. Hadn't he listened to a word she'd said? 'I told you, we don't have a marriage,' she said. 'I'm in love with someone else.' Even if he doesn't feel the same, she added silently.

Their eyes clashed. 'Then I suppose I'll have to stay around until you change your mind,' Max said.

Her temples were beginning to throb. 'Do what you like,' she said wearily.

'Well, I can hardly go back to London on my own, can I? I can just imagine what Suzy and her press gang will make of that.' He gave a martyred sigh. 'I don't suppose you'd consider moving in here with me?'

'No.'

'Then how about dinner tonight?'

'I'm running through my lines with Caz.'

'Lunch tomorrow, then? Surely that won't hurt?'

He looked so injured she had to relent. Max the vulnerable little boy was always more deadly than Max the predator, she remembered. 'I suppose not.'

'I'll pick you up at twelve.' He insisted on walking her out to her car. When she opened the door he tried to kiss her, but she averted her face so he just caught the side of her cheek. 'I love you.'

As she drove away, Annie glanced in her rear-view mirror. He was still there, standing forlornly in the car-park, watching her go. Amazing, she thought. All these years while she'd tried to please him she'd never realised how much a bit of indifference could do for a relationship.

Perhaps I should try it on Nick, she thought, then knew she couldn't. Whatever else she felt about him, the one thing she could never be was indifferent.

As it turned out, Caz had invited Daniel over to help with

her lines, leaving Annie to play gooseberry. She sat huddled in the armchair, watching them curled up on the sofa together.

What was Nick doing now, she wondered. It was all she could do to force herself not to phone him, just to hear his voice. She could feel herself turning into a lovesick teenager.

She'd imagined everything would be so different now. But here she was, still alone, still without the man she loved – it just happened to be a different man.

'Why don't you go out?' Caz eyed her meaningfully. 'I'm sure the others are at the Millowners', if you want to join them?'

'No, thanks.' Any minute now she'll be offering me a fiver and sending me off to the pictures, Annie thought sourly.

In the end she settled for a bath and an early night with the latest Maeve Binchy. Downstairs, she could hear Caz and Daniel whispering and giggling together. They'd abandoned their lines and switched on the telly. She'd never felt so lonely in her life.

Not only that, she was forced to listen to Caz bragging when she finally came upstairs.

'He kissed me.' She bounded on to Annie's bed. 'He actually kissed me! Do you think I could be getting somewhere?'

You mean apart from on my nerves? Annie yanked up the bedclothes. She knew it wasn't Caz's fault that she was so miserable, but her happiness grated.

'I hope you've sent that bastard packing?' Caz changed the subject as she began to undress. 'God, he's got a nerve, trying to wheedle his way in here.'

Annie pulled the duvet over her head and pretended to be asleep. The last thing she needed was another lecture.

She tossed and turned for what seemed like hours. Then, just as she'd fallen into a fitful doze, she was woken up by the harsh sound of the phone ringing. A moment later Trixie joined in the chorus with her frenzied yapping.

'Christ, who's that?' Caz's cropped head appeared from under her duvet. 'What time is it?'

'Ten past five.'

'Bloody hell!' She disappeared again, muttering under her breath.

'I'll get it.' Annie tumbled out from under the quilt, her bare feet sinking into the shag pile.

She stumbled past Jeannie's bedroom door, which was shut firmly. She'd probably taken one of her sleeping pills. With a Temazepam inside her, you could strap Jeannie to the front of the Gatwick Express and she still wouldn't wake up.

She grabbed the phone, turning her back on Trixie's hysterics from beyond the kitchen door. 'Hello?'

'Annie? It's Dan.'

'Dan? *Dan*? Do you know what time it is?'

'Yes – sorry. But I had to ring.' Something in his urgent tone snapped her into wakefulness. 'It's about the theatre –'

Chapter 32

They could smell the smoke before they turned the corner. News had spread and a gaggle of people stood looking up at the building. Some were even taking photos.

'Look at them. Bloody vultures!' Caz started to cry.

Annie put her arms around her. 'Come on,' she coaxed. 'It doesn't look too bad from outside.' She grimaced at the blackened holes where the upper windows used to be.

James was waiting for them by the cordoned-off doorway. 'It happened in the early hours.' His face was grim. His usually immaculate clothes looked as if they'd been slept in. 'They reckon it started in one of the dressing-rooms. Probably an electrical fault of some kind. Luckily some passers-by saw the smoke before it brought the place down completely.'

'How bad is the damage?' Caz sniffed.

'Come and take a look.' James cast them a sidelong glance. 'You'd better prepare yourselves for a shock.'

But nothing could have prepared them for what they saw as they picked their way past the firemen's cordon and into the charred, blackened building. The acrid smell of smoke filled their mouths, choking them. The fire had devoured the foyer, leaving black streaks where its tongue had licked the walls. Its teethmarks were in the charred shreds that hung from the ceiling. It had savaged the staircase, reducing it to ugly, blackened stumps.

The sodden carpet squished under their feet as they walked around, looking at everything. A lump rose in Annie's throat. It had always been a bleak, unlovely building, but it had never really had a chance. Seeing it like this she felt as if her heart had been torn out.

Adam and Daniel were already there, picking their way around the mess. Their expressions said it all. Caz let out a sob and flew into Daniel's arms. Adam hugged Annie. No one spoke.

James led them through the dripping, blackened remains towards the door marked Stalls.

Annie stopped. 'I can't go in there,' she whispered. 'I don't want to see it. Not if it's like this.'

'Come on, pet. It's not too bad.' Adam squeezed her shoulders. 'There's a bit of water damage, but luckily the fire didn't spread that far.'

He was right. It was gloomy, icy cold and the bitter tang of smoke still filled her nose and mouth, but mercifully it was unharmed.

'Does Nick –' No sooner had she started to speak than she saw him. He was on the far side of the auditorium, sitting on the edge of the stage.

'Nick!' Annie immediately moved towards him, but Adam held her back.

'Best leave him,' he said gruffly. 'He's taken it very badly.'

Annie stood still, watching him, tears brimming. He didn't look up. He had never felt so out of her reach.

'It's a bloody mess, isn't it?' Daniel said grimly. 'That old bloke was lucky to get out alive, I reckon.'

Annie's head snapped back. 'What old bloke?'

'That old caretaker guy who's been hanging around here. What's his name –'

'Not Stan?' Annie whispered.

'That's it. Apparently he was in here last night, locking up.'

'Oh, God!' Adam steadied her as her legs threatened to give way. 'Is he – is he going to be all right?'

'No one knows. He's on the critical list, so I've heard. Another few minutes and he would have been a goner.'

Annie felt sick. This couldn't be happening. It was like some terrible nightmare.

They stood silently, looking around, all lost in their own thoughts.

'How long will it take to rebuild it, do you reckon?' Daniel asked the question that was on everyone's minds.

Adam shrugged. 'No idea. At least the damage in here isn't too bad, so we could still open –'

'I doubt it.' James's voice was calm. 'You haven't seen upstairs. It's completely gutted.'

'So you think they'll put off the first night?'

'I shouldn't think there'll be a first night. Or any other night, come to that.'

They turned round. Nick was standing behind them. It shocked her to see how much older he'd become. His face was gaunt and tired, etched with deep lines. She ached to reach out and take him in her arms but he hardly seemed to notice she was there.

'What do you mean?' Caz asked.

'I mean we can't afford to rebuild this place.'

There was an uneasy silence. Then James laughed

nervously. 'Aren't you being a bit pessimistic? Once we get the insurance sorted out –'

'There isn't any insurance,' Nick said curtly. 'I've been talking to the chief fire officer. He reckons the fire was started deliberately. Which means the insurance people won't pay out.'

His words sank into the silence. Then everyone started talking at once.

'Deliberate?'

'But who'd do a thing like that?'

'Your guess is as good as mine.' Nick glanced at Annie. She could see the pain in his dark, hollowed eyes.

'So we're out of a job.' Adam groaned. 'Oh, Christ!'

'But surely if we explained it wasn't our fault –' Caz faltered. James looked at her pityingly.

'Do you really think they'd believe us? This place is in dire financial trouble. Then out of the blue someone starts a fire and burns it down. It's got to look suspicious, hasn't it?' He looked around. 'Mind you, I've got a good idea who did start it.'

'Who?'

'That old fool Stan Widderburn. He could have dropped a cigarette, or spilt something accidentally. He's so old and senile he probably wouldn't even know what he'd done.'

Annie looked at Nick but for once he didn't rise to the bait. He just stood there, his shoulders hunched in weary resignation, letting it all fall around him. They might have lost their jobs, but he'd lost much more. The Phoenix was his dream. And now it had been taken away from him.

She clenched her fists at her sides to stop herself reaching out to him.

'Strange, isn't it?' Caz said as the four of them left the

theatre. James had stayed behind to talk to Nick. 'They say the fire started upstairs, in the dressing-rooms.'

'So?'

'So that's where it started the night Jessica Barron's husband was killed, wasn't it? And that was deliberate too.'

'Oh, for God's sake!' Adam looked impatient. 'You don't think this bloody mess was caused by a ghost, do you?'

'I'm just saying it's strange, that's all. Don't you think so?'

'No,' said Adam. 'I think it's bloody tragic.' He sighed. 'Oh well, I suppose I'd better go and break the news to Becky. I just hope this doesn't send her into early labour.' He plodded off across the square, ignoring the reporters who had gathered around the building.

The three of them stood forlornly on the pavement. 'I suppose it's too early for a drink?' Daniel said hopefully, looking across at the locked doors of the Millowners' Arms. 'I don't feel like being alone at the moment.'

'We could get some breakfast somewhere.' Despite her heart-break, Caz was never one to pass up a dating opportunity. 'There's a café open around the corner, I think.' She turned to Annie. 'Are you coming?'

She shook her head. 'I think I'll wait for Nick.'

She lingered outside the building for nearly half an hour, but he didn't appear. She thought about going back inside to look for him, then decided against it. He probably wanted to be alone.

It was a dull grey morning. As she trudged across the square past old Josiah's statue, Annie was lost in her thoughts.

Surely no one could have started that fire deliberately?

Who could have hated them so much they'd put an old man's life in danger?

She drove home, changed, then headed to the hospital to visit Stan.

Chapter 33

'Are you a relative?' The ward sister eyed Annie with suspicion. 'Mr Widderburn's very poorly. It's close family only.'

No, I'm a phantom hospital visitor, preying on unsuspecting pensioners. 'I'm his granddaughter.' Annie smiled sweetly through an armful of foliage.

The nurse looked doubtful. 'No more than five minutes,' she warned. 'And don't excite him.'

Annie resisted the urge to point out it took her a lot longer than five minutes to excite a man these days, even with a box of Milk Tray and an extravagant bunch of chrysanthemums. Meekly she followed the ward sister down the corridor, trying not to breathe in the horrible boiled cabbage and antiseptic smell.

She ushered her into a side ward. 'Remember, no more than five minutes.'

Annie stopped short. Nick was already at the old man's bedside. They looked at each other for a moment, both at a loss.

'I – I didn't know you'd be here,' she managed to say.

'I thought someone should be with him – in case he woke up.'

'Me too.'

He got to his feet. 'I'd better go.'

'Please don't!' She felt herself blushing. 'Stan would – er – want you here.' Nick hesitated, then sank back into his seat. They both looked towards the bed. Stan lay propped up against a bank of pillows, his face covered by an oxygen mask, his frail body lost under a mass of wires and tubes. A bleeping machine punctuated the silence. Annie's heart contracted with pity. Poor Stan. He looked so thin and old and vulnerable, his bones sticking out from under his wrinkled white skin.

She put down her flowers and pulled the covers up around him. He deserved his dignity.

'How did you get past the nurse?' she asked.

'I told them he was my grandfather.'

'Me too. I suppose that makes us brother and sister?' They smiled warily at each other. Annie looked back at Stan. 'I don't suppose he's got much family.'

'He never talks about them.'

Her throat ached from trying not to cry. 'Have they – said how he is?'

'Not really. You know what they're like. But from what I can gather he's not suffered any serious burns. The main problem is smoke inhalation.' His voice was gruff with emotion. 'The trouble is, he's so old and frail they think he might have suffered permanent lung damage.'

Suddenly the tears she'd been fighting off all day overwhelmed her. She put her face in her hands and wept.

'Shh. It's okay.' She felt Nick close and for a moment she thought he might take her in his arms. Then a crumpled tissue was pushed into her hands.

'I just wish there was something I could do –'

'How do you think I feel? It's my fault all this has happened.'

Annie looked up, mopping her eyes. 'You? Why?'

'I should never have given him the job. I knew he was getting on and couldn't manage it. I only did it to make him happy. And now this –' His face was bleak. 'James is right. He would have been better off in an OAP home.'

'You know that's not true.' Annie dabbed at her nose. 'He would have died a lonely old man. You gave him something to live for, a reason to get up in the morning –'

'And look what happened.' Nick's hands balled into fists. 'My God, if only I could get my hands on the bastard who did this.'

They were silent, both lost in their own thoughts.

'What's happening about the theatre?' Annie said at last.

Nick shrugged. 'God knows. They're holding an emergency trustees' meeting in the morning. I suppose they'll be voting on whether to go ahead with the project.'

He didn't have to say any more. They both knew what that meant. Annie longed to touch him, but she could feel him shutting her out.

'I'm sorry,' she whispered. 'About Max, I mean. I didn't want you to find out like that.'

'I had to some time.'

She twisted her fingers and wondered what to say next. 'Look, I know this isn't easy, but we've got to go on working together,' she ventured. 'It would help if we could stay friends.'

At last he turned his head to look at her. 'That's what you want, is it?'

Of course it's not what I want, she longed to shout. But she couldn't bear being enemies, either. 'I think it would be best.'

He didn't answer. Annie stared at his back, fighting the urge to thump him. She was making an effort. Surely he could do the same?

'Could I – um – get you some coffee or something?' she asked.

'No, thanks. But there's a machine down the hall if you want a cup.'

At least he was speaking to her, she thought, as she pushed coins into the machine. But when she got back he'd gone. She was too tired to feel angry or even upset. She sank down into the chair, the damp tissue still crumpled in her hand, and looked at Stan. He was the one she should be worrying about, not Nick.

'I'm sorry, Stan, I – I didn't mean to sound selfish. I can't seem to do anything right these days.' Her trembling voice echoed around the room, punctuated by the bleeping machine. 'But it'll be all right, you'll see. We'll get the theatre up and running again, and you'll be there to see it.' She tried to smile but her face wouldn't co-operate. 'You can have the best seat in the house for opening night –'

She broke off. The feeble rise and fall of his thin chest was too much for her. With another sob, she rested her head on the bed, her face sinking into the cover, breathing in the sickly hospital smell.

Then she felt something fluttering by her hand, like a moth brushing against her fingers. She looked up sharply. Stan's hand, frail and trembling, was reaching across the bedclothes for her. 'Stan? Stan, can you hear me?' She grasped his fingers and they tightened around hers. 'Nurse! Come quickly.'

As she watched, Stan shakily raised his other hand and

pulled off his oxygen mask. 'The fire.' His voice was barely above a whisper. Annie leaned forward to hear him. 'The fire –' His chest shuddered with the sheer effort.

'Don't try to talk, Stan,' she begged.

'He saw me . . . the smoke . . .'

'Who, Stan? Who saw you?'

'He saw me . . . and he ran –' He started coughing, a cough which shook his body. He collapsed against the pillows, his strength gone.

'Now then, what's all the –' The ward sister came bustling into the room, ready to tell her off. Then she spotted Stan, struggling for breath. 'I think you'd better go now,' she said, shoving Annie out into the corridor.

Annie chewed her nails anxiously as she watched the flurry of activity in and out of the room. Finally the nurse appeared again. 'Is he going to be all right?'

'Yes.' No thanks to you, her look said. 'He has to rest now.'

Annie walked out of the hospital, Stan's words running through her mind. Whoever started that fire had known Stan was there, but they'd done nothing to rescue him. They'd run off and left an old man to die while they saved their own cowardly skin.

Visiting hour had just begun, and the florists and newsagents were filling up with people buying last-minute gifts. Patients in dressing-gowns shuffled down the corridors. The unmistakable smell of hospital food hung in the air. As she passed through reception, Annie's attention was caught by a large slab of polished marble set into the tiles on the floor, in which were written the words: *This foundation stone was laid by Councillor Robert Stone, in recognition of his generosity in funding a new wing of the hospital.*

Annie read the inscription, her anger welling. 'Well, Mr Stone,' she said aloud. 'I think it's about time we met.'

Chapter 34

As Annie headed across the hospital car-park she was astonished to see Max coming towards her. 'What are you doing here?'

'Your landlady told me where to find you. We had a lunch date, remember? An hour ago.'

Annie felt dazed. 'Sorry.'

'Why are you here, anyway?' He frowned. 'Are you ill or something?'

'I had to see someone.'

'You could have called me.'

'I forgot.'

Max looked disbelieving. 'I know what you're up to. You're doing this to punish me, aren't you? I can't say I don't deserve it, but frankly this playing hard to get thing is beginning to get on my –'

'Why does it always have to be about you? Just leave me alone, will you?'

She walked towards her car, Max following. 'Where are you going? What about our lunch date?'

'Some other time.' He would never believe the world didn't revolve around him and she didn't have time to argue.

She got into the car and turned the ignition key. Beryl coughed, then died. Bugger! She tried again. This time the car couldn't even raise a cough. Annie slumped back in her seat. Beryl's timing was impeccable, as usual. Now what was she going to do?

Meanwhile, Max was still whining. 'What about me?' he was saying. 'How am I supposed to entertain myself in this dump?'

Frustrated and angry, Annie stuck her head out of the window to tell him exactly what he could do – and spotted his shiny Mazda parked not far away. Grabbing her bag off the passenger seat, she got out of the car and headed for it.

'I knew it!' Max grinned triumphantly. 'I knew you were just fooling around.' He opened the door for her. 'So where shall we go? I spotted a nice country place not far from –'

'Middlethorpe Golf Club.'

'What?'

'I'll explain on the way.' Annie clicked her seat-belt. 'Just drive, will you?'

'So how do you know this Bob Stone guy will be there?' Max asked, when she'd told him about the fire.

'I called his office on my mobile from the hospital. They told me he always plays golf on Thursdays.'

'Did they know who you were?'

Annie shook her head. 'I said I was from a charity and we wanted him to be guest of honour at our celebrity ball. Apparently Mr Stone likes doing things for charity.'

Max looked at her with admiration. 'Very resourceful,' he remarked. 'You've certainly changed in the last few weeks.'

'I know.'

'I'm getting used to the new you. Actually, it's quite a turn-on –'

'Right at the next set of lights.' Annie diverted him swiftly.

'But you're not planning to tackle this guy? You've got no evidence. You can't just go around accusing people.'

'I've got to do something.'

Max sent her a sidelong glance. 'This place really means a lot to you, doesn't it?'

When they arrived at the golf club, Annie was grateful that Beryl hadn't started. Here in the car-park, amid the Jaguars and the BMWs, she would have stuck out like a vegetarian at a hog roast.

'Are you sure about this?' Max asked again. 'What if he turns nasty?'

'On a golf-course? What's he going to do, clobber me with a number five iron and bury me in a bunker?' Annie looked scathing. 'If you're that worried, you can always come with me.'

'No, thanks.' Max switched off the engine. 'You can make a fool of yourself without any help from me.'

Despite all her bravado, Annie's heart was sinking as she approached the clubhouse. Max was right, she had no proof Bob Stone was involved. What if he did threaten her? She'd already seen the evidence of how ruthless he could be.

The clubhouse was full of middle-aged men dressed in pastel Pringle sweaters. She stood in the doorway, feeling underdressed in her ripped jeans and T-shirt.

'What are you doing here? This is members only.' One of the men, holding a gin and tonic, bore down on her.

'I'm looking for Mr Stone,' Annie said sweetly. 'Could you tell me where I might find him?'

'What do you want Bobby Stone for? He's far too old for you. Wouldn't I do instead?' The man leered, showing off large yellow teeth. 'Why don't you stay and have a little drinkie? I'm sure I could keep you entertained.' The alcohol fumes from his breath nearly knocked her sideways.

Annie lowered her eyes to conceal her anger. 'Some other time, maybe.' Like when hell freezes over, she added silently. 'I really need to find Mr Stone.'

The man sighed. 'He'll probably be on the eighteenth hole by now. I'll show you which way to go.'

Annie fought the urge to turn round and slap his face as he guided her outside, his hand hovering on her bottom. 'Thanks,' she interrupted his long-winded directions. 'I think I'll be able to find it.'

'Sure you wouldn't like me to run you up there?'

Annie shuddered. 'No, thanks.' She surveyed the rolling green, dotted here and there with pastel-coloured golfers. 'Er, how will I know which one is Bob Stone?'

'You can't miss him. He'll be the one with the entourage. Old Bob never goes anywhere without his heavies.'

Annie pictured him, surrounded by a wall of huge black-suited men, like a scene from *Reservoir Dogs*. How reassuring, she thought.

Nearly half an hour later she was beginning to wonder if a lift with Tombstone Teeth wouldn't have been a small price to pay. At least she wouldn't still be walking round in circles. She sat down on a grassy mound to ease her aching feet. Surely a golf-course shouldn't be this big? Had she passed that clump of trees before? Or that big sand-filled thingy? She had visions of wandering for years, her skeleton being finally unearthed from the sixteenth hole some time in the twenty-second century.

Worse still, exhaustion had dissipated her anger. She had a feeling that once she met Bob Stone she would be so relieved to see another face that she'd fall at his feet with gratitude and beg him to take her home.

Then she did see him. As she puffed her way up to the crest of a slope he was suddenly below her, surrounded, as Tombstone Teeth had predicted, by ten other pastel-clad men.

She remembered Stan lying in that hospital bed and Nick, his face drawn with fatigue and strain, and all the anger she thought had gone came surging back in an adrenalin rush that sent her storming, red-faced and breathless, down the hill.

They turned to look at her. All except Bob Stone, who didn't seem to notice her as he lined up his next putt, waggling his stocky hips into position.

As she advanced towards them, a tall, thin man with sparse hair blocked her way. 'Can I help you, young lady?'

'Not you. Him!' Annie jabbed a finger towards Bob Stone. 'I hope you're bloody well satisfied,' she shouted.

Bob Stone calmly watched the ball roll into the hole with a muted clunk. Finally, he turned to face her. 'Not really. I'm three up on my handicap.' The pale sun glinted off his glasses. 'Do I know you?'

'I suppose you know the Phoenix has burned down?'

The hint of a smile crossed his face. 'Oh, aye. I did hear summat about that.' He shook his head. 'Bad business.'

'Don't give me that! You got what you wanted, didn't you?'

His eyes narrowed. 'Are you from the press?'

'No, I'm one of the people you've just put out of work. All so you can hand the site over to your friends the Blanchards and collect your backhander. I don't know how you can sleep at night.'

He was bending down to collect his ball from the hole. Slowly, he straightened up. 'I hope you're not suggesting I had anything to do with that fire?'

They stared at each other. Annie could see why people were afraid of him. That square, blunt face was menacing. Yet there was something familiar about him and his gruff voice. It hovered out of reach at the back of her memory.

She took a deep breath. 'I'm not suggesting anything. I know you did it.'

There was a collective gasp. 'Shall I get security, Bob?' one of the men asked.

Bob Stone shook his head. 'It's all right, Tony. I think I can handle this.' He looked her up and down. 'Look, lass, I can see you're upset. But that theatre's an old building. It wasn't safe. It could have burned down at any time –'

'The fire was started deliberately,' Annie said. 'And you did it.'

'And someone saw me, did they? Someone actually saw me coming out of there with a petrol can in my hand?'

'No,' Annie faltered, 'but –'

'I've got a couple of hundred witnesses who saw me at a civic function last night.' Bob thrust his face close to hers. 'So where's your proof?'

He had the upper hand and he knew it. One of the men muttered something about women with over-active imaginations. 'Over-active hormones, more like,' someone else sneered and they laughed.

Annie clenched her fists in impotent rage. 'So much for

Bob Stone, the caring councillor,' she hissed. 'I wonder if the voters would find it so funny if they knew what you were up to.'

Something inside him seemed to snap. Letting his golf-bag drop, he grabbed her, his fingers biting into her flesh. 'Those are very serious allegations you're making, young lady.' His face was mottled with fury. 'And in front of witnesses too. Now bugger off before I have you for defamation.'

As he released her and turned to walk away, it suddenly dawned on her where she'd seen him before. That short, stocky figure, that brush of greying curls: it all came back to her. Except of course he hadn't been wearing Rupert Bear golfing trousers then . . .

'Thank you, Jeannie Acaster,' she murmured.

The effect was electric. Bob Stone froze, his expression rigid with shock. The others were too far away to hear. He grabbed her arm again. 'What did you say?' he hissed.

Annie smiled. 'Ready for your bed bath, Mr Stone – or should I say Bobby?' She looked him up and down. 'I didn't recognise you with your clothes on.'

His jowly face quivered. 'I don't know why you came here, but if you're expecting me to wring my hands and say I'm sorry the theatre's gone, then I'm not.' Beneath the bluster she could tell he was rattled. 'I made no secret of the fact that I considered it a waste of civic money. And I don't care that it won't go ahead.' He turned away from her and snatched up his golf-bag.

'And don't you care that an old man was nearly killed? You do realise that if old Stan dies you'll be up on a manslaughter charge?'

He stopped. 'Old Stan Widderburn was in that fire?'

'Whoever started it left him trapped in there to die. Don't tell me you didn't know.'

Bob Stone went very pale. 'I had no idea –'

'Your friends the Blanchards must have made it really worth your while for you to stoop to murder.'

One of his cronies stepped between them. 'That's enough! You've had your say and Mr Stone's been very patient with you. Now get lost before I call security and have you thrown off.'

Annie watched them walking away. From the look Bob Stone gave her over his shoulder she had a terrible feeling she might have made a big mistake.

'You must be mad!' Caz looked appalled. 'You actually went to see this guy?'

'I know.' Now some of her white-hot anger had worn off, she felt incredibly foolish. 'I think I might have made things worse.'

'I should say. I wouldn't be surprised if you ended up at the bottom of Middlethorpe reservoir with your DMs full of concrete.'

'Thanks. That thought had occurred to me too.' Along with various other grisly deaths. She'd obviously watched too many Bob Hoskins films.

'And you say this Bob Stone and Jeannie are – you know?' Caz giggled.

Annie nodded. 'Doctors and nurses.'

'Bloody hell! And at their age, too.' She considered for a moment. 'We could always try blackmailing him.'

'I've thought of that, but what good would it do?' It wouldn't bring the Phoenix back. And it certainly wouldn't help poor Stan.

She watched Caz apply her lipstick. She was in tearing

spirits now she and Daniel were finally going out on a proper date.

'I think this might be the night,' Caz had confided.

'I don't know how you can leave me,' Annie grumbled. 'What if he sends round one of his heavies?'

'Then you've only got yourself to blame.' Caz dropped her lipstick back into her bag. 'Now, can I borrow your wonderbra?'

Left alone in the house, Annie tried to comfort herself with a giant bag of Maltesers and an episode of *Casualty* she'd taped from the weekend before. She usually enjoyed spotting her actor friends in the waiting room of Holby City, dripping blood and having seizures. But tonight she couldn't concentrate. Especially when the victim of a gangland shooting was wheeled in.

Would Bob Stone be that unsubtle, she wondered. Or would she just find Beryl's brakes had been tampered with one night?

The phone rang, making her scream. Trixie sprang off the chaise longue and lunged at it, attacking it into submission. It took a while to wrench it from her jaws, by which time it was dripping with doggy drool.

Annie grimaced and held it away from her ear. 'Hello?'

'Are you alone?'

She'd heard the expression about blood running cold, but she'd never believed it was possible until she heard Bob Stone's gruff voice on the other end of the line. 'No.'

'Liar.' He laughed harshly. 'I know Jeannie's out and I've just seen your mate leave with her boyfriend.'

Annie felt light-headed with fear. 'What do you want?'

'I think we should talk, don't you?' There was a heavy silence. 'I didn't like what you were implying this afternoon. You could do me a lot of damage with rumours like that.'

His voice seemed to fill the room. Annie wondered if anyone had remembered to lock the back door. 'So?' she squeaked. 'What are you going to do about it?'

'I think it's time we set the record straight. I've kept quiet about this for long enough. But if old Stan Widderburn dies, I don't see why I should take the blame.' There was a long silence. 'I didn't set fire to your theatre, lass. But I know who did.'

Chapter 35

Annie was already ten minutes late by the time she found James's office, a sleek glass building in the middle of town. Despite her haste, she had time to be impressed. How like James, she thought, as she entered the vast reception area, her footsteps muted by the expanse of tasteful grey carpet.

She wasn't sure if she was doing the right thing, turning up to this meeting. She'd spent most of the night fretting about it. But by the morning she knew she had to go. Someone should be there to tell them the truth.

Her first instinct was to talk to Nick. But there was no answer from his cottage and he wasn't at the theatre. Annie was beginning to feel desperate. She just prayed he would be at the meeting. She didn't think she could do this by herself.

A chic blonde sat behind a sweeping curve of pale wood that looked more like a spaceship console than a reception desk. She looked down her narrow nose as Annie rushed up breathlessly. 'Can I help you?'

'Has the trustees meeting started yet?'

'Are they expecting you?'

'Does it matter?' Annie felt her facial muscles going into spasm. 'I need to be there. I've got something important to tell them.' The blonde eyed her dubiously. 'Look, can you just tell James I'm here?'

'You mean Mr Brookfield?'

Annie could feel a vein in her head about to pop. It was like talking to a Speak Your Weight machine. 'That's right. James Brookfield. Can I speak to him?'

'I'm afraid that won't be possible. He's in a meeting at the moment.'

Annie contemplated grabbing her designer lapels and shaking her. Then she heard James's voice coming from beyond the door to her right. She hitched her bag on to her shoulder and headed for it.

'Wait a minute, you can't go in there!'

Annie ploughed past the secretary's waving arms, pushed open the door and went inside.

The room fell silent as she entered. They were sitting around a long glass table. Annie looked at the strangers' faces and her nerve began to fail her.

James rose from his seat at the other end. 'Annie. What on earth are you doing here?'

'Where's Nick?'

'He hasn't turned up. Couldn't face it, I suppose.' James came towards her. 'I'm afraid you can't stay. This meeting's for trustees only.' He was already shepherding her back towards the door.

'But I've got to be here.' Annie stared at the trustees. Most of them seemed very ordinary. It could have been a meeting of the local parish council. One or two of them appeared quite friendly, although the old dear at the other end of the table seemed a bit Lady Bracknell, with her blue rinse and frosty expression.

'Who is this person, Mr Brookfield?' She peered over her spectacles at Annie.

'She's an actress, Lady Carlton. From the repertory company.' James turned back to Annie. 'I can see you're upset. Why don't you go and have some coffee in reception? We can talk when all this is over.'

'I'm not going anywhere.' She shook him off. 'Not until I've said what I came to say.' She glanced around the room again. 'You need to know the truth, before you do something you'll regret.'

'Annie, you're making a fool of yourself,' James hissed. 'I really think you should go now, before –'

'Oh, shut up, James!' Annie focused on the friendliest face, a bearded man in a hand-knitted pullover. 'I know you're here to vote on the future of the Phoenix,' she said. 'But before you do, I think you should know who started that fire.'

There was a moment's shocked silence. James gripped her wrist. 'For God's sake, you're hysterical –'

'Let her speak.' It worked. The man in the pullover was smiling encouragingly at her. 'If the lass has something to say, I reckon we should hear it.'

'But she has no authority –' James began to protest.

Lady Carlton interrupted. 'I'll decide who has authority to address this meeting.' She turned to Annie. 'So who started the fire, Miss – er –'

'Mitchell. Annie Mitchell.' She took a deep breath. Everyone was looking at her expectantly. She felt as if she was on top of a roller coaster, poised on the edge on a deep plunge, and there was nothing she could do but hang on and hope for the best.

She turned to James, who was still hanging on to her wrist. 'He did.'

There was a long silence, then James began to laugh. 'I

told you she was hysterical. Now perhaps you'll let me throw her out?'

'Just a moment, Mr Brookfield.' Lady Carlton turned to Annie. Her watery blue eyes were full of intelligence. 'I want to know how Miss Mitchell has come up with such an extraordinary idea.'

Annie's chin lifted. 'Bob Stone told me.'

'Bob Stone?' James laughed again. 'My God, this just gets better and better.'

'It's true.' Annie felt her temper flare. 'I confronted him about the fire and he told me what happened.'

'And what did you expect him to do? Get down on his knees and confess?' James retreated behind the table. 'Bob Stone's the biggest crook this side of the A1. He wouldn't know the truth if he fell over it.'

There was a low rumble of laughter around the table.

Annie felt her confidence sinking. He was making a fool of her. 'Maybe not,' she agreed slowly. 'But he's not too pleased at taking the blame for something he didn't do. In fact,' she added, 'he's very, very angry. Did you know Stan was an old friend of his father's?' James paled, she noticed.

'But why would he say Mr Brookfield was responsible? I don't understand.' Lady Carlton frowned.

'Neither do I.' James glared at Annie. 'Look, this is turning into a farce,' he complained. 'I know we're all upset. None of us wants to see the Phoenix fail —'

'Except you,' Annie put in bitterly.

'This is Nick Ryan's fault.' James sent her a withering look. 'Somehow he's made everyone believe I'm the bad guy. Just because I've had to make a few hard financial decisions. The fact that they've been endorsed by the rest of the board —'

'Bob Stone told me you'd been bribing his men to hold up the building work,' Annie cut in.

James's eyes bulged. 'That's ridiculous!' He slammed his fists down on the table. 'What could I possibly have to gain from closing the theatre down? I'm one of the trustees, for God's sake.'

Annie met his gaze unflinchingly. 'You're also Philip Blanchard's son.'

Everyone started talking at once. James, she noticed, had gone very still.

Lady Carlton turned to him. 'Is this true?'

His mouth was a thin line. 'Yes, it's true. But it isn't something I choose to talk about.' He looked at Annie. Suddenly she was glad the table separated them.

'Surely we should have been informed?' Lady Carlton spoke for all of them. 'This is a clear conflict of interests.'

'I don't see why,' James said coldly.

'Your father is head of the company that wants to buy the Phoenix land.'

'That's true. And I agree, it would have been a conflict of interests if I'd had anything to gain from the deal. But I don't. Entirely the opposite, in fact.' Annie sensed the anger beneath his icy calm. 'As I told Miss Mitchell, my mother signed a contract when I was ten years old, relinquishing all rights and claims on the Blanchard family. In return for a certain sum of money she agreed never to reveal my father's identity.' His chin lifted. 'So you see, if I'd declared anything to you, I would have been breaking the terms of the agreement. I'm only telling you all this now under extreme duress.' He stared at Annie with loathing. 'Not only do I have nothing to gain from the Blanchard deal, I also have good reason to resent them for

278

the shabby way they've treated my mother and myself over the years.'

Everyone looked at each other. Then Lady Carlton spoke. 'I see.' She took a deep breath. 'I'm sorry you had to go through all that, Mr Brookfield. I appreciate how painful it must have been for you.' There was a misty look in her eyes.

She's crying, Annie thought. He's played her like a Stradivarius. She caught the glint in his eye. And he knew it too, the bastard. 'If you feel so sorry for your mother, why haven't you spoken to her for the last ten years?' she asked.

James blanched. 'I really don't see what that has to do with you —'

'It's because you're angry, isn't it? You're angry at her for selling your birthright. It's thanks to her and that stupid contract you'll never be able to take your rightful place as a Blanchard heir. No wonder you've never forgiven her.'

'That's not true!' A muscle flickered in his jaw. 'I detest that family and all they stand for.'

'Then why did you offer them the Phoenix site?' There was a collective gasp from around the table. 'That's why you got involved with this place, isn't it? You didn't want to save it from being redeveloped, or to stop Blanchards getting their hands on it. You wanted to run it into the ground so the trustees would have no choice but to hand the lease back to the council.' She took a deep breath. 'You couldn't break that contract, so you decided to wheedle your way back into the family by offering them what they wanted most. The Phoenix.'

James looked as if he was going to explode. 'That's the most ludicrous idea I've ever heard!'

'Really? Philip Blanchard told Bob Stone all about it. He's even kept the letters you sent him.'

Suddenly, James had the look of a cornered animal – a cornered, very dangerous animal. 'I suggest we end this meeting here, since the whole thing had turned into a charade.' He appeared to be fighting for control. 'And as for you.' He turned to Annie. 'I'll see you in court for defamation.'

'And I'll see you there for attempted murder.' They swung round. Nick stood in the doorway. Annie hardly recognised him, he looked so angry. 'Stan Widderburn, the man you left to die in that fire? He's ready to identify you.'

Chapter 36

'You know what the really ironic thing is? Blanchards don't even want the site now.'

They were in the theatre, just the two of them. The acrid smell of smoke still hung in the air.

'You're kidding? Why not?'

'They've invested heavily in a new flagship store in Leeds. They're not interested in Middlethorpe any more.' Nick lit a cigarette. 'I'd like to see James's face when he finds out.'

'I don't care if I never see his face again.' Annie shuddered. A weekend had gone by since the meeting but it still unsettled her. She dreaded to think what would have happened if Nick hadn't been there.

Amazingly, James had somehow managed to keep his cool. He'd gone on protesting his innocence in the face of all the evidence. He'd even accused Nick of organising a personal vendetta against him. Then he'd packed up his papers and stalked out, declaring that no one had any real proof against him and he'd sue them all if they breathed a word of their outrageous lies.

'I should have known it was him,' Nick said. 'The way he was always hanging around here, pretending to be everyone's friend, and all the time he was just stirring up trouble.'

'And letting other people take the blame.' Annie felt sick, thinking how he'd even tried to blame poor old Stan. That was one thing she couldn't forgive him for: not only had he started the fire, but he had left a man to die.

And he might have got away with it, if Bob Stone hadn't decided enough was enough.

'At least he's safe behind bars now,' she said.

'For the time being,' Nick pointed out. 'I wonder if he'll get any of his wealthy friends to stand bail for him?'

'Perhaps he should ask the Blanchards?'

They were both silent.

Annie watched the smoke drifting up from her cigarette. The coldness between her and Nick had thawed slightly since the confrontation in James's office, but nevertheless she could feel an invisible barrier there. Among other things the unspoken subject of Max still loomed between them. 'At least the trustees have agreed not to pull the plug on this place,' she said.

'So what?' Nick's face was bleak. 'How are we going to open in this state? And you heard what they said at that meeting. There's no more money for repairs.'

Annie stubbed out her cigarette. 'But there must be something we can do. Couldn't we raise the funds ourselves?'

'What do you suggest? A whist drive at the local church hall?'

'At least I'm trying to think of something,' Annie retorted. 'I'm not ready to give up yet.'

'Do you think I want to?' Nick's dark eyes blazed. 'Don't you think I've had all the same crazy ideas as you?'

He shook his head. 'I'm just being realistic, Annie. It's not going to happen.'

'Well, I'm not giving up.'

'Why do you care so much?'

She looked up and their eyes met. For a moment she thought she saw her own yearning mirrored in his dark gaze.

Because you do, she wanted to say. And because this theatre is the only thing stopping us from drifting apart. Her mouth went dry. 'Nick –'

'Hello, hello. Hope I'm not interrupting anything?'

They both swung round as Bob Stone stepped out of the shadows, flanked by two grim-looking men. He looked like Mr Toad, with his tweed suit and smug expression.

Nick was immediately hostile. 'What do you want?'

'I've come to look at the damage.'

'Come to gloat, you mean.' Annie pushed her hair out of her eyes.

He ignored her, his spectacles glinting in the gloom as he looked around. 'What a bloody mess. That James Brookfield never could do anything right. I'll tell you summat, if I'd wanted this place burned down it would have been nowt but a pile of ash by now.'

'Disappointed?' Annie asked.

Bob tutted. 'Now then, lass. What have I told you about jumping to conclusions.'

'Oh, come on. You might not have started the fire but you don't care what happens to this place. You want it to fail.'

'Then how come I'm here to help?'

'It's a bit late for that, isn't it?' Nick snapped.

Bob shook his head. 'I'll grant you, there's a fair bit to

put right, but nowt that can't be done by a couple of skilled craftsmen like my lads here.' Annie turned to the shaven-headed men with him. They looked as if they'd be more skilled with crowbars.

'I don't believe this.' Nick shook his head as if to clear it. 'You do your damnedest to put us out of business and now you have the nerve to come round here offering to quote us for repairs?'

'You won't get a better job done anywhere in Yorkshire, I'll tell you that.'

'You're wasting your time. We haven't got a penny.'

'Who says it'll cost owt?' Bob Stone polished his glasses on his waistcoat. 'Look, I know I was against this place reopening. I still am, if truth be told. And I won't deny I've stood in your way more than once. But whatever folks might say about me, I don't hold with doing things the way the likes of James Brookfield do them. Especially when he drags my good name into it.' He looked around, sizing up the damage. 'I still don't think you can make a go of it. But I reckon you deserve a fair chance to try.'

'And you'll do the repairs for nothing?' Annie looked disbelieving.

'Now then, I said I'd help, I didn't say I was Father bloody Christmas, did I?' His eyes twinkled behind his glasses. 'I'm a Yorkshireman, lass. We don't do owt for nowt, you should know that. But I'm prepared to offer you some easy terms. Maybe we could work out a deal so you pay me out of your profits. If there are any,' he added grimly. 'As far as I'm concerned, you've got about as much chance of filling this place as Middlethorpe has of hosting the next Olympics.'

Annie's gloom was beginning to lift, but Nick brought her back down to earth with a bump. 'It's very kind of you,' he said wearily. 'But even if you did do the work for nothing we still wouldn't have it finished in time for opening night.'

'Now that's where you're wrong. We're used to tight schedules. I told you, we're skilled craftsmen.'

'You could be bloody fairies and you still wouldn't get the job done.'

'Who are you calling a bloody fairy?' One of the men took a step towards Nick. Bob Stone held him back.

'We will get it done. We'll work round the clock if needs be.' He stuck out his hand. 'You'll get your theatre for opening night, Mr Ryan. You have my word on it.'

Nick shook his hand. He looked dazed. 'What can I say, except – thank you.'

'Don't thank me, lad. It's this lass of yours you ought to be grateful to. You've got yourself a good 'un there. Even if she is a bit mouthy at times.' He winked at Annie.

'I know,' Nick said quietly.

'Besides,' Bob Stone went on, 'you've made a right bloody nuisance of yourselves around here. People have started to notice this place and they've decided they want to keep it. So I don't suppose it'll do me any harm to be seen doing my bit for the community.'

As Nick discussed repairs with the two men, Bob took Annie aside. 'I hope this means you won't be showing up at the golf club again.' he said. 'I didn't appreciate being made a fool of, I can tell you.'

'Sorry,' Annie said meekly.

'And I hope it's the last we hear of that other little – er – business.' He eyed her meaningfully. 'Jeannie Acaster is an old family friend. That night you saw me – we were just catching up on old times, that's all.'

'Of course.' Annie fought to keep a straight face. 'Don't worry, I won't be going to the press.'

'It's not the press I'm worried about,' Bob said gruffly. 'Bloody hell, I own the local paper anyway. But if you breathe a word of this to my wife –'

'I won't.' Impulsively she threw her arms round his neck. 'Mr Stone, you're an angel.'

'Now then, lass, it's Councillor Stone to you.' He turned slightly pink. 'We don't want your boyfriend getting the wrong idea, do we?'

They spent the next half-hour discussing repairs to the theatre. As he left, Bob turned back and said, 'By the way, in case you were wondering, your pal Brookfield is up before the magistrates this morning. I've got the feeling he'll be in for a nice long stretch.'

'Unless he gets bail,' Annie said grimly.

'Oh, I shouldn't think that's very likely, lass. You see, a good friend of mine just happens to be sitting on the bench today.' With a wink he was gone.

'I can't credit it!' Nick laughed. 'You realise this means we might just make opening night after all?'

'I know. Who'd have believed Bob Stone would turn out to be our knight in shining armour?'

She looked at Nick and realised he wasn't laughing any more. 'Thanks,' he said quietly.

'What for?'

'Bob Stone was right. None of this would have happened if it hadn't been for you. I'm very grateful.'

Grateful! Was that the best he could do? 'You heard what he said. We make a great team.'

Then, suddenly, they were in each other's arms, hugging. Annie clung to him, breathing him in, feeling his reassuring warmth. For a moment it seemed as if Nick might be feeling the same powerful rush of emotions. His arms tightened round her. Then, abruptly, he let her go.

'I'd better go and let the others know the good news.' He turned and walked away.

Annie watched him go, a lump rising in her throat. So that was that. She'd proved how much she loved him and it still wasn't enough. What more could she do?

Chapter 37

'Did you see that? She's limping now. Fucking *limping*, for Christ's sake!'

It was the last rehearsal before opening night and tensions were running high. The rehearsal was supposed to be for the benefit of the stage crew, but as usual Georgia couldn't resist stirring things up.

'I just thought it might bring some reality into the scene.' She appealed to Nick, who sat staring up at the ceiling. 'I mean, it doesn't say in the text that Hero didn't have a limp, does it?'

'It doesn't say Leonato didn't have three heads and walk like a fucking fairy, but you don't see me doing that, do you?' muttered Henry.

'There's no need to be offensive.' Georgia sniffed. 'Tell him, Nick.'

'Lose the limp, Georgia.' Nick sighed.

'I don't see why –'

'Because I say so.' Nick levelled his gaze at her. 'Because we open in two days. This is a lighting rehearsal and it's too late to start making changes.'

Georgia stared at him. After all his soothing and cajoling

of past weeks, it was as if her pet lap-dog had leaped up and gone for the jugular.

'Look, I appreciate your need to interpret the role,' he went on, as her lip trembled on the verge of yet another tantrum. 'But not everyone has your – instincts. They need to predict what's going to happen next.'

'If you say so.' Georgia looked huffy.

'And that includes not suddenly making up your own lines because you can't be bothered to learn your bloody script,' Brendan added in an undertone.

Georgia shot him a pained look as she stalked off back to her spot, her long skirts swishing.

'I'll be glad when she's dead,' Caz muttered to Annie, who was busy adjusting her corset.

'Except she'll probably take half an hour to do it.' They might as well not be on stage when Georgia was there. Even when she wasn't in the scene she was usually ad libbing noisily in the background.

She caught Nick's wry smile and her stomach did its usual backflip. He looked so damned sexy, his black jeans and sweater emphasising his lean body. She found it hard to breathe, even without her rib-crushing corset.

Poor Nick. He was dealing with everything with his usual weary patience, although Annie noticed he was on his fourth Marlboro and was shredding the packet. He looked as if he hadn't slept for a week.

Not that they needed to worry. Bob Stone had been as good as his word. Having decided to embrace the Phoenix, he had put his best men on the job and made sure the renovations were better than any of them could have hoped. He'd also got himself voted on to the board of trustees and insisted on giving the local press a guided tour around the theatre. From the way he talked about 'our' plans, anyone would have thought the whole idea had been his from the start.

But at least it had brought some good publicity. THE PHOENIX RISES FROM THE ASHES, the local newspaper headlines had said. The box-office was doing good business and the theatre had started to attract more than casual glances. For the first time, people dared to believe it might work.

Annie should have been elated, but she couldn't shake off a lingering feeling of depression. She and Nick were still avoiding each other. Meanwhile, Max was refusing to take the hint and go home.

While Dogberry and the Sexton were playing their scene, she and Caz sneaked off to the green-room for a smoke.

Caz was in a foul mood. 'Daniel's wife's coming to the first night. Apparently she thinks they should make a go of it for the kids' sake.' She was an incongruous sight, her cropped hair covered with a lace cap, long skirts tucked up around her, puffing angrily on a ciggie.

'Oh, no!'

'I know why she's really doing it. It's because she's found out about me. She wants to prove she can take Dan back whenever she feels like it.'

'Surely he won't fall for that?'

'Don't you believe it. She's got the kids, remember? Dan dotes on them. As soon as he heard the news he was off to Toys R Us to buy the place.' Her lip trembled. 'How do I compete?'

'You can't,' Annie agreed. 'But would you really want to, if it meant keeping him away from them?'

'I suppose not.' Caz brushed ash off the front of her

crinoline. 'God, why can't I just fall in love with someone who loves me back?'

I know what you mean, Annie thought. She looked up at the monitor, which showed what was happening on stage. Dogberry was in the middle of his comical scene, but the only one she noticed was Nick. He had his long legs tucked under him, watching the actors with a fixed concentration that made her heart lurch.

'You still really like him, don't you?' Caz's voice broke into her thoughts.

'Yes.' She'd given up denying it a long time ago, even to herself.

'So what's stopping you? Why don't you just tell him how you feel?'

'Because I know it's not what he wants to hear.'

'But everyone can see he's crazy about you.'

Well, he's got a funny way of showing it, Annie thought. Sometimes she caught an unguarded look or smile that made her think he might still care about her. But then the shutters would come down and she'd realise they were as far apart as they'd ever been.

'Maybe he's just pissed off because Max is still around,' Caz suggested.

'Don't you think I know that?' Annie's gaze drifted away from the screen. 'I've tried to explain how I feel about Max, but Nick doesn't want to know. I suppose I'll just have to face it. He's not interested enough to care.'

'You're sure you're not letting Max hang around because you're thinking of going back to him?' Caz looked worried.

'Are you serious?' Max was like a Spandau Ballet poster she'd once drooled over but now wondered what she'd ever seen in it. 'It would be a lot easier if I could hate him. But to tell the truth I just feel sorry for him.'

'Sorry? For that selfish bastard? I wouldn't waste my time.'

'I know, but I can't help it. I just wish he'd take the hint and leave.' Unfortunately, her efforts to make him go only seemed to make him more attentive. He sent her flowers and phoned her several times a day. Once or twice, much to her embarrassment, he'd even turned up at the stage door to take her home. Fortunately she'd managed to put him off that one.

'So what are you going to do?' Caz asked.

'I don't know. But I can't stay here.' The idea of leaving was tearing her apart, but seeing Nick every day and knowing they were growing further apart was much worse. 'You know, I don't think I can stand much more of this. If I have to go on acting cool and professional any longer, I think I'll scream —'

She realised Caz was making frantic eye-rolling gestures, turned and saw Georgia, Adam and Nick in the doorway. One look at his rigid expression told her he'd heard every word of her last remark.

'Can you see my nipples?' Annie adjusted her corset and turned to face Caz on the other side of the dressing-room.

It was the first night and the place was in chaos. The surfaces were littered with flowers, mostly from Georgia's admirers. Annie's mirror was lined with cards, including a huge pink satin heart from Jeannie and Trixie, and a more discreet one from Julia, wishing her well and threatening never to speak to her again if she messed this up. The scent of roses and freesias mingled in the air with the nervous sweat of pre-show panic.

'Hard to miss them, in that frock.' Caz didn't look up from her *Marie Claire*.

'That's what I was afraid of.' Annie yanked at the plunging neckline of her gold-embroidered bodice. The dress was beautiful, deep-green velvet that set off her tumbling curls. But either her boobs had grown or Vince had messed up on the measurements, because it was positively indecent.

'At least you can breathe in yours.' Georgia leaned into the mirror, applying a layer of false eyelashes. She looked as beautiful as ever, her dark colouring emphasised by the virginal white of her gown. Never was a costume more inappropriate, Annie thought.

'If you want to breathe you'll have to wait until the interval.' Greta the dresser bustled in with an armful of roses. She looked as if she was wrestling a small shrub.

Georgia looked up expectantly. 'For me? How sweet.'

'Not this time.' Greta smirked as she dumped them on Annie's dressing-table. Georgia had had her running around all afternoon, fetching and carrying her ioniser, her cigarettes and her throat pastilles.

'Ooh, I wonder who they're from?'

'As if we didn't know.' Georgia's mouth twisted. 'He's certainly trying, isn't he?'

Annie threw the card into the bin without emotion. Once upon a time Max sending her flowers would have made her heart race. Now, with a house full of expensive blooms, all she felt was a deep weariness.

It was less than ten minutes to curtain up and from down the corridor came the rich baritone of Henry Adams doing his voice warm-up exercises. Over the tannoy they could hear rustling and murmuring as the audience shuffled into the seats. The show was a sell-out.

And from somewhere, much further away, came another sound.

'Can anyone hear that?' Annie tilted her head, listening.

'Hear what?'

'That music. Sort of scratchy, like a –' She stopped. Like an old-fashioned gramophone. 'It's nothing.' She touched her curls. 'Just my imagination, that's all.'

She could still hear the music, faint but unmistakable. *I'll see you again, whenever spring breaks through again* . . . Strangely, she didn't find it scary any more.

'Is everyone okay?'

She didn't turn round. She didn't need to look at him. It was as if all her senses sprang to attention at once.

'Nick, darling!' Georgia got up and kissed him. 'You look gorgeous.'

Annie risked a glance in the mirror and her heart stopped. He was attractive enough in his rumpled old clothes, but dressed up in an immaculately tailored suit he knocked her sideways.

'I thought I'd make the effort.' He caught her eye in the mirror. 'What do you think?'

What she thought was that she wanted to rip off his jacket, mess up his dark hair and make love to him on the spot, but she managed to control herself. 'Very smart,' she said.

'You look great, too.' For a moment it appeared as if the same thought had been going through his mind. 'I just came to wish you all the best.'

'What do you think of Annie's flowers?' Georgia broke in. 'Max sent them. Isn't he a darling?'

'Very.' Suddenly the softness was gone from his gaze.

'It must be love, don't you think?' Annie willed her to shut up.

Luckily, before she could say any more, Fliss's voice came over the tannoy.

'This is your Act One beginners' call, please. LX and sound operators stand by. Stage staff stand by on OP and Prompt Side doors. This is your Act One beginners.'

Annie rose shakily. 'Well, this is it.'

Nick nodded. 'It looks like it.'

Waiting in the wings, her heart crashing against her ribs, she fought the urge to peer out at the audience, knowing that if she did she would be lost. As the house lights dimmed the heat seemed to drain from her veins.

'Here we go, sweetie.' Henry squeezed her hand. Giving herself a mental shove, like a parachutist about to dive from a plane, Annie closed her eyes and forced her feet forward and on to the stage.

Chapter 38

The moment the curtain went up all her nerves vanished. It was the magic of the theatre, the heady combination of playing to a real audience and the adrenalin that pumped through her veins like a class A drug, lifting her high. Scenes that she'd dreaded in rehearsal suddenly seemed to flow. Even Georgia's atrocious attempts at scene stealing hardly seemed to bother her any more. As feisty Beatrice, she teased her staid Uncle Leonato and tormented her old friend Benedick, giving just the merest hint of her real feelings for him. They circled each other like sword fighters, parrying with words, pretending indifference when deep down they felt anything but.

Just like Nick and me. The thought struck as she and Daniel were in the middle of the emotional scene where Benedick and Beatrice finally break down and admit their true feelings for each other.

"'I do love nothing in the world so well as you, is that not strange?'" Daniel dropped to his knees where she sat, his hand clutching hers.

Stiffly, she withdrew it. "'As strange as the thing I know not: it were as possible for me to say I loved nothing so well as you —'" Without thinking, her gaze lifted, seeking

Nick out in the wings. He was there, as always, watching her intently.

She felt a hard squeeze on her hand and looked round. Daniel was still kneeling in front of her. Beads of perspiration had broken out on his lip. "'But believe me not, and yet I lie not.'" She saw the relief in his eyes as she supplied his cue. "'I confess nothing, nor I deny nothing.'"

Gratefully, he plunged into his next line. Annie glanced up again. Nick had gone.

And then it was all over. Annie stood on the edge of the stage, hand in hand with Daniel, Adam and the others, listening to the thunderous applause echoing through the building as they took their final bow. The lights felt hot on her face. Rivulets of sweat trickled down between her jacked-up breasts. Then Daniel grabbed her hand and dragged her downstage to take her final bow.

As she did, she allowed herself to seek out the faces in the front rows for the first time. There was Jeannie Acaster, a vibrant splash of cerise and orange in the front row, Trixie clutched to her bosom, wearing a matching bow and looking suitably embarrassed. Beside them, in the best seat in the house just as she'd promised, sat Stan, dabbing his eyes. There was Julia, beaming proudly. Further along the row, beside Lady Carlton, was Bob Stone. Annie smiled down at them, tears of happiness mingling with the perspiration on her face. She'd forgotten how good this felt.

She left the stage with the others, the applause still ringing in her ears, and almost cannoned straight into Nick.

'Well done, everyone. Great show.' His eyes swept over them all and then he was gone again.

'Charming,' Caz grumbled. 'My God, two weeks ago we didn't even have a theatre. You'd think he'd be a bit more enthusiastic.'

'He was.' Adam watched him disappear down the corridor. 'Couldn't you see the poor guy was choked?'

'I don't know what he means about a great show.' Daniel glanced back at Georgia as she lingered on stage, extracting the last of the applause from an exhausted audience. 'Did you see how long she took to collapse at the end of the wedding scene?'

'I was too distracted by the speech impediment to notice,' Brendan said gloomily. 'Can someone explain why she developed a lisp in the second act?'

Annie left them chattering and went back to her dressing-room. Her heart sank as she saw Max was lounging in her chair, his feet up on the dressing-table.

'Hi, angel,' he drawled. 'I see you got the flowers.'

'Yes. Thanks.' She shooed him off her chair and sat down.

Max leaned against the wall, watching her. 'I thought I'd get roses. I know they're your favourites.'

'I'm surprised you remembered.'

'How could I forget? You carried them on our wedding day.'

She looked at him sharply. Of course she remembered. Their scent never failed to bring back that chilly grey morning outside Chelsea Register Office. But for all Max seemed aware, she could have been carrying a bouquet of stinging nettles.

He guessed her thoughts. 'I know you think I'm an unfeeling bastard, but there are some things I don't forget.

Like how beautiful you looked that day. And how much I loved you.'

Annie dragged her gaze away, picked up the nearest jar and began applying the contents. Too late, she realised she was smearing her face with hand cream.

'Still, all that's going to change,' he said. 'I realise now how much I need you. I'm a different person.'

So am I. Annie tissued off the cream with a shaking hand. That's the trouble.

'You'll see, once we get back to London –'

'I told you, I'm not going back to London yet.'

Consternation flickered in his blue eyes. 'But you said –'

'No, *you* said. You just assumed I'd go along with your plans.'

'But I don't understand. What's keeping you here?'

What indeed, Annie thought, scrunching up her tissue and aiming it at the bin. It missed.

'Anyway, we don't have to discuss it now,' Max went on. 'I've booked a quiet supper back at the hotel, just the two of us. We can talk about it then.'

'But what about the party?'

'You mean that bun-fight at the local?' He looked scornful. 'You don't want to go there.'

'I do.' Their eyes clashed. Max made a big show of giving in.

'Okay, okay, if that's what you want. We'll go to the party. Just don't expect me to enjoy it, that's all. Making small talk with a bunch of inbreds isn't my idea of a good time.'

'You don't have to come,' Annie pointed out.

'Of course I do. You're my wife.' He came up behind her and squeezed her shoulders. 'You look incredibly sexy in that dress, by the way.' 'I spent the whole first act fantasising about unlacing that corset with my teeth.'

Annie wriggled away from him and got up. 'Do you mind?' she asked. 'I want to get changed and have a shower.'

'I don't mind at all.' Max sat in her vacated chair, his hands clasped behind his head. 'You go ahead.'

'Max!' Annie shot him a look.

'Spoilsport!' He got up grudgingly. 'At least let me help you out of that dress?'

'I can manage, thank you.'

There was a knock on the door. Max strode over and flung it open.

Nick stood outside. 'Annie, I –' His expression froze. 'Sorry, I didn't realise you were busy.'

'Er – Nick, this is Max. My – um –'

'Husband.' Max greeted him in a friendly manner. 'You must be the director. I was just telling Annie how much I enjoyed *Much Ado*.'

'Thanks.' Nick's face, by contrast, had all the warmth of a Siberian winter.

'Did you – er – want me for something?' Annie broke the tense silence.

'I'd like to see you in my office. When you've got a moment.' Shooting Max a final look of dislike he left, slamming the door behind him so hard that all the jars rattled on the counter tops.

'Nice to meet you too!' Max called after him. 'What a fun guy,' he drawled.

Annie didn't reply. She stared at the door, full of sadness.

'Oh, I get it.' A slow smile spread across Max's face. 'You and he are – involved, is that it?' Annie said nothing.

'My God, you really were serious when you said there was someone else. And I thought you were just trying to make me jealous.'

'I've got to see him.' She couldn't leave it like this. Not any more.

Annie stood outside Nick's office for a moment, gathering her thoughts. But as she entered the tiny room and saw him standing behind the desk, his expression was so forbidding that her brain went blank.

'I wanted to give you this.' He picked up a piece of paper off the desk.

'What is it?'

'Your contract.' As she watched, horrified, he tore it slowly down the middle. 'As of now, you no longer work for the Phoenix company.'

'You – you're sacking me?'

'I'm releasing you. Now you can leave.' He watched her closely.

So he *had* heard what she said to Caz. 'But what about the show?' she stammered. 'How will you cope?'

'I'll think of something.' He rasped his hand over his chin. 'That's my problem, not yours.'

'You want me to go?'

'I don't want you if your heart's not in it.' He lifted weary eyes to meet hers. 'Let's face it, you've never really belonged here, have you?'

So this was it. He couldn't have made his feelings clearer if he'd gone round to Jeannie's and packed her bags for her himself.

'I'll make up your pay until the end of the week, if that's okay?' Suddenly he was brisk, discussing the practical details. Annie watched his mouth move but barely heard the words. Was this really the same man who had taken her in his arms in that hotel four-poster and told her he loved her? That he'd always loved her? She fought the overwhelming urge to rush to him, to beg him not to send her away. But it was no use. She had done that once to Max and it had got her nowhere. At least this time she'd escaped with a shred of pride. Although what use that was going to be to her during the long, lonely days and nights to come she had no idea.

She bit her lip, determined to be brave. 'Can I at least have a hug? Just for old times' sake?'

He hesitated for a moment. Then slowly, reluctantly, he lifted his arms to her. Annie rushed into them and for a moment they clung to each other, both knowing it was for the last time.

Max was waiting for her in the corridor outside. 'Well? What happened? Have you two kissed and made up, or what?'

Annie dashed away a tear with the back of her hand, hoping he wouldn't notice.

But Max was too quick for her. 'Christ, Annie, what is it?' Then he saw the fragments of paper in her hand. 'What's that?'

She held it out to him.

As he scanned the words, a slow smile spread across his face. 'Oops,' he said. 'Looks like the end of a beautiful friendship, doesn't it? Cheer up, angel. Now there's nothing to stop you coming back to London, is there?' He put his arm round her shoulders. This time she didn't bother to fight him off.

Chapter 39

The landlord of the Millowners' Arms had never thrown a first night party before, but luckily he was resourceful. Glittery streamers and bunches of balloons bearing the words 'Happy 21st' decked the ceilings. Coloured disco lights flashed, Abba blared from the speakers and, with the champagne flowing, no one seemed to notice that the paper table-cloths all had Christmas trees on them.

'Christ, it's like the school disco from hell.' Max whispered as they walked in. He gripped her hand possessively. It was a novelty after all the parties where he'd dumped her at the door like an old coat while he disappeared in search of booze and some juicy gossip. 'You look stunning,' he whispered. 'You always did look amazing in gold.'

Annie forced a smile. The silk sheath dress had cost a fortune, but it was worth it. It slithered over her body, its rich tobacco colour bringing out the amber of her eyes and the glowing highlights in her hair. But she was painfully aware that she had bought it with another man in mind.

'Don't look now, but the paparazzi are waiting.' Max nodded towards the girl reporter and photographer who huddled together under a brolly outside the pub. 'I suppose it's not often this dump hosts a glittering celebrity event.'

'Who's this, Annie?' The girl called out as they passed.

'I'm her husband.' Annie cringed as he squeezed her hand. 'Max Kennedy.' He peered over her shoulder, making sure she spelled his name right.

'Fancy not knowing who I was.' He tutted as they walked away. 'Don't they have TV up here, or something?'

Just then Bob Stone appeared, surrounded as usual by his entourage, all self-consciously togged up in bow ties and looking like a night-club bouncers' convention.

'Well done, lass!' He gathered her into his arms for a hug as a flashbulb exploded in their faces. 'That was a great show you put on. Absolutely cracking.'

'You really liked it?' She blinked at him.

'Well, to tell you the truth I fell asleep, but the wife enjoyed it. It's an asset to Middlethorpe,' he added loudly, for the benefit of the reporter, who was standing nearby. 'And to think that if I hadn't stepped in at the last minute to rescue the place it might have been lost to the community.' He winked at Annie, then turned away to answer more questions from the eager reporter.

'Alone at last,' Max whispered.

'There's Caz.' Annie distracted him, waving across the room.

He groaned. Caz was sending him the kind of look she normally reserved for something unpleasant stuck to the bottom of her Kurt Geiger sling-backs. 'It looks like she wants to speak to you.' He nodded to where Caz was doing a little war-dance of excitement. 'You go and see what she wants. I'll try and find something decent to drink.'

As he disappeared into the crowd, Caz was already bearing down on her. 'Guess what? Dan's finally split up from his wife.'

'You're kidding? But I thought it was all on again?'

'It was. Until this morning.' Caz jiggled up and down, spilling most of her champagne. 'You know she was supposed to be coming up here for the first night? Well, she rang to say she'd changed her mind. Apparently the car mechanic's come up with a better offer. He's taking them all to Disneyland Paris for the weekend. Poor Dan was furious. I think it finally dawned on him what kind of woman she really is.' She grinned. 'Just think, I might end up being a wicked stepmother.'

'Hang on! He's just got rid of one wife. He might not want another.'

'Just you wait.' Caroline's dark eyes gleamed with a sense of purpose. 'I'll have him up that aisle faster than you can say big white wedding with all the trimmings.'

Only two days ago she was ready to give up on him, Annie thought. When it came to her love life, Caz was as resilient as a bungee rope.

She gazed across at Max. Yet how could she talk? Who could have guessed a few months ago that her feelings for Max would change so completely?

'Is he still here?' Caz followed her gaze across the room. 'You'd better get rid of him before Nick arrives. He'll be furious.'

'I don't think he'll care.' Annie's voice was emotionless. 'He's already told me to go back to him.'

'Nick told you that? I don't believe it! You two were made for each other.'

'He obviously doesn't think so.'

'What about you? Don't you love him?'

'I don't think that really matters —'

'Of course it matters! Do you love him?'

Annie looked at the floor. 'Yes.'

'Then fight for him. Go and tell him how you feel.'

'And what good would that do? I'd only end up humiliated.'

'So you'd rather lose him, is that it?' Caz grabbed her arm. 'Talk to him, Annie. Before you both do something you'll regret.'

She walked off, leaving Annie staring at the sandwiches. The noise of the party drifted around her. Gary Glitter was exhorting everyone to come on, come on. Bob Stone was punching the air drunkenly. Everyone was having a marvellous time, except her.

She grabbed a plastic cup of champagne from the bar and took a swig. It was warm and slightly flat, but it was enough to numb her senses.

Then, from across the room, she heard Georgia's voice.

'So he asked me if I'd consider taking the part on, and of course I said yes,' she was telling Adam and Henry, and anyone else within a two-mile radius. 'I've always felt Beatrice and Benedick were central to the play's theme. I mean, it's their story more than anyone else's, isn't it?' Annie felt a vein throbbing dangerously in her temple. 'And of course I felt I could bring a more sensitive interpretation to the role. I'm not saying Annie isn't a competent actress, but —'

She turned away, crunching the plastic cup in her fist, and walked straight into Julia.

'So this is where you're hiding.' Julia looked distinctly

out of place in a tasteful black Ben de Lisi. 'Why aren't you soaking up all the adulation with the others?'

'I don't feel like it.'

'But you deserve it. You've put this place on the theatrical map. And now what you require is some serious work. I've got a couple of roles in mind that will be perfect for you.'

'Two months ago you told me this was just what I needed!'

'Yes, and I was right, wasn't I?' Julia smiled. 'But now it's time for something more broadening.'

'And what if I don't want anything more broadening?'

'Sorry?'

'I just wish people would stop trying to run my life for me.'

Julia looked blank. 'But I'm your agent. That's my job.' She ploughed on without waiting for an answer. 'Now, I've been talking to an old contact of mine and he reckons they'll be casting for the new Sir Walter Scott adaptation soon. There could well be a part in it for you. I don't suppose you can milk a goat, by any chance?'

'I'm not going to Scotland.'

'Of course you are, darling.'

'No, she's not.' Max sidled up to join them, a cup in each hand. 'She's coming back to London with me, aren't you, angel? We're going to rebuild our marriage.'

'At the expense of her career, I suppose?'

'Some things are more important than work, Julia. Although I don't expect someone like you to understand that.'

'At least I've got her best interests at heart. Let's face it, you only want her back because –'

Annie tuned out as the argument raged around her.

Why did they all think they knew best? Julia, Max, Caz —
even Nick. In all this mess, no one had bothered to ask
what *she* really wanted.

Well, it was about time she told someone, before the
rest of her life was mapped out for her.

She left them arguing and went outside. Across the
square, a dim light glowed in one of the upper windows of
the theatre. Annie headed for it purposefully.

Chapter 40

Annie's heart was beating a salsa rhythm against her ribs as she pushed open the stage door and went inside.

'Hello?' Her whisper sounded like a gunshot in the dense silence.

Then she heard it. Drifting down the stairs, the unmistakable sound of an old gramophone.

'Nick?' she croaked. There was no answer. But from somewhere above her she heard the noise of a woman's laughter.

She froze. Then, slowly, she urged her feet forward down the narrow corridor into the darkness, her hands tracing the cold walls. As she went, she could feel the hairs stirring on the back of her neck, as if someone was behind her.

She walked on stage. It felt strange to look out over the empty auditorium, where only a couple of hours before row upon row of faces had looked up at her. She stood for a moment, lost in thought, remembering the applause ringing in her ears.

'It was quite a night, wasn't it?' She swung round, as Nick emerged from the shadows.

'I'll never forget it,' she said.

'Neither will I.' They stood in silence for a moment, both staring out over the empty theatre. Finally, he spoke. 'What are you doing here?'

'I came to talk to you.'

He rubbed the back of his neck wearily. 'I think we've said all there is to say, don't you?'

He started to turn away from her but Annie grabbed his arm, dragging him back. 'No,' she said. 'So far everyone else has done the talking. Now it's my turn.'

His face darkened. 'What –'

'Don't!' Her voice echoed around the empty theatre. 'Don't you dare say a word until I've finished.'

He sighed and sat down in a carved chair at the side of the stage, his legs stretched out in front of him. 'Okay, then. Let's hear it.'

She took a deep breath and stared out at the rows of empty seats, unable to look at him. 'I just wanted to know what I've done wrong,' she said. 'Why do you hate me so much?' Nick opened his mouth to speak, but Annie silenced him. 'Okay, so I made a mistake and fell in love with you. It's not such a great crime, is it? You didn't have to fire me.'

'What did you say?'

She ignored the interruption. 'I mean, now you've made it clear you don't feel the same, I can respect that. I think I'm grown-up enough to move on. And I hope I'm professional enough to –'

'Annie!' She turned round and he was there, standing right behind her, close enough to touch. Close enough to kiss. 'Why the hell didn't you tell me all this before?'

'I tried, remember? When Max came back. But you wouldn't listen.'

'I thought you were just trying to let me down gently. I

310

was so upset and furious that I wasn't in the mood to listen to anything.' He looked her straight in the eyes. 'You really mean it?'

She never thought she'd see that look on his face again. But at the same time she couldn't resist teasing him. 'I think I should,' she said. 'If only to stop you giving my part to Georgia and making the biggest mistake of your life.'

'I've already done that,' he admitted. 'The biggest mistake of my life was letting you walk out of here.'

'Then why did you?'

'Because I thought I knew how you felt about Max. When he turned up, I assumed you'd jump at the chance to go back to him.'

'So you pretended you didn't care?'

'I did it before, when you married Max. I thought I could do it again.' He paused. 'I was scared to tell you how I felt, if you must know, in case you didn't feel the same.'

'I can understand that.' Hadn't she been through the same agonies herself?

'Only this time it wasn't so easy. I nearly cracked tonight after the show. That's why I came to see you in your dressing-room. I was going to tell you how I felt, lay my cards on the table. And then I saw him with you and I knew I couldn't do it.'

'I wish you had.'

'So do I,' he admitted. 'That's why I stayed away from the party. I knew if I saw you together, again I'd end up punching him, or making an even bigger fool of myself. I let you go once and I ended up regretting it. I don't think I could go through losing you again.'

He took her in his arms and kissed her for a long time.

This time there was no thought of letting each other go. This was where she belonged.

'What about my contract?' she asked, when she finally came up for air.

'I've been thinking about that.' Nick grinned his old familiar lopsided grin that made her heart lurch. 'As a matter of fact, I wondered if you'd consider taking on a new one. Something different. I thought we could go down to the register office and get one drawn up?'

She controlled her shiver of excitement. 'I don't know,' she said. 'I'll have to get Julia to check it over. Will it involve a performance every evening?'

'Almost certainly.' His smile was devastatingly sexy. 'And probably a few matinées too. And absolutely no chance of an understudy.'

'Sounds perfect.' She grabbed his collar and pulled him towards her for another kiss.

As they stood in each other's arms, a spotlight suddenly picked them out in the middle of the stage. And from somewhere up in the gods came the distant sound of applause.